CROWN OF THORNS

Doris Leslie

CROWN OF THORNS

Published by Sapere Books.

24 Trafalgar Road, Ilkley, LS29 8HH

saperebooks.com

ISBN: 978-0-85495-199-4

For God's sake, let us sit upon the ground
And tell sad stories of the death of kings:
How some have been deposed...

Shakespeare, *Richard II,* Act III, Scene ii

FOREWORD

In writing this life of Richard II I have carefully authenticated all the known facts of this unfortunate king's reign.

There are few modern biographies of Richard II, but I am deeply indebted to Harold F. Hutchison for his informative and admirable life of Richard II, *The Hollow Crown* (Eyre & Spottiswoode, 1961).

Other authorities consulted are:

Richard II and the English Nobility, J. A. Tuck, Edward Arnold, 1973.

The Chronicles, Jean Froissart, translated by John Bourchier, Lord Berners, edited and abridged into one volume by G. C. Macaulay, MacMillan & Co. Ltd., 1904.

History of England, G. M. Trevelyan, Longmans, Green & Co. Ltd., 1926.

A History of France, Andre Maurois, Jonathan Cape, 1949, translated from the French by Henry L. Binsse.

Also several extracts from contemporary French and English eye-witnesses' chronicles.

No character or name of a character is fictitious, and all excerpts of speeches made by Richard and Henry Bolingbroke (Henry IV) and others are authentic.

DORIS LESLIE

ONE

'Checkmate!'

The boy whose fingers hovered uncertainly over king's knight glanced quickly up at that triumphant shout and stayed his hand.

'Too late!' cried Henry. 'You should have moved your castle and saved your king — not that I wouldn't have beaten you as I always do, even without a queen. You'll never be a player. You mustn't think only of what's on the board. You have to think ahead of what your opponent is going to do. A chessboard's a sort of battlefield. A good chess player will make a good fighter. My father told me that my uncle — your father — was always a good chess player, even when he was younger than you and me. He was only about sixteen when he won his spurs at Crécy.'

Said Richard, 'I didn't know my father played chess at our age — or any age.'

'Much you know about your father! You hardly ever see him, at least not until lately when he came home sick from the wars and is waiting here to die.'

A sharp indrawn breath tore at Richard's throat.

'All you ever think about — if you ever think at all,' Henry went on, watching the colour ebb from Richard's face at that painful reminder of his father's illness, 'is trying to write your silly poems about knights and dames like that fellow Chaucer you're always following around.'

'Chaucer isn't often h-here for me to f-follow around. He's either in Italy or s-somewhere nowadays, but we used often to see him when we l-lived in K-Kent.'

'When you l-lived in K-Kent,' jeered Henry, mimicking Richard's stammer, which was always worse when Henry teased him. 'You couldn't have had sight of him when you were a baby in arms. You are still a baby, but without arms, for you can't *carry* arms — can't even joust or ride a horse of any mettle — only that old grey mare of yours thought to be safe for a mother's darling milksop! Hey! *No!*' For Richard, goaded by Henry's taunts, had swept his hand across the board, tumbling the chessmen helter-skelter.

Henry sprang up, fury reddening his face. 'Look what you've done! God damn you!' He was down on his knees in the rushes where the chessmen had fallen. 'You've lost a king's head. Not the first king's head to be lost, if you ever wear the crown, and that'd be the ruin of England which my father — and yours — fought to save, and which *I'll* fight to save when I — if I ever wear the crown, given the chance!'

'Richard!' Sir Simon Burley, his tutor, stood in the doorway. 'Your father summons you to his chamber … Henry, what are you doing with those chessmen? Get up!'

Henry scrambled to his feet. 'He's thrown them down,' he panted, 'broken 'em to spite me because I beat him. See what he's done to this king — *my* king. He knows I always play with red. They are *my* set. My father gave them to me last birthday.'

'Come along, Richard.' Sir Simon was not disposed to waste time on the squabbles of the two youngsters when bent upon the order of his going from his prince.

Richard, safe in the custody of the tutor, poked his tongue at his cousin, Henry Bolingbroke, Earl of Derby. Although two or three months younger than Richard, Henry looked two or three years older, a handsome ruddy-faced boy, son of John of Gaunt, Duke of Lancaster, brother of the Prince of Wales.

In direct contrast to Henry's gipsy-dark hair and eyes, Richard had his mother's flax-gold hair and shell-like purity of skin. Yet while he lacked his father's magnificent physique, he had inherited the beauty of both parents.

Sir Simon's surname aptly described this rubicund stalwart companion-at-arms of Edward, Prince of Wales, the hero of Crécy and Poitiers, whose latest victory at Najara had returned him to England and a sickbed in his manor of Berkhamsted.

The prince had appointed Sir Simon as his son's tutor together with Sir Guichard d'Angle, both valiant soldiers and favourites of the Black Prince, but Sir Simon was not only a good soldier, he was a cultured man of parts seldom encountered outside the walls of a cloister. His library was reputed to hold more than twenty volumes, the contents of which he imparted to his young pupil. Thus Richard when barely five years old had assimilated, if less soldiering, more scholarship than many a child of his age or even an adult whether prince or commoner other than the priesthood or those intended for a political or ambassadorial career could have known in those Middle Ages. By the time Richard had left Bordeaux where he was born he could speak and write fluent French, some Spanish and a smattering of Latin more than learned in the Mass.

His mother, known as the 'Fair Maid of Kent' before her marriage to the Prince of Wales, was the heroine of several ex-marital adventures that ended in divorce from her first husband, Sir Thomas Holland. This necessitated a dispensation from an indulgent Pope to enable her to marry the heir to the throne of England.

Froissart, author of those incomparable *Chronicles* that have survived six centuries, gave his eye-witness reports of the endless wars between France and England. To him we owe his stirring account of the Peasants' Revolt, in which the young King Richard played his part that has rendered him the hero of every schoolboy studying the reigns of the mediaeval kings.

It is from this same Froissart we have the somewhat equivocal description of the Princess of Wales, that she was *la plus belle et la plus amoureuse* of women. This extravaganza, extolling her beauty with a suggestion that she was desirous as desired, may have enhanced her attraction to all men who knew her in or out of the Court — all, that is to say other than the ladies who may have been the wives or would-be wives of her admirers.

Joan, no longer a 'maid' but always 'fair', bore to her first husband Thomas Holland, later Earl of Kent, two sons respectively seventeen and fifteen years older than their half-brother Richard. By her second husband, the Prince of Wales, she was delivered of another son, his first-born Edward. He, to his father's lasting sorrow, died when Richard was too young to have remembered more than his brother's name, so often on his father's lips.

This baby Prince Edward, even in his tenderest years, had shown a tendency to follow in his father's warlike steps. Before he had lost his milk teeth he was playing with tin soldiers, storming toy fortresses and uttering the war cries taught him by his prideful father.

But Richard, the second son, evinced none of the warrior prince's qualities whose victories at Crécy and Poitiers must have been crooned to the infant Richard by his nurse Dame Mundina of Aquitaine when she rocked him in his cradle. His father's famous exploits in the ceaseless wars with France held no interest for him. His tastes, to his father's dismay, leaned towards the arts. He loved to daub parchments with incredible knights in armour or ladies in conical tall headgear with floating veils under a startling bright red sun; or he would lisp rhymes based on poems of Chaucer as taught him by Sir Guichard d'Angle, the poet's 'gentle perfect gentle knight', and he would write them on his parchments, decorated with numerous blots from the ink and an attempt at illumination of the lettering from the box of colours his doting mother had given him.

'An artist and a poet!' she would delightedly declare. She was always ready to encourage his aesthetic tastes for, 'I am sick of wars,' she would tell her prince on his rare visits to Bordeaux.

'And sick of me?' he would jestingly ask.

'I do not see enough of you,' she would remind him, 'to be sick of you who are more infatuated with Mars than with Venus!'

And this while Dame Mundina would be scrubbing Richard's hands and face that bore some of the contents of his colour box, equally divided between himself and his artistry.

'Crucify me!' she deplored, 'for the mess you've made of your prettiness. A pretty boy you were — and now look at you!'

'Too pretty for a boy,' his father swung round to say. 'He should have been a girl. His mother prayed for a girl, and now she's got one — all but its necessary parts!'

'You've put s-soap in my eyes!' whimpered Richard, jerking away from Dame Mundina's ministrations with a soap ball.

'And vermilion all over your nose,' grumbled the dame.

Trotting alongside Sir Simon in answer to his father's summons, striving to adjust his short legs to his tutor's lengthy stride, Richard recalled how his father would always remind him — and everyone else — how different he was from the brother he had hardly known, and how shameful to be 'pretty' like a girl! And what did his father want of him that he must be hurried to the chamber where his father lay sick, and to which he was seldom invited. Was he more ill, or dying? 'Oh no!' he cried, 'not that. He is not … is he?'

Sir Simon, halting his stride, asked, 'What did you say?'

'N-nothing … much,' was all Richard had time to say as they came to the entrance of the sick room, where a page guarding the door bowed to Sir Simon and Richard and announced them to the prince.

Propped on his pillows in his four-poster bed hung with heavy tapestry lay the 'Flower of Chivalry', as extolled by Froissart; yet there was nothing flower-like in the wasted face of the nationwide-vaunted Black Prince.

The last of the June sun filtered through the stone mullioned window to allow a cooling breeze to fan the sweating forehead of England's hero. His sickness, diagnosed by the Court physicians as dysentery contracted during the recent war with Spain, might well have been an intestinal cancer with which medicine in the Middle Ages was virtually unknown. As his son, at a whispered command from Sir Simon, knelt at the bedside, his father's hand was outstretched to meet the boy's lips, grown suddenly cold as he heard the prince's words, so low he must strain ears to hear them.

'I sent for you, my son — my only surviving son.' An effort was made to overcome the weakness of his voice and to tell him, 'It is my wish that you shall be entrusted to the care of the King, your grandfather, when I —' that weakened voice gained strength to say — 'when I am no longer — here.'

'Sir!' A stammering cry of, 'D-don't say you w-won't be…' was interrupted by a gesture to Sir Simon and the words, 'A scribe … my scrivener…' But as Sir Simon turned to go, 'Come back with him,' he was told, 'and stay to witness what he writes to be my … Last Will and Testament to the effect.'

A frowning pause for recollection and an effort to raise himself brought Richard from his knees to assist his father. He was waved aside. 'This is what I intend to leave him who will replace me. All my property to my son Richard … my manors, my lands — no, Simon, don't go, I want you to hear so you can prompt the scribe should I — forget. This goddam poppy seed my doctors dose me with for pain … make … all is to be Richard's except my titles, Duke of Cornwall, Earl of … what? Damme if I can remember the rest of 'em, and a lot o' use were they to me when I was cutting up Frenchmen!' A flash of that sudden mischievous humour, part of his and his son's endearing charm, lightened the pallid face of him who had been the nation's pride. 'But this one,' he stroked back a silken lock of yellow hair that had strayed into Richard's eyes, 'all that is mine will be his along with my titles … but I can't leave those to you in my will, Richard. Parliament will have to grant them to you … in due course. Is that not so, Simon?'

His friend and devoted follower choked back his tears as his head bowed a silent assent.

'But you, Richard, won't be interested in conquering the French who would attempt to seize my land … this England. You care nothing for wars and the triumph of victory … do you? Had your brother lived he … but you would sooner wield a pen than a sword … don't cry, lad.' He gave a tug to that lock of hair. 'Maybe a pen, or even a paintbrush, could be mightier than a sword in the right hand to use it, eh? Not your fault if you hate war, or … don't you?'

'It isn't that I h-hate war,' Richard managed to articulate, 'it is that I don't like k-killing people.'

'You'd rather they killed you than fight to defend this land which will be yours some day, or some other day … and may a father's curse be on the head of any who dares steal England from you!'

Many years later Richard had reason to recall his dying father's words.

The death of the Black Prince plunged the people of England into mourning. Never had a Prince of Wales been more greatly loved and honoured to the detriment of his heir of whom few had ever heard, much less seen.

It was a gloomy year for the child heir presumptive to the throne who followed his father's cortège to his burial in Canterbury Cathedral; but the Black Prince had been lost to England barely three weeks when the 'Good Parliament' summoned Prince Richard to attend them in Westminster Hall to be proclaimed Heir Apparent to the Throne.

Why this Parliament should have been named 'Good', unless it were the best of successive 'Bads' — including the worst of them rightly named 'The Merciless', has never been explained. However, it was the 'Good' Parliament which presented their future king to a vast assemblage with the third son of King Edward III, John of Gaunt, Duke of Lancaster, much in evidence who it was believed would act as regent to the child king and might also attempt to take the throne.

That there is no concrete evidence to involve John of Gaunt in any such treacherous connivance did not deter the Commons from condemning this third son of the ageing King Edward with their wholly unfounded suspicions. Far from bringing disaster to his nephew, the future King of England, Gaunt, who had so gallantly fought beside his brother, the Prince of Wales, although never called to act as regent, watched over and guarded the young king during his early minority. Nevertheless the clouds of suspicion from a Parliament composed of barons and knights each seeking to secure for himself high governmental control during the child king's formative years, shadowed Gaunt's life, until heartily sick of the ineptitude of those in power and the wholly unfounded allegations directed against him even though none had the temerity openly to voice them, Lancaster eventually retired to his vast estates and left the Commons to their own 'Good' selves, for better or for worse.

So for the next five years an incompetent government was totally unprepared for and quite unable to cope with the catastrophic crisis that took them all by storm. It was a boy king of scarcely fourteen who proved himself a worthy successor to the throne of his grandfather.

That for the future; for the present we may be permitted to follow Richard on his journey from Berkhamsted to Westminster in answer to a summons from Parliament to attend a meeting especially called in order to proclaim him indisputable heir to the throne.

In a conveyance euphemistically styled a carriage, but in these Middle Ages little better than a cart on wooden wheels despite its lavish interior upholstery, we find Richard seated between his mother, the widowed Princess of Wales, and his nurse, Dame Mundina, who had not yet relinquished sole charge of her nurseling. Unaccustomed to the discomfort of travelling over deep rutted lanes embedded in mud or smothered in dust on that sweltering June day, bumped and jolted, bruised and bone-shaken, Richard gave vent every now and then to bursts of that Plantagenet temper inherited from the first of them.

Soothingly chid by his mother who could never see a fault in him: 'Darling, I know these roads are dreadful but we, Dame Mundina and I, are used to them. Your dear father used often to complain that something should be done to —'

'It isn't the roads,' Richard interrupted, ''tis this horrible wagon that is bumping me black and blue. I don't *want* to go to London. Why should I? And if you and the dame don't mind being bumped black and blue — w-well, I do!'

'Only about ten more miles, my love, and we'll stop at the next inn and you shall have a nice posset and a stick of barley sugar to suck while we rest the horses.'

'Don't want barley sugar,' sulked Richard, 'and 'tis a shame to bring the horses all this way just so's I attend Parliament. What has Parliament to do with me? Why can't they leave me alone instead of dragging me from my home?' Then, seeing a tear roll down his mother's cheek under the black veil pulled aside to allow a slight breeze to cool the heat of the dust-laden vehicle, he was instantly contrite. 'I'm a beast to mind —'tis not your fault, my dearest dear, 'tis that goddam government or whatever they are — calling themselves "good" — about as good as a devil's horn!'

'Where does he learn to speak and swear like this?' his mother checked a tear to ask.

'From Lord Derby, his cousin Henry, on the few occasions he comes to visit us. Even if only once a year,' glumly replied the dame, 'it is too often for Richard's good.'

The uncomfortable journey having at last brought them to Westminster Hall, Richard's travelling suit was removed in a private apartment of the Chapter Hall, his face and hands scrubbed with Dame Mundina's ubiquitous soap ball, his flax gold hair brushed to fold under into his neck; and when dressed in a brand new tunic of mourning black velvet with purple trunks and black hosen, he was as pretty a boy as could ever be seen, for whom his mother in her idolatry thanked God…

In the Great Hall Richard was presented to Parliament by a herald in crimson and gold. In the five years since he left Bordeaux he had lived a cloistered life in his father's country manor, or his mother's seat in Kent; and other than his cousin Henry he had never known a child of his own age. And now to be announced to a vast assemblage of gentlemen in their heavy mourning robes of black and purple, was an experience of wonder and not a little unease to Richard who inclined to ask them, *What you staring at? Me? As if I'm some sort of freak? Silly old fools!*

His new velvet tunic, where the silver braid of its edging chafed his neck, caused an uncomfortable itch. His fingers strayed to scratch, when one of the gentlemen was on his feet … *And who's this old 'un?* Richard asked himself, twisting his neck to relieve the itch.

This 'old 'un' was Sir Peter de la Mare, Speaker of the House, and possibly the only loyal and disinterested member of them all.

Stentoriously he announced to his lords and gentlemen on that day of 25 June 1376: 'May all present see and acknowledge the Noble and Honourable Prince Richard, the very Heir Apparent and second only in the kingdom to His Grace, the Mighty King Edward…'

At which those many lords and gentlemen rose and bowed heads to knees … *at whom? At me?* marvelled Richard, as the first knowledge of what all this might mean crept into his bewildered mind.

Was he, Richard, second only in the kingdom to his deaf old grandfather the King of England? On the few visits to his palace he had always been accompanied by Sir Simon, when his grandfather's wheezy old voice would address him in a tone of surprise as if he had never set eyes on him before. 'Is this boy Richard, my son?' to be prompted by Sir Simon, 'Your Grace's grandson, Sire.' And where *was* Sir Simon? he wished to know, searching that sea of bowing heads.

Sir Simon, with Sir Guichard, was waiting for him when Parliament, having done with him, he had been led from the hall and all the 'old fools'.

'Now you know what I have endeavoured to impart to you,' Sir Simon said, taking his hand to conduct him to the coach, 'that one day, we cannot tell when, for none of us leaves this earthly kingdom for the Kingdom of God until we are invited, you will rule this England as the one and only rightful successor to the throne … in God's good time.'

'Amen to that,' sepulchrally uttered Sir Guichard.

'And the next time you come to Westminster Hall,' continued Sir Simon, 'it will be at the command of His Grace, the King.'

And the next time he was summoned to Westminster by his grandfather, was not to the Houses of Parliament, but to the Palace of Westminster on Christmas Day 1376.

He was conducted to the great banqueting hall wearing a new suit of clothes and, although still in his mourning of purple and black, was no longer scraped to itching from silver braid at his neck for he wore a gold chain falling from his velvet collar over a tabard of black velvet embroidered with the royal arms of the leopards of England and the lilies of France. He knew that England, always at war with France, had conquered part of it and that the Plantagenets quartered their arms with those of France.

So here he, Richard Plantagenet, had been brought to sit in the place of honour beside the King at the head of the long banqueting board above all his uncles, the bishops, archbishops and many grand gentlemen he had never seen before in their robes of purple and black and hung about with gold chains.

A much greater assemblage was this than those before whom he had been brought to sit in the Houses of Parliament; and Richard was quite relieved to see among them his uncle Gaunt, Duke of Lancaster, whom he knew better than any of his uncles unless it were the Earl of Cambridge who was always kindly, and also the youngest uncle, Lord Thomas of Woodstock, later to be created Duke of Gloucester by Richard himself — for his undoing. There were also his brothers, John and Thomas Holland; he did not know them very well as they were so often away at the war fighting the French. It was John, younger than Thomas, whom he knew and loved the best. He had only these two brothers to love with no friends of his own age; the only boy he ever saw, and him very seldom, was his cousin Henry Bolingbroke. But these brothers, John and Thomas, Sir Simon had told him, were only half-brothers as they had a different father from his own, the Prince of Wales ... Richard crossed himself and uttered a prayer for his father's soul, as he remembered his father, having died, had gone directly to heaven, he hoped, and was not one of the souls in purgatory waiting to be received by St Peter at the Gates.

A very devout little boy was Richard. And seeking that crowded board for a familiar face, he saw his favourite half-brother John screwing up his nose and grinning as if to say: *Fancy young Richard sitting there all grand beside the King — so mind your manners!*

He was minding them dreadfully because his cousin Henry, seated beside his father, Richard's uncle Gaunt, was making ugly faces at him and behind his hand Henry cocked him a snook, thumb to nose, and if Richard were not seated at the head of the table beside the King, he would have retaliated with an uglier face and a cocked snook at Henry.

The king was speaking … and now what?

'Now what', as he told his sons, was: 'Your Graces, my lords and gentlemen…' A wheezing cough caused resort to a lace edged handkerchief into which the King noisily spat, interrupting his speech — a momentous speech as it proved to be.

'Your Graces,' recovering, the King began again, 'my lords and — ech-ech-ech — pardon me — I am come here today to present you to — ech-ech — the Prince of…' (with an aside to Richard: 'Stand up, boy. Don't sit there like a dummy!') Richard stood up and the King, rising, said, 'You see here my son' — with a wheeze, hastily corrected — 'my grandson Richard. (They are all looking at you. Bow!)' This was accompanied by a bony finger poked in Richard's ribs under his velvet tunic while the King wheezily proceeded, 'My sons, lords and gentlemen hearken what I say that the young Prince Richard —' another and quite hurtful poke — 'shall be king after my death, and I adjure you all — ech-ech —'

The king's finger left Richard's ribs to point it at all those listening faces — all, that is to say, except Henry's face, for he had dived under the table, presumably to retrieve something dropped but obviously to hide his giggles at the old king's spitting and coughing, so that Richard was hard put to it to hide his own giggles as the King meandered on.

Having at last interpreted his grandfather's announcement (*Lord save us, Richard mentally soliloquised, me to be king! Don't laugh!*) he knew that Sir Simon had sometimes prepared him for what might happen to him after his father's death, but he had never taken it to mean that he, Richard, would... *(And if he goes on poking at me I'll be black and blue!)*

'My grandson Richard, Prince of Wales — ech-ech-ech' — spluttered the King, 'henceforth will be known as second — ech-ech — only to myself. I know he is not yet of age —' another poke and a mutter: 'What's your age, boy? How old are you?'

'I'm nine, Sire,' Richard achieved, controlling another giggle.

'You're what?'

'I said I'm nine, Sire, rising ten.'

'I told you to rise. Don't sit 'til I tell you to. Your age, boy!'

The king inclined a less deaf ear to Richard, who thought, *He hasn't had his ears washed for a month at least, and full of dirty grey hairs!*

'I said I'm nine, Sire.'

'Mine? What do you mean, mine? Not *my* age — yours. So my lords, my sons, and all my bishops — ech — archbishops — heed me that you see before you him whom you must hom — ech-ech — damn this cough! — homage as your future king and do swear before God Almighty to be faithful and true to Edward — no, not Edward, Richard, Prince of —' Again a mutter at Richard in a further effort to remember: 'I was thinking of your father, God rest him ... Duke of Corn ... wall. What? And Earl of — who?'

'Earl of Chester, Sire,' prompted his son, John of Gaunt, seated second only to the Princess of Wales who, between tears and laughter, was on the verge of hysterics at this honour to her best beloved, publicly proclaimed Prince of Wales by the King.

'Chester?' triumphantly wheezed King Edward, wiping from his nose a dewdrop that was trickling into his straggly white beard.

'What do you think of *that*?' chortled Henry when the monarch had retired and the guests were permitted to disperse. 'I thought he'd never have done with his wheezing and coughing. 'Tis likely you'll be more than Prince of Wales come next Christmas Day!'

'Don't be too sure,' was said in a drawling voice from Henry's companion, a tall, handsome lad somewhat older than the pair of them and very elegant in a purple velvet tunic and a tabard depicting a coat of arms headed by a crest and coronet. He had auburn hair clubbed under into his neck, as was the fashion for young mediaeval boys and pages.

'Of course we can't be *sure*,' agreed Henry, 'creaking doors last the longest, I've been told ... Do you know Robert de Vere?' He indicated the young Earl of Oxford.

'N-no,' stammered Richard as Robert de Vere took his hand in a warm firm grasp with the words, 'You will know me next time — and I hope it'll be soon, for I've always wanted to know *you*!'

Richard was flattered; he blushed to the roots of his hair, and hopefully thought that at last he had found a friend, one who had wanted to know him and wouldn't despise him for beating him at chess — even if, like Henry, he played without a queen — and also because he couldn't joust, at any rate not yet. But he *would* joust when his mother would let him ride a younger and more mettlesome horse than his dear old Blanchette, and if this Robert de Vere would be allowed to visit him at Berkhamsted ...

He surprised himself by saying, and with no stammer, 'Yes, I hope next time *will* be soon. Perhaps you'll come and visit me — us — my mother and me, at our home in … wait, there *is* my mother!'

She was talking to a rather stout lady in the customary purple and black, her neck encircled with jewels and, despite her Court mourning, diamonds sparkled all over her corsage; she had very pink cheeks, very bright gold hair, and Richard noticed that, in speaking, she smiled a great deal and showed rows of dazzling white teeth.

'Yes, there's your mother,' said Henry, 'cornered by the Perrers.'

'Who,' asked Richard, never having seen this lady before, 'is the Perrers?'

'Alice Perrers, our senile old grandfather's Lady of the Bedchamber,' Henry told him; and both boys, he and Robert, fell to laughing.

Richard didn't see what there was to laugh at in the King having a Lady of the Bedchamber. His mother had *three* ladies of the bedchamber, but perhaps it was more usual for a king to have a Lord of the Bedchamber, like his father always had when he was at home in Berkhamsted.

He made for his mother and, politely apologising to 'the Lady Ferrers': 'Excuse me, Madame, if I interrupt, but — Mother, may Robert de Vere come and visit us at Berkhamsted?'

It would be the first of many visits from Robert to Berkhamsted, and the beginning of a lifelong friendship between King Richard and the Earl of Oxford.

The day before Richard returned home with his mother, he was again commanded by his grandfather to attend him at Westminster Palace. It was Sir Guichard now who accompanied him to the King's private apartments and who told him, 'You must remember that the King is very old and although he has been a great and mighty monarch and a courageous leader of his armies, under whom I had the honour to serve, you must understand that he is now in his declining years, so that if you find his conversation a trifle, er, confused and difficult to follow, it is because he is somewhat hard of hearing.'

Richard did find his grandfather's conversation not only confused, but so hard of hearing that much of what he said was not conveyed to the King, constantly interrupted by his unpleasant catarrhal cough and the promptings of the Lady of the Bedchamber, who was present throughout the whole proceedings.

To Richard she offered a hand bejewelled to the knuckles and with a great display of teeth not entirely her own, she exclaimed in a loud, shrill voice, 'So here we have our Grace's beloved grandson Richard, Prince of Wales! You may kiss my hand, my lovely boy!'

Richard did not much like kissing her hand, for the many rings pricked his lips as he bowed to obey, nor did he at all relish being called her 'lovely boy'.

She, Alice Perrers, was an endless source of friction between King Edward and his Parliament, and having gained complete control over the King in his dotage she was not only a menace to his government but to his sons, for after the death of their mother Queen Philippa, it was evident that the Perrers, the King's mistress, had every intention of becoming the King's wife.

After Richard had extracted himself from the lady's rapturous reception, 'So now,' said the King with his throaty cough, 'you know who you are and who you'll be when I ... give me, *mon adorée*,' this to the smiling lady, 'a pastille. This goddam cough — ech-ech — I can't bring it off my chest.'

The lady, seated beside the King's chair, took from a gold box on the table at her elbow a jelly-like substance and popped it into the King's expectant mouth while he sucked at whatever it was with much dribbling and the inevitable wheeze.

'So now,' he repeated, 'you know who you are and who you'll be ... I don't believe what they say of my son Gaunt ... What *do* they say, eh?'

This to the Perrers who answered, 'That your son Gaunt...' She wiped a dribble from his mouth and a drop from his nose with a silken handkerchief taken from her wide sleeve, saying 'Blow, my poppet.' Obediently her poppet blew his nose into the handkerchief while the lady continued, 'I said that Gaunt is like to steal the crown from this angel boy's head, but he won't...' So emphatically did the lady toss her own head that all her golden curls tossed with it, and one of them, held by a jewelled pin, slid along her very pink cheek. 'Drat my woman!' she cried. 'I'll dismiss her!' And leaning down to Richard who stood uncertainly between them, 'Always remember that when — God send, I mean God forbid — your precious dear grandfather is no more, *you* will be king and *I* will be queen to you, my blessed boy, and to me you will turn whenever you want advice and loving guidance. Never mind your uncle Gaunt of Lancaster who will try and take from you all that —'

'How old are you?' croaked the King, who had heard no word of this.

'I'm nine, Sire, almost ten.'

'I asked your name, not your age,' his grandfather testily replied.

'I'm Richard —' he faltered. 'Richard P-Plantagenet,' he shouted to the King's inclining ear.

'What? What's your age? How old are you? Can't you speak English? Where do you live? Who the devil *are* you?'

To which the lady soothingly told him, much to Richard's relief, 'He is Richard, Prince of Wales, my angel.'

'Prince of — how can he be Prince of Wales? My son Edward is Prince of — my handkerchief, woman! Must I ask you twice?'

Another handkerchief, not over-clean, was taken, this time from the King's sleeve, and handed to His Grace with more soothings. 'There, there, my love. I have bought you a dozen new handkerchiefs, finely wrought and for which you owe me fifty marks…'

'Fifty what?' Again the King inclined an ear. 'I asked his age — it can't be fifty!'

'Not his age, my pet. I told you I paid fifty marks — marks,' she capitalised loudly. 'The price of the handkerchiefs. You use two dozen a week.'

'The queen! Where is she?' The king half-rose from his chair and then sank back again. 'And why are you asking me for money? The queen buys me all I need. Where is she?' The aged dotard, retreating to the past in his muddled mind, searched the chamber with his old bleared eyes, tear-filled. 'I can't see her. I never see her … where is she?'

'She is here, my darling.' The lady fondled his blue-veined skeletal hand outstretched for her comfort. 'I am your queen, or as good as.' And sharply to Richard, 'Don't stand there staring! Can't you see the King is…' She significantly touched her forehead under the bright gold curls. 'He is not quite … it's his age. You must go now. You have tired him.'

Richard, thinking it was not he who had tired the King, thankfully prepared to go, and bowing before his fuddled old grandfather was caught roughly back by the Perrers. 'You must not go until you are fetched. You would never find your way out of the palace alone.' And, going to the door, she flung it open. A page kneeling, ear to keyhole, sprang to his feet and received a hearty cuff to the offending ear.

'The next time I catch you at it,' declared the lady showing her teeth, but not in a smile, rather in a snarl, 'you'll have a sore bottom for a week. Go now and find Sir Guichard and tell him the prince is ready to leave.'

'Is the King not very … or perhaps…' panted Richard, as Sir Guichard hurried him along many stone-walled passages and out into the tree-embowered gardens of the palace. At the gates one of the King's coaches waited to drive him to the Tower where his mother was lodged until he would be taken back to Berkhamsted. 'Perhaps,' he continued, 'he has lost his memory. He kept mixing me up with my father, and asking me first my age and then when I told him almost ten, he asked who I was.'

'The king your grandfather, our beloved sovereign,' Sir Guichard sententiously pronounced, 'is — *was* one of the most brilliant and spectacular monarchs during these last fifty years of his reign.'

Chaucer's 'perfect gentle knight' was disinclined to discuss his sovereign's senility with the heir to the throne of the 'Great King Edward', as his loyal knight and many of his subjects knew and still believed him to be.

'The lady seems very fond of the King,' Richard pursued. 'And she told me that I must always go to her for advice and "loving guidance". But why should I go to the King's Lady of the Bedchamber for guidance, and living such miles away from Westminster, while I have my mother to turn to for guidance — and not to her, a stranger to me?'

Sir Guichard stayed his steps, and as Richard also halted, gazing enquiringly up at his tutor, he said, 'You will always, please God, have your mother, the Princess of Wales, to guide and care for you; and also Sir Simon and myself, your faithful and loving mentors. Now here is the King's coach to drive you to the Tower, where Her Highness awaits you in the Wardrobe to take you back to Berkhamsted after these Christmas festivities.' Resuming his walk Sir Guichard told him, 'I have left you the transcript of a chapter in the first book of Horace, for you to render into English. We have already gone through it together, so you should be able to give me a passably good translation … Sir Simon and I will rejoin you at Berkhamsted next week. So, farewell, my prince.' Again the tutor halted, and taking the boy's hand raised it to his lips. 'And know that to none but your mother and your tutors must you turn to seek advice and guidance in Your Highness's good cause, whatever in the future it may be.'

Then, to Richard's surprise and not a little to his embarrassment, for until this visit to the King's palace neither Sir Guichard nor Sir Simon had ever treated him other than as a pupil regardless of his rank, Sir Guichard knelt, and bowing low to the prince, he murmured, 'May God bless and keep Your Highness… *Sed libera te a malo.*'

The Christmas festivities were followed in the New Year of 1377 by further honour bestowed upon Richard by his grandfather, the King, that he should open Parliament in the sovereign's stead.

The Londoners at once seized the opportunity to welcome the Heir Apparent with a magnificent banquet in the hope that his ascendancy to the throne would soon be forthcoming and so put an end to the dominance of the Perrers, the King's rapacious and detested mistress.

However brilliant and spectacular (according to Sir Guichard) the 'great King Edward' had been in the past, he was now no more than a senile dotard, regressed into second childhood.

In order to celebrate their joy in the hope of a near future monarch, no matter were he barely out of the nursery, the citizens of London offered an even more resplendent banquet than that provided by the King for his grandson on Christmas Day, when he had announced Richard as second only to himself, God's Anointed.

Never had been seen such jubilation in the City of London to the wonder of the hitherto nurseling, virtually unknown to those Londoners who homaged him with such an extravagance of food and drink that not only his head but his stomach swelled with many gastronomical delights.

Fountains of wine poured like water in Cheapside, where oxen were roasted whole, and those who still had room to eat a slice of beef took that one extra cut before passing out. Scarcely a man and few women stayed sober. As for Richard he, having had more than a taste of everything offered from oysters in aspic and neat's tongues to innocuous syllabub to say nothing of beakers of wine, while his mother anxiously watching, so one eye-witness amusedly had it, 'took good care of him'. As also did Sir Simon when, seeing his pupil stagger and fall in the midst of a dance of the mummers, especially arranged for the prince to take part if he so wished, and he did wish … to be picked up and carried from the revels by his tutor to have his head bathed in cold water and his stomach relieved over a basin.

When sufficiently revived to insist he rejoin the fun, an indulgent touch was reported that games of dice were carefully loaded so that the prince would always win.

As for Gaunt, suspect of conniving to seize the future throne of his young nephew, far from being the 'Wicked Uncle', as almost the whole kingdom including the King believed him to be, it was this would-be usurper of the Heir Apparent's inheritance had himself instigated that joyous welcome to the child Prince of Wales. Not only for his beauty but for his warm-hearted response to the people's loyalty did they pay tribute in direct contrast to the aloof superiority of the once magnificent King Edward before he, in his dotage, had become completely dominated by the Perrers. She was loathed by the Londoners who saw her pass in the royal coach, covered in jewels that had been held, as they thought, in safe keeping for the lovely fair-haired child they hailed as their future king.

Richard, well recovered from his part in the celebrations, was staying with his mother at the palace at Kennington, a village on the outskirts of Westminster. It was a few weeks after his tenth birthday when sounds, not of revelry but sinister boos and howls of execration could be heard across the Thames from the City of London.

Richard rushed to a window, facing the river and with his nose glued to the casement, for this palace of modern construction boasted panes of glass unlike the empty apertures of the grim Norman castle of Windsor and his manor of Bordeaux, he saw, approaching, the barge of his Uncle Gaunt. It flew the Lancastrian colours and its oarsmen rowed as if their lives depended on gaining the shore at Kennington, as indeed did the life of John of Gaunt.

In flight from a furious mob of his enemies in London, those who had always suspected him of treason if not of intended murder in his greed for the future throne of his nephew, Gaunt was seeking shelter in the safety of Kennington Palace and the apartments of his brother's widow, the Dowager Princess of Wales.

She had always shown affection for and trust in her late husband's favourite brother and comrade in arms, and loyally disbelieved the rumours of his treasonable motives against her boy.

'Look, Mother!' Richard swung round from the window to say: 'My Uncle John's barge is drawing up at our landing stage. I thought he was on his way to Spain.'

She had thought so too, and uneasily wondered at his change of plan since he had meant, as she knew, to retire to Spain and avoid the menacing discussions and virulent opposition to Gaunt's support of the scholarly reformer Wycliff. He had earned the furious opprobrium of the clerical administrators who abhorred this 'upstart' Wycliff's temerity in attempting to reform — 'reform', if you please — the traditional Catholic Faith of the Church!

Joan, beside her son, uneasily watched the descent of John from the barge, wading ankle deep in mud after the recent snows of February and a thaw that rendered the bank where he slipped in the slush almost impossible to find a footing.

The power of the great John of Gaunt, whose father King Edward endowed him with lands and castles in almost half of England, had been challenged by the clerics and laymen of bureaucracy and by their leader, William of Wykeham, Bishop of Winchester. He had viciously directed an attack against

Wycliff, and also against Gaunt. A staunch supporter of the Lollard Wycliff he had defiantly resisted the influence of Wykeham. Once a struggling clerk of all works Wykeham had been recently raised by the Commons not only to a bishopric but to the office of Chancellor. This, much to the disapproval of Gaunt and other feudal barons who saw in this self-made man of the people a menace to themselves, their lands and all their legal rights.

The fat was in the fire, fuelled by the hot Plantagenet temper of Gaunt that poured wrath like boiling oil on the heads of false administrators and the loathly parvenu Wykeham. That same ungovernable temper, smouldering in the dormant subconscious of the young Richard, would burst into flame when he, as the second King Richard, scorned or opposed those of better — or maybe worse — control in the affairs of state.

That for the future; for the present this child Plantagenet watched his uncle's escape from a murderous mob that had assembled outside St Paul's Cathedral.

Wycliff had a strong following in London and after continuous debates and discussions a trial was opened by his adherents before the heads of the Church held in the precincts of St Paul's. This was attended by Gaunt in support of Wycliff along with the Earl Marshal Henry Percy, and their retainers.

The bishops were divided in their admiration for the scholarly reformer Wycliff and his courage in facing the storm he had aroused; at the same time they were equally antagonistic to the barons, and Gaunt in particular for his support of Wycliff who defied the orthodox clergy.

The atmosphere was highly explosive; and Percy's aggression brought a final flare up to the burning undercurrent which soon became a riot. Gaunt and his satellite Percy were ignominiously forced to retreat scrambling through a jeering hustling crowd in St Paul's churchyard. The Londoners had borne a long-suffering grudge against the feudal supremacy of the barons who had taxed them dry of what little lands and money they possessed.

Pursued by infuriated citizens throwing stones and brickbats and volleys of abuse at them, Gaunt and Percy battled their way through a frenzied mob out for their blood. And blood flowed freely, not only from a gash on Gaunt's cheek but from the attackers' own injuries sustained by their fellow rioters.

The riot assumed its ugliest proportions with a raid on the Marshalsea prison and the escape of prisoners who joined in that hurtling crowd. Gaunt and Percy eventually managed, God knows how, to get to Lancaster's barge, while Wycliff got himself safely to Oxford.

Of this convulsive turmoil, Richard knew nothing; yet when he turned from the window having seen his uncle drag his mud-bespattered self up the slush of the river bank with Henry Percy in similar disorder, Richard was met by his uncle who entered, or rather staggered, into the room. The princess, with her son at her heels ran to meet him, her face ashen.

'Good God, John!' she cried. 'What does all this —' Before she could finish she was waved aside while Percy following Gaunt stumbled and bumped his head against the door-post; he already had a great blackening bruise above an eye and blood dripping from his nose.

'If you want to know what "all this" means,' Gaunt replied between clenched teeth, 'it means that our loyal Londoners,' his sneering mouth jerked out the words laying a hand on Richard's flaxen hair, 'who have adored this boy and all he represents, are in revolt not only against an intelligent reformer but also against me' (he capitalised) 'whom they want to have out along with my dying father and this one in.' Whereupon he retched as if about to vomit.

Richard hastily retreated; and Dame Mundina, emerging from a recess in the apartment where she had been waiting with two or three pages, came bustling out. To a page, 'Fetch me a basin,' said she, 'his lordship sickens.'

'Small wonder if I do,' muttered Gaunt. 'But I don't … See to Sir Henry,' he told her, 'he's in worse case than I from blue fright. He's more at home in the safety of Northumberland taxing his tenants than fleeing from London's bloody rebels.'

'And a bowl of water,' continued the dame, with a cuff to the ear of a hovering page as she leaned over the prostrate Earl Marshal. She felt his pulse, laid a hand on his head, and to the page who still lingered rubbing his ear, 'Go you — and all of you. Don't stand there gaping. And you, Highness,' to the pale princess, 'give me that flask,' pointing to a bottle on a small nearby table. 'You'd think the French was storming London, with me Earl Marshal in a faint and me Lord Gaunt in sick panic. As for you, my chuck,' this to Richard, 'go to your room. I'll attend to you later.'

Her 'chuck' sneezed.

'And wipe your nose,' she bade him, who obeyed with a damp and none-too-clean handkerchief. 'I'll have you to your bed and your feet in hot mustard when I've done with these two.'

Reluctantly he went as she called after him, 'I knew you'd be catching cold going out in the rain yestermorn with that de Vere boy, your hosen soaked to your trunks and you so prone to chill to have it on your chest … there, then,' to Percy, 'take a sip o' this.'

Percy obediently took a sip of that from the silver flask she held to his lips; and to Gaunt on whom she rounded, 'A drop o' stronger water for you, me lord, to brace you … wonder 'tis you didn't call out the King's guards to quell them ruffians better than a lot o' rantin' bishops … fetch me,' she called to another page, 'a bandage for me lord's face. He's bleeding like a pig.'

The princess came forward to assist.

'Not you,' she was told. 'Go to your boy and see that he's gotten to bed. I'll soak his feet in hot mustard and dose him with camphor. I don't want him chilled to his lungs, God forbid!'

As a result of her ministrations, both gentlemen recovered from what she had likened to 'sick panic', reclothed and, if not yet in their right minds were not too far out of them to discuss how best to deal with the city's disturbance where far distant howls from the racket at St Paul's could still be heard.

Their controversial discussion in the presence of the princess who stayed silent, not understanding half of it, was interrupted by a messenger in hot haste from the Palace of Westminster.

At once their conclave was halted by an urgent summons from the Lord Chamberlain to Her Grace, the Princess of Wales.

The poor lady, beset with anxiety not only on behalf of her brother-in-law who had become embroiled with an infuriated mob, but because of Dame Mundina's insistence that Richard's severe cold had put him in a fever, the princess, having read the Lord Chamberlain's message, breathlessly announced, 'The King! He's sent, I mean the Lord Chamberlain … that Richard must come at once … but he can't with his feet in hot mustard, and Mundina says … o, God, that it should be *now*! And when I visited him at Sheen only two days ago he was up and about and eating a pork pie, and him with this nasty chest cold!'

This coherent speech interpreted by Gaunt and Percy, their differences forgotten, they sought Mundina and found Richard on his bed, his eyes streaming from vaporous mustard.

'Up with you!' his uncle commanded, and to the dame, stubbornly defiant, 'Dress him. He is to go to the King. No time to be lost!' Then, as she continued to object, 'Do you want to have his death on your conscience?'

'Not *his* death, but one of far more consequence,' said Gaunt; and from Percy, 'Don't argue, woman! Take his feet out of that mustard. God's truth,' he snuffled, ''tis strong enough to kill more than a cold.'

'I'll not have him moved from here,' declared the dame, her arms akimbo, 'unless over my dead body.'

'Then let it be over your dead body.' Gaunt swept aside the loudly protesting Mundina and, ignoring the protestations of the tearful Joan, he hauled Richard from the edge of the bed where, in his shift, he sat dabbling his feet in the bowl of hot mustard water. He was dried, wrapped in blankets, and dragged by his uncle to a dressing room.

Mundina endeavoured to snatch him from Gaunt who, without her assistance, clumsily robed him in a crimson velvet tabard, one arm in and one out of his shirt, while Mundina hammered on the door that had been shut in her face, shouting, 'Let me in! He is not to leave here without me!'

In the haste with which Gaunt had dressed him, Richard — lost of a shoe and sneezing, coughing, noisily complaining — was bundled into a coach, and driven through pouring rain to the palace at Sheen where the King was in residence that summer. Seated between his uncle and the Earl Marshal, talking in whispers over his head, each time Richard sneezed Percy sniffed at a vinegar-sodden handkerchief and muttered, 'Damme if I don't get his (unprintable) cold!'

At length after a long drive through downpours of rain — for it had been an unusually wet June — they arrived at the palace of Sheen near Richmond. Richard was dismantled of his wrappings although still bereft of a shoe, unnoticed in the haste of his departure. But even as he entered the hushed chamber, the once Great King Edward, with a hideous rattle in his throat, breathed his last.

Those of his Household gathered round the canopied bed covered their eyes, heads bowed.

Uncomfortably aware of his shoeless foot, Richard limped to the bedside where a tapestried coverlid enveloped that motionless form. His long white beard flowed over his chest, and the bloodless Plantagenet face with its high cheekbones and two filmy streaks of grey behind the half-closed lids, looked as if carved from marble in the majesty of death.

Richard, his heart in a tremble, knelt; his hand strayed to make the sign of the Cross, and a voice in that silent room rang out:

'The King is dead. Long live … the King!'

TWO

When on 21 June 1377, in the fifty-first year of his reign, Edward III died, none mourned him save a few friends who had not deserted the victor of Sluys and Crécy, where his son, the sixteen-year-old Black Prince, had won his spurs. But the once-great King Edward was glorified in death as in his dotage he had been forgotten.

It was Edward Plantagenet's tragedy that his closing years were darkened by the shadow of his rapacious mistress for whom he had sacrificed his name and honour. It was said she even robbed his corpse of its jewels when he lay in state in the chapel at Westminster Abbey where they brought him to be buried beside his queen.

The eagerly awaited coronation of his grandson, to be held with unseemly haste barely a month after the death of the King, was to ensure that no obstacle to the succession should deprive Richard II of his throne. The suspicion, however wrongfully attributed to the new king's uncle, John of Gaunt, still rankled in the minds of many of the late king's subjects, who were determined that none other than the son of their beloved Black Prince should succeed to the Throne of England. They had suffered too long from a senile dotard's absorption in 'that bitch' as in taverns over tankards of sack the abhorred Perrers was discussed *ad nauseam.*

'Thank God,' they muttered between swills of drink, 'that he's too young to go lechering after a woman.'

'So here's to King Richard the Second!' gulped one, raising his tankard amid cheers from those who stood around the trestles, and a buoyant repetition of 'Here's to him,' from the landlord whose till was full of a whole week's takings in one night...

As for him under discussion in taverns, in Parliament, and the royal Household, we have no doubt he was far less jubilant at the prospect before him of kingship than were his future subjects.

We may believe that when with his mother he was lodged at the Tower a few weeks prior to the day of his crowning, he bitterly complained to Robert de Vere, Earl of Oxford, the one and only friend of his age, or near to it, who had been allowed to stay with him at the Tower on and before the dreaded day, 'Just imagine,' was the recurrent litany. 'I am being dressed and redressed, measured and fitted all day and every day by an army of tailors and upholsterers as if I were a window to be curtained! As for that thing,' pointing to the crown that had been left on a stool when found to be too large for the King's small head, 'it's so huge and heavy, they'll either have to make another or fill this up with s-sawdust or something so's it doesn't fall over my nose!'

With Robert kneeling beside him on the window seat overlooking the courtyard of the Tower where his bodyguards paraded, rehearsing their performance for the coronation, he let forth his fear of the coming ordeal.

Although ever since the death of his father he had been primed by Sir Simon of the future to which he was ordained, he had not entirely imbibed its full import until that moment at his grandfather's deathbed when he heard himself name 'the King'.

'I h-hate,' he told Robert, the stammer uppermost, 'the very th-thought not only of being cr-crowned but of being king. I don't want to be k-king of England.'

'And part of France,' prompted Robert, who rather envied him, 'and Lord of Ireland, Duke of Cornwall and God knows what else.'

'Whatever else,' grumbled the King, 'I'd rather remain what I am, just Richard of Bordeaux or one of those down there.' He pointed to a group of pages who so soon as the soldiers on parade were dismissed, had evaded their master to play at catch ball, 'than,' he continued, 'to be second to none in the kingdom. Who'd want to be a king, bowed to, knelt to, and told what to do and what not to do by a lot of fat-headed old women in or out of Parliament? Just imagine!' The litany began again. 'I am still being bathed in a wooden tub having my ears scrubbed by Mundina, my nurse. At least *you* don't have your ears scrubbed by a nurse.'

'I used to have,' Robert morosely remembered, 'until I was your age, when my father died and I became an earl.'

'Better to be an earl than to be me,' grumbled Richard. 'I'd gladly change places with you if I could.'

'I'll wager you wouldn't,' returned Robert, 'and I'd never want to be *you.* It's bad enough to be saddled with an earldom and estates and having to hear long recitals from my agents or sheriffs or whatever they call themselves who come to me with grievances of tenants and farmers and Lord knows what … But as far as you're concerned, you don't have to be bothered with a kingdom for another eight years until you come of age. It's eighteen for a king and twenty-one for me, yet I still have to sign papers and read long incomprehensible documents as I've no uncles to do it for me, and listen to complaints brought to me by tenants about their taxes. It's *we,* the nobles, who tax them while we go free.'

Richard shook his head. 'I call that very unfair. Why should the p-peasants be taxed by you or by what you say are — the nobles? Why don't you pay your own taxes? Making them work for you on your lands, as I suppose they do and then if you pay them you take it away in taxes. If ever I have a say in Parliament I'll not tax the poor, I'll tax the rich!'

'You won't be allowed to do a damn thing,' Robert reminded him, 'unless Parliament allows it.'

'They will *have* to allow it! I've been given a seal and have had to read all that tiresome business to do with taxation, but it doesn't say a th-thing about taxing the poor only about things like s-salt and — and things,' he finished lamely.

Robert nodded. 'Yes, they keep quiet about that. Time enough for the peasants to start rioting about their taxes like the Londoners did over that fellow Wycliff trying to reform the A. But you don't have to bother about your tenants — in this case your subjects — yet. You'll have to go back to your schooling and have your head stuffed with Virgil and Horace and Plato and all those old Greeks. Thank goodness all my tutors stuff me with is how to joust and fly a falcon. Your tutors never take you hawking, do they? No, I thought not. All they do for you is to fill you up with Greek and Latin. As for what I've learned from my tutors it has never got me further than Alpha Delta Beta ... and a fat lot o' use that is to me!'

'Which it isn't,' chuckled Richard, 'since it's plain you haven't even learned the alphabet in Greek. That's where we get the word alphabet from. Alpha, Beta, Delta...'

'That's enough from you, Master Know-all! What I've learned is of more use to me than transcripts from Horace or the Bible in Greek, which it never was when Jesus gave it to those dirty old fishermen — the apostles, I mean,' he corrected hurriedly, for he knew Richard took his religion and his faith very earnestly. 'As for those bits of poetry you write after —

very *much* after — Chaucer and his boring tales of knights and dames and nuns and all sorts on their way to Canterbury…'

A knock at the door preceding the entrance of a servant followed by Dame Mundina, left Robert's dissertation in mid-air.

'Here then, my chuck,' Richard winced at Robert's hoot of laughter at Mundina's address to her nurseling. (As if I were two instead of ten and King of England, he inly seethed.) 'Master Walter Witley,' Mundina told him, 'is come to measure you for your robe of state. 'Tis too wide, he says, at your bottom.'

'He hasn't got a bottom!' giggled the irrepressible Robert. 'He's flat fore and aft as a girl!'

'How now, me Lord Robert,' the dame gave him a withering look, 'leave him be. He's not half through his growing, and better for him to grow slow than too fast and too tall as a maypole as some I could name.'

'Your Grace,' hastily put in the tailor, with a conciliatory bow to Richard, 'I was alluding to the *hem* of Your Grace's robe.' And to Mundina, 'Off with His Grace's tabard, dame, if you please. We must have this robe correct. It is too wide at the bot — at the edge of the hem,' he swiftly corrected at another hoot from Robert, 'which will be finished with a band of ermine.'

Long-sufferingly Richard submitted to Master Witley's measuring and chalk markings in the folds of velvet until he expressed himself satisfied. 'And I will attend Your Grace, my Lord King, for a final fitting on — shall we say this day week?'

And on that day week which was the eve of Richard's coronation when, relieved of manifold fittings and cuttings and a final adjustment to the padding of the much too large and heavy a crown, he was put to bed by Mundina, tucked in and kissed by his mother, the tears running down her cheeks as she pressed her lips to the silken gold hair on his forehead, saying, 'God bless and keep you, my darling … O, to think that my baby, for you will always be my baby to me … is my King!'

'I d-don't want to think of it,' stammered Richard. But his last waking thought, as sleep descended, was: *Now I* am *king, to be crowned king tomorrow, I'll forbid that old dame to call me her chuck and to scrub my ears.*

He may have assimilated the vernacular in common use among the gentlemen of the Household and equally by the pages, since his ears, whether scrubbed or not, were never hard of hearing.

With the first rose-tinted clouds of dawn, on that sixteenth day of July 1377, came Dame Mundina, stealthily to approach the bed and look down at him who slept the sound untroubled sleep of childhood.

With a stifled sob at the thought that she must lose him whom she had nursed from his birth, she realised that with his crowning as God's Anointed, he must rule not only his kingdom but his subjects from the lowest to the highest, although not yet would she relinquish her nurse's kingdom. *He has eight years to go,* she told herself, *before he will be called upon to fulfil his sovereign's duties. Shame 'tis to wake him…* She wiped tears from her eyes as she smoothed a stray lock of hair from his closed eyelids.

Sleep-dazed, startled at her touch, his eyes opened as he asked, 'What's to do?'

'There's much to do, but first, your tub, my chuck.'

Which roused him, fully alert now, to say, 'I'm not your chuck!' Indignation sharpened the words. 'N-never no more — so now you know!' And to the page who entered carrying a wooden tub, 'What *you* g-grinning at? Who do you think I am?'

Not very sure himself who he was when, having been tubbed and scrubbed despite vehement objections, and mounted on a splendidly caparisoned gelding, the quietest to be chosen from the royal mews, Richard rode through the shouting streets to Westminster. Recent riots and turbulent unrest of inflamed citizens a few months before had sent John of Gaunt and Percy, Earl Marshal, fleeing for their lives to the safety of Kennington Palace to be sheltered by the widowed mother of this boy who had known neither why nor wherefore they had fled. Nor could he have foreseen an even more serious revolt which he would be called upon to quell, failing the support of his elders in authority.

His mother, her heart swelling with pride on this great day of days did not ride beside him, escorted by his bodyguard. She rode behind him with his uncles, Gaunt, Duke of Lancaster, the Earl of Cambridge and the youngest of them, Lord Thomas of Woodstock. But his own half-brothers, the sons of the Princess of Wales by her first husband, Sir Thomas Holland, were absent from this day of their young brother's coronation; they, both hardened warriors, were at the seemingly endless Hundred Years' War in which Richard's father had taken his valiant part.

The cheers and jubilation of the crowds hit the sky at sight of their beautiful child king. None had ever seen or heard the like of it within living memory, nor even in the knowledge of those who had acclaimed this boy's grandfather more than half a century ago.

This young successor to a once-great king, astride his tall grey horse with its scarlet and gold trappings and the jingle of its bridle bells heard only by those in the forefront of that sea of faces for the clamour of bell-ringing from every church steeple near and far, must have been likened to a sunny dawn in a frost-bitten orchard that had blossomed overnight, so fresh a contrast was this sprig of a boy to his senile old predecessor.

Details of eye-witness accounts have been preserved through the centuries to record this Second Richard's crowning. One may wonder how so delicate and young a boy could have borne the long traditional ceremony or understood its spiritual meaning; the taking of the oath, the Archbishop's anointing, the placing of the much too heavy bejewelled crown, and the dramatic finale of the King's Champion riding into the hall to challenge any who dared oppose their Sovereign King's right to be the one and only *Ricardus Secundus Rex*...

When all was over he, thoroughly exhausted, had been carried in the arms of Sir Simon Burley to be put to rest in the care of Mundina before the coronation banquet held in Westminster Hall. There was one more ceremony to be performed before the banquet: the creation of three new peers at the instigation of Richard's uncle Gaunt.

Sir Henry Percy was created Earl of Northumberland; Richard's youngest uncle, Thomas of Woodstock, given the earldom of Buckingham later to be raised to the Dukedom of Gloucester ... for Richard's undoing. The third peerage in the coronation honours was the earldom of Huntingdon bestowed upon Sir Guichard d'Angle, Richard's tutor, a title rightly or wrongly attributed to the legendary Robin Hood during the reign of the first King Richard Plantagenet.

Another earldom recently inherited from the death of an elder brother, was that of Tom Mowbray, Earl of Nottingham, a boy of Richard's own age who, until that moment, he had never seen and was to become Richard's intimate friend. He would have wished his much-loved tutor, Sir Simon Burley to have received an earldom, but when he asked him: 'Sir, why is not your name in the list of honours my uncle has given me?' Sir Simon took the boy's chin in his hand and gazing down into those wide-apart blue eyes: 'I have refused to accept the offer of an earldom,' said he, 'because I want only and always to be your devoted and loyal King's Knight...' As so, to his life's end, he remained.

This first investiture that Richard held in the Great Hall of Westminster must have given him his initial taste of power. Although he had bravely undergone the long and wearisome ordeal of his coronation he had scarcely realised the solemnity of his anointing which had made him not merely, as were all men, the sons of God, but God's personally selected Sovereign Lord, blessed by the Archbishop with more than kingship, with power ... yes, *power!* He, Richard of Bordeaux, hitherto unknown by the multitude of his subjects who, in the dawn of that day had acclaimed him their King, had been given the power and sole right to endow his fellow men with high rank and lands, the lands, of *his* kingdom! It must have been a lightning glimpse of all in the taking of his vows he represented and in the years to come he would be called upon to use: that God-given power, the Divine Right of Kings, for good ... or ill.

A gleam, a flash between a second and a second of illumination, as swiftly fading, was merged into the overwhelming present to be himself again, Richard — trying to catch the eye of Robert standing among his peers, for none in that exalted company must sit until the King should command them, 'Pray be seated.' Then all sat at that festive board. We know this was not the first ceremonial banquet over which Richard had presided, but that was when he had been a prince and not a king ... He succeeded at last in catching Robert's eye and saw his left eyelid droop in as near to a wink as made no matter; saw also that the Earl of Nottingham had surreptitiously purloined from a gold dish in front of him something that made a suspicious bulge in his cheek … *King or nothing,* Richard may have told himself, *why shouldn't I?* He did, and took, we may even suggest he grabbed, a stick of marchpane from one of the dishes before him, and even though a lackey was at his elbow with the offer to him at the head of that festive board of 'Larks' tongues, Your Grace?'

'No, I don't like eating the tongues of l-larks,' he managed to articulate while his own cheek bulged as did Lord Nottingham's. *And what have I done now?* he wished to know, seeing his uncle Gaunt frown at him and recalling his last instruction: 'Take nothing from a dish on the table, wait to be served. You will always be served first, and remember who and what you are…'

He had little chance to forget who and what he was in the two weeks following his coronation when he had to receive a succession of foreign diplomats and ambassadors who had come to be presented to the King of England at Westminster.

Robert, Earl of Oxford, was promoted to be King's Lord Chamberlain by Richard's uncle Gaunt; a gesture possibly devised by Gaunt not only to gratify Richard but to assert himself as nominal regent by drawing up his own honours list.

Unsympathetically did Robert listen to Richard's complaints of 'all this bowing and scraping from a lot of greasy foreigners. And how they stink of garlic! Breathing it all over me. Why can't you — now that you're my Lord Chamberlain — receive them for me?'

'Not on your life! King's Chamberlain my arse!' was Robert's inelegant rejoinder. 'I didn't ask to be your chamberlain and do your dirty work for you as if I were your chamberman — or chambermaid! Your uncle is only throwing his weight about as your guardian or — let's face it — your keeper so as to tell the Commons or Parliament or whoever's jostling to take over the regency what to do — or what not to do with you. None of them wants *him* to be regent because they all believe he thinks to get you out and himself in?'

'Why should they — or you — think that? 'Tis cruelly unjust! What have you against my uncle?'

'What a good many others have against him and his son — your precious cousin Bolingbroke. I've no use for those Lancasters. And as for you who smell nothing worse than garlic under your nose, with Lancastrian sewage stinking to high heaven, the sooner you get one of the Court surgeons to attend to your nasal organ the better!'

'I suppose you've been hearing what Sir Simon calls "the slanderous gossip of Westminster", which he says is like blowflies feasting on g-garbage,' said Richard, hot in defence of his uncle Gaunt.

'A pretty fancy, God wot,' drawled Robert. 'But don't say I didn't warn you.'

'I'll thank you to keep your w-warnings under your tongue lest it be cut out!' retorted Richard.

He had reason to heed Robert's warning too late.

Back at Berkhamsted life for Richard resumed its former orderly routine. Occasional weekly visits from Robert and a new friend, Tom Mowbray (Lord Nottingham) enlivened the monotony of the days following the excitement of his coronation which must have been a chilling anti-climax. With Robert or Tom Mowbray he would ride and now, under the supervision of Sir Guichard, the recently created Lord Huntingdon, he soon became efficient in falconry. The mews at Berkhamsted still contained his father's famous hawks, for the Black Prince had been a notable falconer. Among newly hatched fledgelings Richard found one that was to prove his favourite peregrine. She would come to his call and perch on his shoulder when he sat on the terrace overlooking the grounds of the manor; and would take titbits from him, a small piece of calf's liver or raw beef.

In October of that year the first Parliament of his reign met at Westminster and was opened with customary pomp and regality by the monarch.

If Richard were too young to have understood much of the long and for him tedious debates and discussions, he was certainly impressed by the powerful oratory of the Speaker Peter de la Mare. He in the past had outshone many of his contemporaries and astonished a committee of the Lords by his attack on the late king's mistress, the Perrers and, indirectly, on the King himself who had encouraged her in her extravagance, had showered her with jewellery and all she demanded, and grasped from the Treasury.

And now again it was de la Mare who, as Speaker in the new Parliament, finally obtained the disgrace and dismissal of Alice Perrers before she could have any possible chance to corrupt or intrude upon the young king's guarded privacy.

Led by de la Mare, the Commons determined to reduce or prevent a recurrence of the Court's former extravagance under the influence of the loathly Perrers. To this end they formed a council composed of the more efficient feudal lords, with a list headed by the Duke of Lancaster.

This was an evident attempt to dispel or at any rate subdue the current suspicion of treachery towards Gaunt's young nephew's Divine Right of Kingship, as hinted in the Archbishop of Canterbury's opening speech. Gaunt, however, had no intention of accepting any such appeasement, which he realised was merely a conciliatory measure from the majority of the Commons and all inside or outside the Court who chose to regard John of Gaunt as the 'Wicked Uncle'.

His unpopularity may have been induced during the last few weeks of the late king's life when he had declared the dukedom of Lancaster a Palatinate and had rendered to Gaunt not only the administration of the County of Lancaster but the feudal rents therefrom. In addition, the dying Edward III had been persuaded by his son to give him almost half his kingdom. The heir to these manifold gifts was Gaunt's son Henry Bolingbroke, to whom these great powers and privileges would eventually pass as a curtain raiser to the tragic drama of this second King Richard's life.

Small wonder that the name of Gaunt stank in the aristocratic nostrils of his peers as much as in the sewerage or, as Froissart puts it, *the Servage of the Villeins* who serviced the lords of the lands and hoarded the grievances of those who sooner or later would rise to leave a poignant and lasting impression in the pages of history.

When offered this untasty *bonne bouche* from the Commons in the hope of disguising their hostility to him who had caused, as Sir Simon told Richard, 'much slanderous gossip', Gaunt determined to refuse it and openly to deny any such unwarranted and totally unjust accusations. To Richard's embarrassment his 'Wicked Uncle' fell upon his knees before the enthroned boy king and in a loud impassioned speech implored his nephew to 'hear the defence of my honour and my challenge to all those who accuse me of what amounts to treason to you, my nephew and my king! I now swear before God that never in word or thought have I harboured any treacherous intent but have endeavoured in my love and loyalty to the son of my noble and heroic brother to fulfil that which I regard as my duty in *loco parentis* to my beloved nephew and Sovereign Lord. I therefore challenge my accusers to come forward and openly confront me with their foul unworthy accusations in the name of chivalry.'

For Richard this dramatic announcement may have caused, other than embarrassment, a not unwelcome if theatrical relief from that, for him, dreary debate. As he later reported to Robert and Tom Mowbray, both vastly entertained and regretful since, although they were peers, they were minors and had no word in the proceedings and were not yet among the lords and prelates who, when Gaunt flung in their faces this staggering gauntlet, he said, 'They were only trying to excuse themselves —'

'"Of feasting", as your Sir Simon so prettily put it,' interposed Robert, '"like blowflies on a garbage heap".'

Tom Mowbray chortled approval and added: 'If I were king,' (he had not yet become accustomed to being a peer,) 'I would have them all out, I'd dissolve them — I believe that's what it's called when a king throws out his government. I'd not have them insult my uncle if I had one.'

'I may be a king,' said Richard glumly, 'but I've no more to do with the government of my kingdom than if I were *this.*" He stooped to lift in his arms a greyhound puppy, a gift from his head groom who had chosen the best of his bitch's litter to give him.

'Well,' Robert yawned, 'I've had enough of Parliament's rights — or wrongs — which, thank God, I've naught as yet to do with them, so let's go hawking.'

Across the Channel, Froissart, that indefatigable scribe, was watching the boy King of England who in a few more years might follow in the victorious steps of his late father. Froissart and France had reason enough to watch him and wonder if he would achieve the splendid successes as warrior in parity with those two elder Plantagenets, his grandfather and father, during the ceaseless wars between their two countries.

As for Richard, his early years of monarchy must have been as uneventful as they were boring to him, only just beginning to understand the significance of his birthright.

His life was one of isolation and monotony, save for the occasional visits of Robert de Vere or Tom Mowbray, since Tom, who was also undergoing strict tutelage at his home in Nottinghamshire, could seldom come to Berkhamsted.

Richard rarely left the precincts of his acreage, where accompanied by his dog he would wander alone but guarded at a distance by watchful servants and one or other of his tutors. Never must their precious charge be left to a possible chance of importunate intruders or exposed to his uncle's intentions whether fair or foul towards the child whose throne half the country unjustly believed to be threatened.

Yet when Richard rode into or out of the village he had no inkling of suspicion rife among his subjects or his relatives. His mother, devoted as she was to her youngest and best beloved son, had not yet reached the age when the gaiety of Court life had ceased to attract her nor, as the once 'Fair Maid of Kent', if no longer a maid, still preferred the admiration of the men who sought her in the Palace of Westminster to the homage of and gaping stares of Berkhamsted's squires or bumpkins.

Richard's early paintings, in which he would endeavour to recapture the brilliant green of April, his favourite springtime month, often represented the familiar landscape of his almost solitary rides or his strolls along country lanes with his dog. And he would frequently complain against 'this scurvy trick of fate when God — or the devil — caused me to be born, or at least to have made me a king … I have no liberty or free will. Why you, Matt,' (short for Matthew the pup, now full grown) 'are less watched over than I…'

He would stay his steps and gaze up at the sky as if he addressed God in his heaven while Matt adoringly gazed up at him, and resuming his walk, or his ride, he would pass youngsters at their games on the village green and would envy them their gleeful shouts as they chased or rough and tumbled each other in their play and — miserably — would see how they stopped when they saw him and would doff their caps and bow while the girls bobbed in curtsies. And as with a jerky inclination of his head he acknowledged their recognition of him, their king, he was reminded how different *his* life was from theirs.

I'm as much a prisoner here in my home, he would tell himself, *as if I were in the Tower…*

Sometimes when loneliness beset him as he rode in his park where he knew every tree, every bush, every landmark, he would cry aloud to startle the grazing deer, 'God! Why can't you let me be born again as other boys? Why have I nothing to look forward to except incessant bowing and scraping, even from the village lads no older than I? And when I have to go to Westminster — too often if only once a year — I get the same bowing and scraping and meaningless polite "Your Grace this" or "Your Grace that", as if anything they had decided upon to do with Government or Parliament was worth less than a fiddler's bitch to me!' And where could he have learned that singular expression, unless from remarks of groomsmen overheard when he ventured to sneak into his stables to see the horses or to give his own dearly loved Blanchette a titbit?

'I know,' he would soliloquise for, failing audience other than Matt, he would often talk to himself, 'that my father wished I were more like my brother who died before I could remember him, because he — Edward — was what my father, the nation's hero, called a born warrior and I'm just a nobody who hates war and killing men to win great battles. I *hate* war and I hate myself for being what I am. And what am I? A nonentity, and although I've been crowned king I'm no more a king — at least not for five years ahead — than are you, Matt, d'you see?'

If Matt saw, the only sympathy he could offer was to lick the hand Richard had clenched at his side in exasperation at his unhappy lot.

So we have it that Richard's minority was bleak enough to wish himself anything other than the lonely boy whose desire for his life to end might not have been unreasonable in widowed, friendless and childless old age, yet was surely exceptional in a boy of thirteen with his whole life and a kingdom before him? But as a sudden sun-flash in a storm-clouded sky came unexpected relief from the daily monotonous routine of tutelage....

It was Sir Simon who informed him of the serious economic crisis that Froissart had observed and gloomily predicted *great mischief and rebellion among the common people*, by which England *might be lost without recovery*...

Of this prophetic doom Richard's government had little or no suspicion until it was too late to prevent the disaster that, like some torrential undercurrent, upsurged to flood the land as if with a tremendous tidal wave. And but for the fearless courage of a boy scarcely known save by name and seldom seen by the common people, Froissart's doom might irrevocably have fallen upon the King and his threatened kingdom...

He was as usual in his study at Berkhamsted on a wan grey morning in the autumn of 1380, engaged upon a translation into the original Greek from the second chapter of St Luke's Gospel, when his tutor bade him, 'Put aside your transcript, Richard. I have somewhat of importance to tell you which is directly of your concern. It is incumbent upon me,' he sententiously continued, 'to inform you of the precarious condition that threatens the country due to the third and bitterly resented poll tax.'

'What is a poll tax, sir?' Not that Richard was a-thirst for knowledge, but glad of any opportunity to postpone or evade the dreary morning's work on St Luke; the appalling spelling of his Greek had already caused confusing erasions in blue chalk by Sir Simon on his parchment.

'I will explain that to you later. I am remiss,' an anxious frown appeared between Sir Simon's grizzled eyebrows, 'not to have enlightened you before now, for despite your youth —'

Why do you and everyone keep dinning into me my youth? said Richard; but this he did not say aloud. What he did say was, 'No one has yet enlightened me, not you, sir, nor Sir G-Guichard — I mean Lord Huntingdon — on anything to do with the country which is mine — my k-kingdom in which I am no more use than a fiddler's bitch!'

'Richard!' Sir Simon rapped a ruler on the table littered with scribbled parchment wherein occurred at frequent intervals erroneous ill-spelled words and verbs in Greek. 'How and where,' demanded the shocked Sir Simon, 'can you have learned such a vulgar expression?'

'In the course of conversation, sir,' was the reply with an upward glance of cherubic innocence.

In truth Richard had of late endeavoured not only to overcome his stammer that might account for the perpetual reminder from his elders of his youth, but also more colloquially to adapt his speech as spoken by stable boys on his visits to the horses, if with no intent to horrify his tutors at least to make him feel less different from others of his age, even were they village boys training to be grooms.

'You forget to whom you speak out of your turn,' Sir Simon told him sternly. 'I was about to say that Lord Oxford in his capacity of Lord Chamberlain has been advised by me to prepare you of the parlous condition of your kingdom's exchequer which, although I consider him too young for the office of Lord Chamberl —'

'Youth seemingly,' came the gentle interruption, 'is an offence, sir, is it not?'

This query brought another rap of the ruler, narrowly escaping the pupil's knuckles, and was withdrawn in time to save the vexed knight from assault that could, in the letter of the law as applied to the sovereign, be considered treason.

'I was about to say, if I am permitted to speak in my turn and not yours,' achieved with an effort of irony, 'that Lord Oxford may have given you some idea of the crisis due to higher taxation which is reaching its climax with the third poll tax.'

'Robert did tell me that the Treasury, or rather the Exchequer which is mine,' Richard said, 'or ought to be — were I not t-treated like the village idiot — that the Exchequer is at rock bottom or —' mindful of Robert's quip a few years back when the King was being measured for his coronation robes — 'if that skinny old Chancellor Arundel has *got* a bottom — you see, sir, I'm not quite so d-deaf and dumb as you and Lord Huntingdon would have me!'

'I am hard put to it,' Sir Simon's patience was rapidly declining, 'not to set you five hundred lines for, let us hope, unintentional impudence. However, I am bound to tell you, after this much interrupted preliminary, that Parliament desires that you, having reached years of discretion at the ripe age of thirteen, should proceed to London as resident in your capital in view of any riotous disturbances or revolt that might arise, which your presence as monarch, should and *must* endeavour to suppress.'

Richard, genuinely interested at this belated acknowledgement of his regality in that he was desired to return to his capital to suppress *(fancy* me *to suppress what those stupid old fatheads can't suppress for themselves!)* was his unvoiced opinion of his government's inefficiency to deal with the revolt of his subjects as against — 'what are they revolting against?' he would have asked; yet rather than risk a rebuff, and having reached the 'years of discretion' at the age of thirteen — 'and a half', he murmured as he got up from his chair and made for the door saying, 'Sir, I am ready to leave for London now!'

'Sit down!' Sir Simon pointed to the vacated chair. 'You will continue your transcript of the second chapter of St Luke, and when Lord Huntingdon and I have made the necessary arrangements for your departure, you will remain here at your studies until further notice.'

Further notice, as Richard had hoped, was not immediately forthcoming; indeed some several months elapsed before he was summoned to his capital to take his place as monarch in order to suppress, as he had been advised, that which dangerously threatened his kingdom … Indeed in various parts of the country from the autumn of 1380 well into the following year, and in particular in Essex and Kent, the peasantry and many of the villeins were gathering in their thousands to declare their inflammatory propaganda on village greens and in marketplaces to protest against this latest poll tax that as a spark to dry tinder blazed to involve every adult above the age of sixteen. The previous tax had limited the age of the taxpayer to fourteen, but now this increase offered as a soothing concession affected every sixteen year old and over, every working man, ploughman or peasant and even the milkmaids who must pay one shilling to the Exchequer in lieu of the original fourpence demanded. Not even those who fuelled it, could have foreseen the devastation of the fire whose first fatal spark they had ignited.

In the early spring of 1381 it was evident to the harassed Commons that the third poll tax drained from the already impoverished peasants to whom a shilling represented a whole week's wages, far from aiding the Exchequer, looked to plunge the Treasury into bankruptcy.

The cities and towns were prepared to unite with the suppressed wage earners; and soon the rebels had amassed a formidable army that if it lacked skilled men-at-arms, had weapons enough ransacked from the manors of their enemies, the lords of the lands.

Their numbers were increased by the many ex-soldiers who, discharged from the wars as redundant, were ready to join the rebels whom they could instruct in the use of any such primitive arms as they could muster.

Many who embarked on what to them was an adventurous mission, even as the legendary Robin Hood who robbed the rich to give to the forbears of those who saw themselves enrolled in a similar vocation, gave wholehearted support to the agitators.

Among the gangs of beggars, mummers, vagrants, wayfarers, all sorts, there were many fanatical evangelists prophesying eternal hell fire to the damned who had brought honest wage-earners to the extreme of poverty. Many of these itinerant friars and priests were poor curates acting as chaplains to the lords of the manors on a niggardly stipend. The wealth of the

Church lay in the cathedrals, the abbeys and monasteries. Of some such priests voicing God's wrath to all who misappropriated the rights of the unfortunates was one John Ball.

He, the head and front of the uprising that marched in thousands throughout the eastern and southern counties, had a power of oratory which had caught the attention of contemporary chroniclers, including Froissart. Not that he at his vantage point across the strip of water that held England islanded from would-be invaders had either sight or sound of this John Ball, but Froissart was never daunted by the lack of proximity to any man — or woman — whom hearsay or eye-witness could offer evidence for his voluminous chronicles.

According to Froissart we are told of 'the imagination of a foolish priest in the County of Kent', and of this 'foolish priest's' address to the people going to and from Mass in Canterbury Cathedral.

To the 'good people of England', he spoke of 'matters that goeth not well to pass until we may all be united together and the Lords be no greater masters than we'.

Was this the first inception of Tom Paine's battle cry, *The Rights of Man,* four centuries later?

Ball goes on to remind his listeners who surrounded him where he stood in the Cathedral's close that, 'We all come from the same father and mother, Adam and Eve…'

His loud-voiced oratory reached the ears not only of his crowded spectators but of the Archbishop at the window of his palace. Shockingly dismayed at these incendiary utterances from the vehemence of this down-at-heel and out-at-elbows priest, much of what he heard he stored for future reference and chastisement.

'Who can say that the lords be no greater masters than we who labour for them and are kept in servage at a pitiable wage or no wage at all? Does not our Lord Jesus tell us that every labourer is worthy of his hire? And what is *your* hire? This dastardly poll tax of one shilling for all men and women over the age of sixteen? You go in the poorest of rags,' the Archbishop ragefully heard, whose rubicund face may have rapidly resembled an albino beetroot, 'while your masters are clothed in purple and fine linen, in velvet and furs ... They drink wine and eat good bread while we drink water and are forced to eat rye, bran, or straw...'

We can assume that more than good bread was eaten at the lavish board of the Archbishop, and at the equally well laden tables of lords of the manors. As for wine only the choicest Rhenish, Burgundy and other luscious fruits of the grape were imbibed by the nobles — and the Archbishop — while lesser mortals drank water according to John Ball.

It is certain that water may not always have contented him during his mission which covered all the southern counties where the oppressed suffered, as did the whole country whose labourers were 'bondsmen', a favourite expression of the ubiquitous Ball.

This 'foolish priest's' virulent denunciation of those he named their 'Masters' who, if the bondsmen did not readily serve them, would have them flogged and their wretched wage confiscated to swell their coffers...

'There be none to whom we can complain,' vociferated Ball, 'and none will hear us nor do us right ... But we have a king. We know he is young, yet let us go to our king and show him what slaves we be, and let all peoples in bondage follow me that when the King shall see us we will be made *free*!'

This was the first mention of the King in Ball's speechifying and it is possible that many insurgents did not know the name of their king, nor that he was young, since only their elders knew of an aged monarch who had reigned for fifty years. Indeed few younger than forty could have known of the existence of the present sovereign. He had been kept in strict seclusion seen only by a small majority of country folk and the citizens of London who had watched him ride through the welcoming streets of his capital to his crowning, not five years since.

Ball's suggestion that his followers should take their grievances and themselves to the King was met with uproarious approval and triggered off that vast army of rebels, estimated at some sixty thousand as they marched in massed formation of four or six abreast along the King's highways.

Incited by John Ball they were joined by many inhabitants of towns and villages, each voicing their infuriated outcry against the hated third poll tax.

The Peasants' Revolt had begun.

THREE

News travelled slowly in those days and while the fisher-folk and impoverished labourers of Essex were the first to take arms of whatever primitive sort they could lay hands on, they were soon outnumbered by the men of Kent, desperately prepared — if needs must — to raise no bloodless revolution, but a bloody one!

Sir Simon Burley and his fellow tutor in charge of the King decided that Richard should be taken away from Berkhamsted at once. 'These ruffians,' Sir Simon told Huntingdon (the former Sir Guichard), 'are ransacking and pillaging all manor houses along the road to London. Richard should and must be in London and at the Tower. You may remember that barely a year ago Parliament insisted that Richard, having (ironically) reached years of discretion, at the age of thirteen should take upon himself his monarchical responsibilities. But now —'

'Yes, now,' interrupted Huntingdon, 'I think, if put to the test, he would assume his sovereignty to better purpose than do those who call themselves his regents.'

'All and sundry,' Sir Simon sourly remarked, 'excluding his Uncle Gaunt who, by right of heritage as second to his brother, the late Prince of Wales, should have been joint regent with the Princess of Wales.'

'There is no nominal regent,' agreed Huntingdon. 'The care of the King, no longer in his nonage, has been given to us, and I — we — have no wish to relinquish our charge. Yet it is evident he should be in his capital and not here, although we are not in the direct line of the insurgents' march to London.'

'I hear they are already at Gravesend,' Sir Simon said gloomily.

Not only were they at Gravesend but, joined by a Kentish contingent, they waylaid the princess, who had been visiting her two elder sons, the Earl of Kent and John Holland, both home on leave from the interminable wars with France and Spain. Realising the likely danger of her presence if not to her person to her Kentish estates inherited by her eldest son Thomas, both he and John decided to accompany her to London, a wise decision in view of the threatening hostility of crowds who followed her coach from Canterbury. With her two sons, Joan arrived at the Tower on the same day as did Richard with his two tutors.

If John Ball were the leader of the men of Kent, one of greater significance, who has lent his name to the revolt, was Wat Tyler.

There is no doubt his trade was that of a tiler, hence the name by which history knows him, but whether an outcast from an indignant father of some social standing, or a redundant ex-soldier from the interminable wars with France and Spain, who had joined the ranks of rebels at Essex against the loathly poll tax, has never been decided. But he was indubitably an inspired militarist at whose command men followed him as their captain, with his two lieutenants, John Ball and a newcomer, Jack Straw. He attached himself to the insurgents from Essex as they neared London. It is said he came from one of the northern villages on the outskirts of the capital, more likely the village of Hampstead where to this day an inn carries the name of Jack Straw's Castle.

With the two other leaders, Jack Straw was destined to end as a martyr to their cause…

The princess must have been in frenzied anxiety concerning her youngest son since, on her way to London we have it from Froissart that she was in 'great jeopardy' when an infuriated mob intercepted her coach, 'and dealt rudely with her whereof the good lady was in doubt they would have done some villainy to her and to her damsels'.

Shrieking curses on her, as none could have realised she was the mother of the King — or, seeing the coach with the coat of arms on the panels of the doors, they might have believed the lady inside it to be the wife of a wicked baron who doled them a pitiable wage or no wage at all — we can imagine a haggard woman with a baby at her breast yelling at the horrified Joan a volley of hate. 'You! Whore of Satan! You, dressed in the finery and jewels that are the devil's wages of sin, worn by such as you who've brought us to starvation! We who have to eat roots dug from the earth that we have tilled for you! See my babe,' (a skeletal pigmy) 'dying for want of my milk — I've none to give him, starved as am I and all of us, while you eat of good bread and drink wine … May God damn you to hell who tax us of the shilling that would keep any one of us well housed and our children fed on the fat o' your lands!'

Some such vituperative howls from the women, and threatening fists from the men, with occasional stone-throwings at the vehicles of the royal entourage regardless of the coachmen's lashing whips and the scattering of crowds by the mounted body guards, accompanied Joan and her terrified 'damsels' along the dusty sun-baked roads to London.

Richard's journey from Berkhamsted on that hot June day had not met with any violent interruptions, and Joan's joy at finding him safe and sound compensated for the horrors of those eight hours since dawn of that awful day.

Fearing to cause him further anxiety in view of the perilous conditions he and his Court endured while incarcerated in the Tower, including the Archbishop of Canterbury, Joan refrained from more than the lightest allusion to the cause of her belated arrival, since it had been expedient to take a roundabout route to the capital rather than encounter belligerent armies from all quarters bent on pillage, invasion of houses, or — murder!

Next morning when it was evident that the rebels from Kent surrounding the city were at the very gates of London, Richard for the first time in his reign felt or knew himself to be the ruling monarch — at the age of fourteen!

The thought gave him confidence to meet whatever his subjects, rightly or wrongly, might demand of him. He must make his own decision in this formidable crisis to judge if their revolt against taxation, the head and front of the offending, were justifiable. A shiver passed through him as he faced the alternative: to condemn them for refusing to accept Government's passing of this third poll tax, or that they must pay the penalty for treason — to the King. And treason, he knew, spelled death!

Six months before, when murmurs of discontent from the 'Common People' — as Froissart designated the persecuted peasants —began, the government, roused from its *laissez-faire* complacency, came to realise that any dissatisfaction — even if by wayside demonstrations from unauthorised persons, with their evil influences on simple yokels — might lead to a serious eruption and the necessity to acknowledge that the kingdom had a king.

The suggestion the year before to shift responsibilities to a fledgeling of thirteen had stirred Sir Simon tactfully to remind Richard that in the not far distant future he might be called upon, while yet a minor, to undertake the duties which

Parliament, 'if not comatose and snoring', he had disdainfully reported to Huntingdon, 'would choose to enforce upon him…' And now the explosion had fallen not only upon London but on Kent, Sussex, Bedford, from the western counties to the turbulent northern shires, spreading like an epidemical infection with the worst of it centred in the capital city.

The time, decided Sir Simon, had come to bring the King to London.

When on their way from Berkhamsted to the Tower, where the Court was already assembled, Simon tackled this critical situation with Huntingdon, while Richard, seated between them in the coach, feigned to doze and was all ears for their undertones over his head.

'This Wat Tyler is no doltish yokel. He has nursed his grievances, stirring them in a cauldron of hate, since the first of these infamous taxes was imposed even on adults — as they called them — over fourteen.'

'And from all accounts,' Huntingdon reminded him, 'there is another — or rather two of them — one a ranting priest, the other with the name of Jack Straw. He comes from the village of Hampstead and is, I believe, a menace. I heard of him from an old aunt of mine who lives there and is scared for her life — or rather the lives of her cats. She has four, or did have until this ruffianly fellow took and killed one of them — skinned it alive to make himself a fur cap, according to the village folk.'

'Oh, no!' Richard started up, fully alert now. 'If he's *that* sort of rebel who wants to see the King, well he'll see him for sure, with a brick in his eye as a gift from me for cruelty to a cat!'

'That's the style, Richard.' Huntingdon patted his shoulder. 'Have at the whole blood — the whole disgraceful lot o' them,' deftly substituting the word 'bloody', since only that morning he had admonished Richard for 'using so vulgar an expression'.

'It isn't vulgar, sir,' mildly had contradicted Richard. 'It derives from "by our Lady" as I have been given to understand.'

An amused glance passed between the tutors with the unspoken thought from Huntingdon: *He's nothing so soft as his mother would have him be.*

Nor was he, as the next few days were to prove.

The next morning from a turret in the Tower, Richard, with his cousin Henry Bolingbroke, and his closest friend Robert de Vere, looked down upon the hordes of men storming the Tower gates that had been barred against them by William Walworth, Mayor of London. Armed sentries paced back and forth behind the gates while those of the rebels who had come from Kent or Essex had straggled away from their leaders, massed three or four miles beyond the city at the Black Heath.

In the far distance above the Surrey hills shouldering the sky could be seen reddened clouds, the reflection of fires where the insurgents had pillaged and burned the manors of their oppressors, the lords of the lands.

'They burn our houses!' they yelled as they watched the mounting flames destroy their hovels. 'We will rebuild them for ourselves and our wives and children who go roofless, seeking shelter from the cold and rain in the hedges on the lands where we toil while a *shilling* is robbed from us by our masters to pay this bleeding poll tax!'

'*We* are the masters now!' shouted one, a sturdy giant. 'Yes, we are the brotherhood of man — all equal in the sight of God. Brotherhood, Equality, Fraternity!'

John Ball's rhetoric had not fallen on deaf ears, nor did he know, any more than did his followers, that he was voicing the trumpet call of revolutionaries in centuries to come.

'These fools,' said Robert in his lazy drawl, 'have no arms, only pitchforks and spades or rusty old weapons looted from the houses of those who fought in the crusades, as did your ancestors Richard, and mine.'

'Yes, the King, Coeur de Lion, came back to England before he had entered Jerusalem, to prevent his brother John from stealing the throne … I read all about it in the original French that Sir Guichard — Lord Huntingdon — gave me of one of Coeur de Lion's minstrel boys, Ambroise, who was an eye-witness of the King's Third Crusade.'

'You can't surely believe,' said Henry loftily, 'all that was written of the king they called Lion Heart because he was supposed to have torn out the heart of a lion that attacked him! All that stuff about your or anybody else's ancestors is simply folklore handed down by a lot of ignoramuses two hundred or more years ago.'

'Is it folklore that my ancestor, William Duke of Normandy invaded England and killed the last of the S-Saxon kings at the Battle of Hastings?' retorted Richard, incensed by Henry's scornful denunciation of all he had learned from Sir Guichard of his kingdom and its kings.

'All history,' Henry continued in his superior way that always raised Richard's gall, 'is founded on folklore … even the Gospels you are so fond of quoting.'

'Don't you dare —' began Richard hotly, and was interrupted by Henry as if he had not spoken.

'Pity my father isn't here. He would have stopped them from getting near London. He'd have had all those he could have caught, hanged, drawn and quartered. And if you,' to Richard, 'were to do what you have been brought here to do instead of standing there gaping like a numbskull and talking about your ancestors...'

'If your father *were* here,' Robert cut in, hot in defence of Richard, 'instead of lording it at the embassy in Scotland, he would find his head rolling in the dust on Tower Hill and the rest of him under the axe on the block! He plays for safety, as far away as he can get from the rebels who have asked for Richard, their king. They want to see and speak with him, and now he has come in answer to their call!'

'And what does he think he can do for them now he *is* here?' asked Henry with smiling spite. 'He might as well address a herd of grunting swine as to speak to that lot with his s-s-stutter!'

Robert's fist shot out, but Richard took on his ear the blow intended for Henry. 'Sorry, Richard! I didn't mean...' Robert knew that none must assault the King, even if he were his dearest friend.

'That's all right, Rob, 'twas my fault. I don't intend to parley words with Henry. As for my stutter, under Sir Simon's as-assistance I've got rid of most of it and have practised my speech to the mob, though I misdoubt me it will be as much use to them as the bark of a fiddler's b-bitch!'

Henry, retaining his smile, said with exaggerated mimicry, 'The rendering of your English — the King's English — charms me. Did you learn that d-d-delightful ex-ex-pression from Sir S-S-Simon or your c-c-cronies, the st-stable b-boys?'

Ignoring him, Richard turned to Robert. 'I had better go down to the gates and let them see me. They ought to know I'm here.' He dodged Robert's arm, outstretched to hold him back.

'No, Richard, don't go yet. Not until your brothers or the Archbishop can go with you.'

But he was already at the top of the narrow winding stairs from the turret. After him went Robert, shouting, 'I'll come with you. I'll not have you go alone…'

Yet even as Richard gained the last step, the mayor waylaid him. 'Your Grace,' he panted; he had obviously been hurrying. 'The rebels have sent Sir John Newton, whom they have captured. He is — was — the Governor of Rochester Castle. They have taken the castle and are holding Sir John as hostage. They send him with a message to Your Grace that they will see none but the King … Sir John is here.'

He drew aside as Sir John Newton came forward. Well known at Court, he had fought with the Black Prince at Najara. Having ridden non-stop from the rebels' camp, stationed at a place on the banks of the Thames between Greenwich and Rotherhithe, he was hot, dusty and dishevelled; his fine clothes torn and soiled from rough handling.

'Your Grace, the rebels have sent me from their camp on the banks of the Thames, but thousands of their followers are massed at the Black Heath.' And, kneeling at the feet of Richard who stood at the foot of the turret stairs, he bowed his head. 'Your Grace, my Lord! I beg forgiveness for having brought this unpardonable message from the leaders of the revolt. They seized me at Rochester, captured the castle and brought me chained and fettered to the Black Heath where they hold me as hostage, also my wife and family, until I have Your Grace's assurance that you will speak with them. They rode with me to the Tower — guarded against my escape. I am assured — if their word is to be trusted — that my Lord King will come to no harm. Will Your Grace return with me — and them — to the Heath?'

'Of course.' And to the mayor, standing behind him and in a state of acute unease: 'Please to fetch Sir John Standish' (his gentleman-in-waiting), 'and tell him to bring my servant with riding clothes and my groom with my horse.'

'Indeed, Your Grace,' said the mayor, in a panic at this ready agreement to accompany the rebels' hostage. They might well hold the King himself as hostage. God alone could know *what* they would do if they laid hands on the King. 'I beg Your Grace that you will not ride to the encampment outside the city. I pray my liege to go by barge and speak with them from the river.'

'Yes, Richard,' Robert put in his word. 'Do as the mayor suggests. It is a trick to get you to go with Sir John to their camp on that heath. Their leaders will be waiting for you to fall into their trap. They have sent some of them to the river banks to make you believe they are there with their leaders.'

'You are right, my lord,' the mayor agreed with Robert. And Sir John, rising from his knees said, 'I heartily endorse my Lord Oxford's suggestion and the mayor's advice. The head — or rather the *three* villainous heads of the revolt — are assembled at the Black Heath. But some hundreds are near here to induce you to believe that their leaders are with them. Listen to them!'

As he spoke, howls and shouts of, 'The King! We want the King … we are ready and waiting for him!'

'You see?' Robert took Richard's arm. 'It's a blind to get you to this black — or blasted — heath! Why is it called the Black Heath?' he asked Sir John.

He shook his head. 'I have heard among the peasants thereabouts — that the black soil and the thick heavy oaks surrounding the heath did centuries ago cover a mine of charcoal…'

Sir John Standish, who had just then arrived, told Richard, 'Your servant awaits Your Grace in your apartment. Also your brothers, Lord Kent and Sir John Holland.'

'I'll go with you,' Henry said; and Robert, 'So will I. We will all go.'

When the three boys came to Richard's suite in the Tower, his two half-brothers were there and Thomas, Earl of Kent, said, 'You are to go by barge, Richard. We and some of the Court will be with you — but not either of you,' he addressed Henry and Robert. 'You can follow with the others who will attend the King in four barges. You, Sir John,' to Newton, 'will remain in safety here in the Tower with the princess. The king's guards,' he said grimly, 'have dealt with your escorts, Sir John. They are held' — he pointed below to the Tower's dungeons — 'in the same fetters and chains with which they captured and brought you to the King!'

So far so good. The Holland brothers had conferred with Archbishop Sudbury of Canterbury and Sir John Hale, the Treasurer, and had decided that at all costs Richard must not be brought to the rebels' encampment on the Heath.

Within less than an hour the King's barge was sighted by the crowds on the banks of the river. Richard had been ceremoniously dressed by his servant under supervision of Sir John Standish. He wore a tabard embroidered with the golden leopards of England and the silver-and-blue lilies of France. His blond hair was bound with a golden fillet; the royal barge carried the King's standard. As he turned to give an order to the bargemen: 'Row close to the banks of the river but avoid the willows. I don't want to lose this,' his hand went up to the jewelled fillet, 'if the willows catch hold of it!'

'Pardon me, Your Grace,' Archbishop Sudbury intervened. 'I advise you to order the bargemen to keep to the centre of the river.'

'Yes, Richard, on no account must you go too near the bank. Stay within hailing distance of them,' said Lord Kent; and John Holland capped it with, 'I doubt if they will give you a chance to get a word in edgeways.'

From the massed crowd on the Rotherhithe and Greenwich banks a murmurous hum, as of swarms of bees, rose to an uproar as the royal barge retreated to the middle of the river.

'The King! We want our King! He will see us righted!'

'Answer them!' urged Kent. 'Tell them to go back to the heath and you will speak to them there.'

This was the first time and indeed the last that a king of England had addressed his subjects from the River Thames. As the royal barge plied slowly back and forth, those hundreds assembled on the banks howled their disappointment that the King would not land within nearer sight of him and to mingle with them. 'We must have the King with us!' they yelled. 'If not we will demand the heads of the Archbishop, the Treasurer, and all the nobles who dare defy us!'

'Come, Richard, you must return to the Tower.' His brother Kent must also have feared for his head.

'I won't go,' Richard demurred, 'not until I have spoken with them. They have asked for me — I can't refuse to speak to them. I must be rowed nearer — they will never hear a word from me here.'

'Make a trumpet of your hands,' John Holland advised him, 'and shout at them. Your voice will carry that way.'

Bidding the bargemen row nearer to the bank Richard stood forward in the bows of the barge and raised his hands in a cup to his mouth with the words, 'See me now! I am your king — and your leader. Ask what you will of me!'

His voice, loud and clear, unhesitantly floated on the warm still air and was greeted with a roar of triumph and yells of, 'Hearken to our king! Although young, as one of our own sons he will not fail us. He will see us righted!'

But the roars of triumph at having, as they thought, brought the King to them in answer to their appeal, were drowned in groans and hisses as they saw the royal barge turn and retreat towards the Tower, followed by a volley of stones, brickbats and a flight of arrows from those who had looted any weapons, old or new, from houses they had ravaged; but while they aimed at the escorting barges care was taken to avoid attack on the King's barge. Nor did any of the missiles find a target. All fell harmlessly into the water with no worse damage than fountains of river spray from the fall of heavy bricks or stones.

In the nearest escorting barge Robert shouted, 'Shoot back at them, Richard! Your barge must have weapons aboard — and tell them you will have them hanged if they dare to threaten —'

'No!' Sir John Salisbury, Knight of the Household, who was beside Robert in his barge, cut him short. 'There must be no retaliation from the King; they trust him. We must not betray that trust.'

'If I had my way,' Richard sulkily informed his brothers, 'I would go to them. It is not my wish to b-back out of meeting them face to face. I'm not afraid of them — they want me to speak to them. You heard how they greeted me.'

'Don't be foolish, Richard,' said Thomas Kent, the elder Holland. 'These fellows are savages. God knows what they might do to you if they can't have what they demand and are near enough to get at you!'

Followed by belligerent shouts from the masses on the banks, the barges moved resolutely forward; and when distance subdued the clamour from the crowds gathered to watch the barges retreat, that riverside conference, the first ever of its kind, was summarily dismissed.

So ended that fatal day of 13 June 1381.

FOUR

The effect on the rebels concentrated on the banks of the Thames, frustrated of their demand to meet with and speak to the King, at once brought a massive attack from the terrorists upon the King's capital.

This their momentous protest — not against their sovereign on whom they had set their hopes of freedom from what Froissart called their 'Servage', but against the government who had refused to allow them the King's support.

They who were encamped upon the Heath swept down upon the city in their thousands to join their fellows from the riverside, and as they marched they chanted their battle cry: 'To arms! March on! We will be serfs no longer. We are of the Brotherhood of Man, in Liberty, Equality, and Freedom.' (They had been well primed by John Ball.) 'March on and seize what is our right by the laws of God ... march on to *victory*!'

While the King, with his mother and his Court, were comparatively safe within the walls of the Tower, the vast army of rebels were gathered from the impoverished peasants and villeins of the home counties, among them many aldermen and sympathisers with the revolt. And they, who had been waiting for their contingent on the riverside to confer with the King who, as they thought, had abandoned them, stormed across London Bridge, bent on seizing the Tower and all within, including their sovereign lord.

Walworth, the mayor, staunchly loyal to the King, notwithstanding that some of his aldermen and many of the citizens were on the side of the rebels, held a particular grievance against John of Gaunt who had supported the religious reformer Wycliff some years before. And now, pending this calamitous crisis and the present descent upon London, Gaunt had wisely removed himself to the embassy in Scotland, for he guessed that he and his palace in the Savoy would come in for what the rebels were pleased to call 'rough justice'.

Walworth was uneasily aware of the overwhelming numbers that had joined the rebels from north of the river and were now in possession of London Bridge.

Conferring with the Holland brothers, whose chief concern was for the safety of their young half-brother, the mayor agreed with Lord Kent that since all communications from outside the city were cut off, these vast numbers of insurgents would have difficulty in feeding themselves.

'Let's hope they will starve,' said John, the younger Holland. 'At least we have enough here in the Tower to feed Richard and the Court.'

'Providing,' Walworth said grimly, 'they do not force entrance here.'

'How can they?' demurred Kent. 'You have raised the drawbridge. They can't get across.'

'Unless they swim the moat,' the worried mayor pessimistically opined.

'God!' The Princess of Wales, since the moment that Richard and her two elder sons with their entourage arrived at the Tower, had never left Richard's side. 'What if they *do* swim the moat? We — and this one here —' she hugged Richard close to her — 'will all be massacred.'

'They won't harm him,' Kent comforted his mother. 'They pin their hopes of the tax repeal on him. They are unlikely to go for the King as they will go for all of us. But we had best remove him to one of the dungeons. They won't go for him there.'

Sir John Newton, the rebels' hostage who had been safely housed in the Tower, came forward. 'That is the best course to secure the safety of His Grace,' said he. 'The king's guards are holding the rebels' prisoners below, and if the King is in one of the dungeons and in care of his bodyguards he will come to no harm. 'Even if they could force entrance they would be far too busy —' a thin smile twisted his lips — 'disposing of us, to search for and release our prisoners.'

'Yes,' agreed the anxious mother. 'The king's guards are holding the prisoners below. He will be safer there than here.' And to Richard, 'Go with Sir John, my darling. I'll have no peace until I know you are safe in one of the dungeons.'

'Good heavens, Mother!' Richard, who during this discussion had held himself in, now let himself out. 'What do you think I am? A cowardly cur to go hiding in one of my own dungeons? *Me!* Their king! And they have asked me to see them righted, and I *will* see them righted! I didn't *want* to come back here with the rest of you. I wanted to be with them — to speak with them! If my father were here would you believe *he* would run away from the enemy? They are not *my* enemies. They are my friends as I am theirs. They have asked me for justice and they will g-get it. Am I a rat to go hiding in a cellar?'

'If your darling father, God bless him, were here,' said the tearful Joan, 'yes, he would have gone to meet them, for he was a valiant soldier, but you, my angel, are no soldier, you are only a young boy.'

'I am my father's son! And although no soldier and only a boy, I am the King'. I take no orders from — from you, my mother, nor anyone. I myself will go down to the men who have asked for me and I will hear their grievances and help them to ob-obtain the justice that is their right. I'll leave no men, women or children to starve. No! Nor boys of my own age either, being made to pay tax of a shilling — a whole *shilling*, which is as much as twenty marks would be to us! We, who have everything we want — and don't do a hand's work for it!'

This speech brought from John Holland, 'Bravo! that's the spirit! You *are* your father's son, God bless you!'

His mother turned on him. 'Don't you encourage him in this foolhardy mock heroism. He is but a child. Would you have him sacrificed to these villains — and murdered, God forbid?'

'It's no sacrifice, Mother,' Richard said stoutly. 'And I am no child. I'm fourteen. Why, the Jews — I've been studying their history with Lord Huntingdon — are adults at *thirteen* and of marriageable age, so I am going down to the gates to meet them!'

To which his brothers, Archbishop Sudbury, and older wiser heads than this intrepid youngster's, decidedly objected. He saw not only an exciting adventure in taking the initiative against a vast army of insurgents, but was spurred by that allusion to the father whom he remembered had always deplored his disinterest in warfare that was the breath of life to the Black Prince. And now the opportunity had come to prove the mettle of his son ... *I'm not just the girlish nincompoop my father would have me be,* was his innermost thought as he asserted himself as ruler of his kingdom for the first time in his short reign.

To those who watched and heard him he seemed to have gained stature. The sun's rays from the aperture of the Tower room's window lightened the gold hair as the halo of a saint seen in the frescoes of a church.

Away with sentiment! the Earl of Kent may have told his inner man as he resigned this young brother to what he believed to be his fate. *The lad's a king every inch of him,* was his consoling thought.

And even while his elders had misgivings that he should take upon himself the monarchical duties of his realm, a message was brought by a rider on a horse stolen from one of the manors they had ravaged that they, of the encampment on the Heath, intended now to hold a conference at Mile End; they demanded the King be brought forthwith to keep faith with them according to his word.

The Mile End was an open space on the outskirts of the city where Londoners held their sports, and simultaneously with Richard's forced return to the Tower had come the direful consequence of his retreat. Howling vengeance on Archbishop Sudbury and all the nobles of the Court who held the King in their custody, they ran riot. It was a holocaust of pillage, arson and indiscriminate murder of any in defiance of their cause.

'In defying us,' they yelled, 'they defy the King! He is *for* us, not against us! We will take Sudbury and all such who oppose us!'

Their next objective was the Marshalsea Prison facing the Bridge of London; also the King's Bench on the south bank of the river. Both were stormed and raided. In the maelstrom that ensued with the release of prisoners not only from Marshalsea but from the Newgate and Fleet gaols their numbers were enormously increased by jubilant and murderous supporters.

The rebellion had now become a carnage of butchery, of bleeding corpses done to death for no reason other than they were out to vanquish the monstrous poll tax and the government that had passed it, of which the majority, especially the teenage victims of either sex, knew nothing. They followed their leaders like herds of wild cattle. The houses of the great and not-so-great, or of any whom they did not wait to prove were for or against them, were burned to ashes. A bonfire of what had once been the magnificent mansion of John of Gaunt in the Savoy that outrivalled in its splendour the King's Palace of Westminster, blazed to the skies, its treasures destroyed. The Manor of Hales the Treasurer at Highgate, north of the city, may have been Jack Straw's target, as it was a mile or two from Hampstead. That soon became a roaring flame, and the shrieks of those within it who could not escape their hellish death may have satisfied Jack Straw that the Treasurer was one of them…

No sooner had the messenger delivered the rebels' intent to hold a conference at Mile End and that the King should speak to and for them there, than Richard, hearing the thunderous clamour rising up from all quarters of the city, left the apartment where his mother and many of his Court were huddled in quaking fear.

Resisting all efforts from his brothers and those who sought to detain him, he cried, 'Let me be! I am in charge now! I will go down to them at the gates. I want them to know that I will come to — where is it? — this Mile End?' And he rushed from the room, banging the door in the face of Robert who ran after him saying, 'I'll go with you!'

'No! Not you, Rob. First I want to see from above what they are doing. I smell smoke from the windows…'

On a topmost turret of the Tower he stood and saw the raging furnace of his uncle's palace in Savoy, distinguishable even through the pall of smoke that enveloped the city. At a step behind him he turned to see his cousin Henry, breathless with hurry and furiously red.

'They have set fire and burned to the ground my father's palace ... It is *I* who will go to Mile End and speak to these murdering devils! What is it to you that they have destroyed my father's house and property — *my* house and property? I am the heir of Lancaster, and don't you dare to take from me what is mine — my right!'

'You have no property,' rejoined Richard, fighting his stammer to speak calmly. 'All of this kingdom and all in it is mine by right of my Crown ... Crown p-p-property. Anything you or your father has, is given to you by the King.'

'*Was,* you mean given by our grandfather to my father, his favourite son. *He* ought to have been king — and not you!'

'If given by the King, the King can take away. Your father and the lords of all the manors in the lands — *my* lands, belong to *me.* I am the King!'

He hardly knew he had uttered the unutterable, sowing the seeds of enmity between his cousin and himself, to reap the fruits of a Lancastrian dynasty. Yet it was as if he were possessed of some spiritual force that, although he knew it not, would rule his kingdom and his life to its bitter end.

When dusk fell on that flaming city, swarms of infuriated rebels were at London's gates. Despite the ineffectual efforts of the few of the King's guards that were not on duty at the Tower, Aldgate had already fallen to the men of Essex, who had now joined forces with the men of Kent.

Although the thousands invading the city were undisciplined, had only the crudest of arms and were unskilled in any military knowledge, Richard realised that the Tower and all within it were at the mercy of incalculable numbers of ruthless and savage hordes. He knew, too, that he and he alone was immune from vengeful attack. They had hailed him as their leader and their king; in him they put their trust. He would not fail them, but his heart was wrung in fear for his mother and his friends, who were powerless to save themselves against those thousands of insurgents.

The bulk of his army was in France, Portugal and Spain. Only his bodyguard were stationed in the Tower, and although trained soldiers they would be entirely outnumbered by the rebels should they invade the Tower which was their present sole purpose.

The lives of Archbishop Sudbury, his Treasurer Hales, and all who were known to oppose them, were in jeopardy. Any hope of escape diminished while the narrow streets of mediaeval London were filled with violent demonstrators. Even were military aid available they would have been powerless against half the kingdom's population.

After Henry left him Richard still stood there, undecided whether to go down as he had intended and speak to the crowds at the gates, or wait until dawn for his mission to Mile End.

From the turret he could see the camp fires where the marauders had settled for the night. The roar of multitudes bent on revenge were now replaced by hilarious and possibly inebriated choruses of triumph at having so far achieved their uninterrupted pillage and their intention to besiege the Tower and assassinate or take prisoner those within it other than the King, whom they believed or had reason to know, would act on their behalf.

They must have looted the wineshops and taverns, was Richard's not unlikely assumption, *and won't be in any state to listen to reason or anything else. Far better wait until dawn before I attempt to speak to them.* Having come to that conclusion he prepared to descend the spiral stairway of the turret and met his brother, John Holland, hastening up.

'We've been hunting for you everywhere,' he panted, 'we thought you had gone down to the gates, and when we couldn't find you there we believed they might have seized you and done God knows what to you! Henry only told us a while ago that he left you up here … he said you were threatening to do away with him and all of us. Have you taken leave of your senses?'

'No, I have only just come to them,' Richard said calmly.

'Does that mean you are setting yourself up to defend these murderous devils?'

'I am not defending them, and I haven't threatened Henry or anyone else, not even the rebels, but I must know what they want of me. There must be some reason why they and almost the whole country have risen against us — or against those who govern them. Not against me. They have said they are not against me. But it is a sort of war — civil war as it is called — isn't it?'

'*Un*civil, I should call it,' John said drily. 'Yet it hasn't come to that — so far,' he added unconvincingly. 'And although they have no arms, or none to speak of, some of our own people here in London and almost all the merchants and trades guilds are with them.' John took his arm. 'Don't go bothering your head about your rights and their wrongs. Come along to Mother. She is frantically worried about you, and you are of no age yet to undertake the responsibilities of your kingdom. Not that I don't agree that you should know what this ghastly insurrection means to you as King, but you are not to face them alone. We will all be with you.'

Richard shook his head. 'No. I *must* face them alone.' He swallowed a lump in his throat that had forced unshed tears to his eyes. He brushed a hand across them. 'I feel — proud, if you like, that though I am as you say of no age — that they should look to me for help. I am m-moved that they should ask me to take sides with them considering they know no more of me than that I became king when I —' he smiled crookedly — 'still had a nurse! I was barely nine then.'

'Yet you are still the youngest king in Christendom,' John reminded him. And with John holding his arm in a firm grasp they came to the apartment in the Tower where their mother and the Court were assembled. Richard found them in a state bordering on panic and all his mother's ladies in hysterics.

It seemed that some of the rebels' leaders surrounding the gates had invaded the lower passages, killed a guard and held another prisoner while they threatened a similar fate to Archbishop Sudbury, Hales, and any others whom they thought to be their immediate enemies.

'Which means,' sobbed Joan in tears of thankfulness at her errant son's return, 'that they will kill all of us if they can get in here.'

'They won't get in here,' Richard assured her. 'And at present they are all too drunk — at least those encamped outside the city — to start an invasion of the Tower. But I advise the Archbishop,' he turned to Sudbury, whose pallor reflected the horrified anxiety of them all, 'that you make your escape while it is still dark. Can you not go out by the Water Gate, in disguise if need be?' And to his elder brother, Thomas Kent, 'Tom, could you not go with the Archbishop — as his bargeman — and row him upriver to somewhere safe, rather than risk leaving him and others that are howling for whom they threaten to — you know.' He tactfully avoided saying they howled for the heads of the Archbishop and Hales in particular, if not of them all.

It is difficult to believe that the refugees besieged in the Tower relied on the courage of this one lad who had taken command of the situation that meant life or death to them, not excluding himself, despite his confidence that the rebels had declared they were ready to come to terms with him and none other.

The ruse by which he had suggested that Sudbury, Hales, and those incarcerated in the Tower might manage to escape, disastrously failed. Aided by Kent who at his advice had commandeered a barge at the Water Gate and although wearing servants' liveries, they were spotted by the wife of one of the Essex men. She was out for blood and had joined the revolt to vindicate the death of her baby from want of the milk dried in her starven breasts.

At once the fugitives realised that there was no hope for them. The woman had reported her findings and a body of vengeful rebels stormed after them. They got away through an underground passage where the river sucked at the moss green walls, only in time to prevent a violent death.

Back in the comparative safety of the King's apartments there seemed nothing they could do but pray for deliverance from their inevitable end.

Richard's attempts to assure them that they would come to no harm while they awaited the result of his conference at Mile End with the leaders, Wat Tyler and the others who were in command of the revolt, did little to persuade them that their lives were not endangered. The infuriated mob at the gates yelling for the heads of Sudbury, Hales *et alia,* did nothing to lessen their conviction that they would not see the dawn of another day.

Richard's advice that they should take some rest, since it was evident there would be no invasion of the Tower during the night, was met with instant agreement in the forlorn hope of avoiding escape from immediate death. Richard also needed rest, but was too excited to relax from the tension that had kept him keyed up from the moment he took command as king. *Their* king!

But Sir John Standish, his gentleman-in-waiting, who had unobtrusively guarded him while he was in the Tower, did persuade him to retire. Yet, even while he submitted to the removal of his outer garments ('so that you may lie on your bed, Sire, even if you do not sleep,' said Sir John), the door of his room was unceremoniously flung open to admit Dame Mundina, now the wife of Witley, the royal tailor.

She was in parlous plight, her hair dishevelled, her head-dress awry, her robe torn, her face begrimed as, between laughing and crying, she rushed at Richard, exclaiming, 'I had to come!' And with scarce a pause for breath she went on, 'They raided Witley's shop tore down bales of cloth only just bought from the Flemings those ruffians tried to detain me but Witley had got an old lance God knows how and pointed it at them saying he would drive them all to the gallows with it in their guts but they heeded him not and trampled on rolls of velvet Witley was making for Sir Guichard's new suiting — I should say Lord Huntingdon — found dead in his bed has been ailing these two weeks the doctor said heart but I say a fit being so anxious about you my chuck as are we all and as for you Sir John,' she turned to Standish, hard put to it as was Richard to follow this tangled recital, 'how could you let His Grace go out among those murdering devils and look at your face your chuck my king it can never have had a soap ball on it for a week my own neglected darling who I nursed from its birth…' Floods of tears followed this announcement with an instant burst of hysterical laughter.

'Did you say,' gasped Richard disentangling this much of it, 'that Sir Guichard is — *dead*?'

'As a door nail, my angel,' sobbed Mundina, 'and gone to heaven where none of us goes 'til invited, and now I'll to Her Highness your sainted mother. Sir John! Instead of standing there staring put his chuck My Grace to bed and not leave him here half naked, and him with his chest too…' And as she had rushed in she rushed out.

'Lord Huntingdon d-dead?' which was all Richard had grasped of Mundina's rigmarole.

'I fear so.' Sir John stooped to retrieve from the floor the shirt that the King, in disrobing, had let fall. 'I heard of it only yesterday, but did not tell Your Grace lest it add to your anxieties in all this turmoil. Lie down now and put up your feet. There are four hours yet till dawn.'

Although sleep was far from him while he lay on his bed, he recalled Mundina's frenzied account of the raid on Witley's shop, which concerned him less than the news of his tutor's death. *If he had been ailing these two weeks,* he reflected, *that is why I have not seen him since he left Berkhamsted with us. I did not worry about him because I knew Sir Simon had gone to Rochester to round up rebels who had raided the castle, and I thought Sir Guichard would have gone with him searching for others who … and I know that Sir Simon did take some of the guards from the Tower…*

Pondering sadly on the loss of his tutor, sleep claimed him at last and as dawn broke John Standish, who had been keeping watch beside him in a doze, was rudely alerted by Thomas Kent.

'Up, Richard!' he shouted as he entered the room; and to Standish, 'I wonder you let him sleep so long. He should have been on his way to Mile End by now.'

'Indeed, my lord, I had hoped to have kept His Grace from that dangerous conference. This is work for a man not a boy.'

'He may be a boy,' Kent retorted, 'but he shows more courage as a king than any one of us!'

'How right indeed you are,' was Sir John's trite rejoinder, and Richard, starting up from the bed fully awake now, cried, 'What are you two muttering about? Have I been asleep? Get me my clothes, Sir John, and my hosen, my trunks. Why did you not wake me? And my sword. I must have my sword. I hope,' he added slyly, 'I m-make good use of it!'

As the King rode out from the Tower on that Friday morning of Corpus Christi, having attended Mass served by Archbishop Sudbury, he was accompanied by Lord Kent, John Holland, Chancellor the Earl of Salisbury, Robert de Vere and others of the Court. Not until well on the way to the pleasant fields of Mile End, where a large concourse awaited him for the conference, did the rebels, who had watched him and his retinue leave the Tower, take the opportunity to storm the gates.

The few soldiers left behind on guard were powerless against the hundreds of bloodthirsty insurrectionists. All the previous day they had yelled for the heads of the Archbishop and Hales. Now they were determined to put an end to the chief offenders of their liberties, their rights and their 'servage'.

According to Froissart he recounts that Wat Tyler, Jack Straw, and John Ball, that 'prating priest' with hundreds of their followers entered the Tower and broke up chamber after chamber.

There is no evidence that Wat Tyler, Jack Straw or John Ball led those whom Froissart names the 'Gluttons', as the instigators of this raid on the Tower; not that they led the said

'Gluttons' to commit their villainous crimes, since the chief leaders were organising the final meeting at Smithfield where they had planned their ultimate victory.

That they were bent on destruction and the murder of any whom they knew to be their masters, keeping them in bondage all their miserable lives, was vouched for by Froissart. He dispassionately tells us: *These Gluttons fell upon Sudbury and Hales and slew them and four others and strake* (sic) *off their heads, also beheaded a friar, Master of Medicine to the Duke of Lancaster...*

Their grievance against the good old Archbishop Sudbury was that he had deputised as Chancellor pending the Earl of Salisbury's promotion to that office. John of Gaunt might also have been victimised had he not removed himself to Scotland, since he guessed that the rebels regarded him as their enemy and as the instigator of their 'bondage' to rob them of their livelihood in order to sustain the great estates left him by his father, the late King Edward.

Richard, aware of the murderous hostility held against his uncle, had left his cousin Henry, Gaunt's son and heir, with the princess, his mother, thinking he would be safer in her company than with him and his retinue at Mile End. He was mistaken: not only did the 'Gluttons' succeed in making a shambles of each chamber where they forced entry, they did not spare the bedroom of the King's mother.

The Princess of Wales suffered the terrifying ordeal of a ruthless searching of her bed. They dragged off the coverings, probed the covers with their swords thinking to find hidden traitors to their cause. Satisfied there was none in the bed of the princess to be murdered, they triumphantly paraded the streets with heads of the decapitated on pikes, and stuck them on the railings of Temple Bar.

Fortunately Richard did not know of the destruction of the Tower rooms, nor of the hideous deaths of the Archbishop and others, until his return from Mile End. By that time Standish had conducted the terrified Princess Joan and her ladies to the Wardrobe, where they were joined by the badly shaken Henry. He was furious with Richard for his refusal to let him go to Mile End.

'I suppose,' he fumed, 'he wanted to leave me here to be murdered.'

'For shame, my lord,' Standish sternly reminded him, 'the King thought only of your safety in advising you to stay with Her Highness. I and others of the Court were left here to guard the princess and yourself. This would have been the wish of your father, the Duke of Lancaster, well aware of the hostility these rebels hold against the Duke.'

It was estimated that about sixty thousand men of Kent, Bedford, Suffolk and those of the western counties, were massed to meet the King at Mile End.

Richard's foresight and initiative which, despite his youth, outweighed the ineptitude of his elders to cope with this formidable crisis, decided him not to take immediate action. Rather than surrender to the rebels' demands he would act upon a subterfuge.

Waving aside his brothers and his retinue and even Robert de Vere, he called to him, 'Keep back, Rob. I must tackle them myself. I know what to do.' What he did was to advance alone and address that multitude, many of whom were undecided whether to make short shrift of him, a potential enemy and the King and overlord of all who had suffered under the Sovereign's Right and Might. But at sight of that slip of a boy, his yellow hair a wind-blown tangle, mounted on his mettlesome charger — not now his gentle mare, lest she take fright at these enormous crowds — his first words in a shrill young treble dispelled any doubt of his intent. Never, in those verdant meadows reserved only for recreational sports or fairs, had been seen such a concourse of men and some women assembled to demand their rights. None but this lad had come there at their command to hear their petitions.

'Such a bonny boy,' murmured the women among themselves, wondering to see one so young to face them alone and unafraid.

'And pretty as a girl,' said another, luckily unheard by Richard.

Froissart must have sent his own scribe to report these upheavals in England as he was not in London at that time; yet he gave an intensive and, as historians of centuries later believe, authentic account of that conference. As Froissart gives it: *The king entered among them saying, my good people, you see me here, your king. What do you want of me?*

One who understood his cultured English that differed as in a foreign tongue from their rustic dialect, came forward to answer, 'We want you to free us from the lands of the lords on which we labour, taxed to our last shilling of the pittance we earn in bondage.'

Not then, nor until later did any of them know that Wat Tyler, who was absent from the preliminary meeting at Mile End preparing for his final conference at Smithfield, intended to take upon himself the title of 'Lord Tyler' and confer an archbishopric upon John Ball, 'that prating priest', while retaining 'Good King Richard' as the sovereign of England who, from that time forth, would be nothing but a figurehead, a king in name only…

'What you ask of me,' Richard answered, 'you shall have.' And with scarcely a stammer he continued, 'And as I am willing to grant all you want, I request that you return to your homes and villages and I will cause writings to be made in my name to confirm what I have said, and will seal them with my seal.'

A pause while he hastily bethought him of what he had so rashly promised. *No, I didn't actually promise, did I? But they must be got away whether I did or I didn't.* In any case he knew that whatever he had told them would have to be decided by Parliament and not by him.

His conscience eased on that score, 'Sirs,' he said, 'you men of Kent, Bedford, Essex, Sussex' (*and of hell,* he added to himself), 'you shall have my b-banners brought to you, and if you follow my banners I will pardon all that you have done so that you go back to your homes in peace.' To be rid of them at all costs was his chief concern.

This, 'sweetly spoken' as Froissart gives it, was greeted with cheers from the men and god-blessings from the women, and more admiration for his 'prettiness', and never mind that they had tramped many weary miles through the nights, footsore and starving without bite nor sup for hours, just to see and hear him.

So, in thankfulness and peace they went their homeward ways.

'Good for you, Richard!' Robert rode forward to tell him amid clouds of dust kicked up from the marching feet of the retreating rebels and the hooves of stolen horses.

Thomas, Earl of Kent, who had kept well in the background since the men of his county were in the forefront of the agitators, was disinclined to receive brickbats, stones, or any other token of their grievances flung at him.

'It is all very well for you, my boy,' he told Richard when he had watched the rebels safely out of sight, 'to promise them all they ask but do you not realise that if they are freed from what they call their "bondage", besides the repeal of the poll tax, it would lead, if not to the murder of all of us who rightly own our estates, but also the confiscation of…'

'What I have said I have said,' interrupted Richard, soothing his fretting horse. 'All's well, dear lad, we've finished with them. Home now to your stable and a good bran mash.'

Yet the concessions on the part of Richard that had contentedly dispersed the masses who attended the conference at Mile End, did not content Wat Tyler, Jack Straw and John Ball. They, with thirty thousand behind them, were assembled at Smithfield preparing to bring to its grand finale their revolution which would give their leaders full government and dictatorship of his kingdom and people.

Was this an embryonic conception of the maniacal dictatorship that, seven centuries later, threatened the destruction of England and the whole of Europe? If so, in successfully averting a catastrophic dissolution of the rights not only of man, but all that the feudal barons had persistently sought to sustain unconquered since the Norman invasion, it was due to the courage of a fourteen-year-old boy who had faced single-handed those thousands of desperate rebels…

Richard found his mother safely housed in the care of Standish at the Wardrobe, though not quite recovered from the horrors she and her women had endured in the ransacking of their rooms and the princess's bed. Walworth the mayor who had been supervising the ruins of the houses the rebels had demolished in the city, rode out with Richard early the next morning.

His success in disposing of the rebels at Mile End the day before had a stimulating effect upon him, and also upon his retinue who seemed to have awakened from their laconic — we must not suggest craven — attitudes to the dangers of the situation with which none but this boy had the courage to cope.

As Richard passed through the ruins of London to Smithfield by way of Lud Gate and the Inns of Court, he was met with the horrifying spectacle of the heads of his good old Archbishop Sudbury, of Hales, and others stuck on spikes at Temple Bar. After the first shock in sighting these gory trophies of the rebels' hideous revenge, Richard determined that whatever murderous risk he ran, he would seek vengeance on those who had done these awful deeds. Spurring his horse forward he cried, 'I don't care what the Gospel said — but vengeance is *mine*!'

Mayor Walworth caught up with him saying, 'Sire, vengeance rightly is yours, yet none save God Almighty can and will claim it in His own good time.'

Richard offered no reply to Walworth's mild reproach, but before pursuing the road to Smithfield, a market for horses and cattle, he turned towards Westminster followed by his escort to hear Mass in the Abbey. The monks greeted him with joyous thanks to God for his deliverance from the meeting at Mile End. At the Shrine of Our Lady in her chapel, Richard burned candles to the Blessed Virgin, and when his orisons were done he remounted his horse and rode on through the now comparatively quiet streets to Smithfield.

Henry, who was among the lords of his escort, gained his side as they passed the smouldering ashes of what had been his father's palace in the Savoy and: 'Look!' he cried, 'what those devils have done to my father's house and property! They, whom you pardon and send home to their dens with fair promises and your banners to be doled out to them with your documents signed and sealed! Lucky for me that I was not one of their victims as you doubtless intended when you refused to let me go with you to Mile End, knowing they would storm the Tower!'

'P-precisely,' agreed Richard with sardonic calm. 'I left you here to be murdered along with my mother, her ladies and all my friends at Court.'

'I knew it!' blustered Henry. 'As Lancaster's heir you know how these villains thirst for his blood — and *mine*! — and you also know that I — my father and I — are the rightful heirs to the throne for which that senile dotard, our grandfather, named you, as persuaded by his woman, the Perrers, because she was well aware that if my father, the King's favourite son came to the throne she would be flung back to the gutter where she belonged! And 'tis *you* who stir up this revolt against the Lancasters — yes! Against *us* who rightfully should own and rule England, which is *not* yours! You were not even born in England when your father was fighting the French. You couldn't speak English when you first came to our land — *you* are Richard of Bordeaux, and not Richard of England any more than is that Flemish horse you ride, a bastard born of a —'

At this, Richard's temper boiling, 'Hold your lying tongue,' he flared, 'lest it be cut off!' With one hand he reined back his startled mount and drew his sword from its sheath, saying, 'along with your head as those bloody swine have taken the heads of four great and honest men,' a sob tore at his throat, 'and one of them my g-good old Archbishop! As for you,' he re-sheathed his sword, "'tis not for me to ask God Almighty why he allowed those four — and one His Archbishop — to suffer their hideous deaths and not yourself.'

His brother Kent, having heard and seen this altercation overtook them, ranging his horse between the two heated youngsters. 'Richard, 'tis you should lose your tongue since it would seem you have already lost your head in this senseless brawl. Henry is justified in thinking you were too easy with your pardons and promises, which I hope you don't intend to keep!'

'That,' Richard replied coolly, 'remains to be seen.'

As was seen when, arriving at Smithfield Market just beyond the New Gate of the city, the King and his party halted, backing their mounts in front of St Bartholomew's church. Under the King's banners waving in the breeze, the rebels had massed themselves in those wide-open spaces, devoid that day of its usual sale of horses and cattle.

Richard, turning to Walworth, the mayor, bade him, 'Summon that fellow Tyler to me.'

With brazen effrontery Tyler rode forward. From its rich trappings it was evident that the horse had been stolen. His greeting to the King was a deliberate attempt at *lèse-majesté.*

Addressing him familiarly, 'Brother,' he said, 'you see here some thirty thousand of my followers. All are commanded by me to uphold our cause in faith and trust. And, in defiance of my orders, you have sent my armies at Mile End back to their homes with your promise to free them from your hateful bondage. Why then, young sir, do you not return my men to their homes with the writings you have promised to those others, and with the banners yonder?' He pointed to the brightly coloured flags bearing the King's standard with its gold leopards of England and the blue-and-silver lilies of France. 'Did you intend to send these thousands away with naught but false promises, and without your letters and the banners which you agreed to give to every house and village of all my trusted followers?'

To which Richard, with consummate cool, replied, 'What I have said I have said, and any such promise I have made depends upon my agreement to your claims. You have not yet p-presented me with any just cause for your rebellion against me and my kingdom.'

'Our claims,' returned Tyler, his insolence unabated, 'are not made against you who are king but in name and still a child. Aha! That pricks your pride, since you see yourself a man! Yet I grant you are like to be a better man than your own kind when you reach more years and can dispense with the authority of the lords your uncles, and others. Nor have we any wish to dispense with monarchy even a monarch so young as King Richard the Second.'

'That,' Richard said with gentle irony, 'I gratefully appreciate. Pray continue. State your claims.' A clock from the church's tower chimed twelve strokes. 'It is now midday and I have other and more important concerns on my time than to dally with your demands.'

'My demands,' retorted Tyler, 'are of more immediate concern to you than all else that your masters, who school you in your kingship, have any right with which to interfere. Hear then my claims.' He edged his horse nearer to the slim young lad mounted on his richly caparisoned gelding.

Richard, looking through him as if he were a window, noted the face of the man who dared take upon himself the leadership and governance of half Richard's subjects.

A rugged face was this, with a dome-shaped intelligent forehead, square-jawed, uncomely, but the aquilinity of its prominent nose and the firm well-moulded lips betokened a birth and breed superior to that of a bricklayer or tiler of roofs, hence his name.

'I claim,' said he — his voice held little trace of rustic accent — 'no lordship save that which I owe to my king, boy though you are, for I see in you a sensibility that acknowledges the drastic measures we undertake for our just cause as fellow beings in equality with our overlords, the barons, who have made of us their serfs. I claim the disestablishment of Church property to be divided equally for the benefit of the people and the brotherhood of man, as God intended when in His Son's name He bade us "Love our neighbours as ourselves".'

'Is that all?'

'If not enough,' he retorted, stung by the boy's quiet irony, 'I am empowered to claim more should those who rule you not agree to my rightful demands! I would claim not only the brotherhood but the *soul* of man as they, who destroy our souls, have starved our bodies and robbed us of all that makes life bearable, taxing us of the daily bread Our Lord's Prayer gives us!' He passed a hand across his throat and gestured to one of those who crowded close. 'Give me to drink. I thirst.' A cup was brought; then, after draining it to its dregs, what remained in his mouth he spat in the dust at the feet of the King's horse.

An angry murmur rose from among Richard's retinue, and the mayor, who had been fretfully chafing at the fellow's lack of courtesy, swore below his breath, 'God damn you! You stinking thieving knave!' so Froissart gives it. And spurring his horse to confront Tyler, 'Hold!' he cried, 'I arrest you in the King's name for contempt!'

'Do you! Then take this for contempt of me and *us*!'

Drawing a dagger from his belt Tyler struck at Walworth, who parried the thrust and with his sword sliced open the man's head. At the same time Standish, having left the princess and her ladies at the Wardrobe in the care of others of the Court, rushed his horse forward to stab Tyler to the heart. He fell from his saddle and was dragged across the marketplace, his blood reddening the dust.

His followers, although too stupefied to realise that their leader was dying or dead, drew their bows in one last effort to kill the boy who had led their enemies, the overlords, to strike down their captain. But Richard, dauntless of danger to himself, shouted: 'Don't shoot! Let *me* be your leader. Trust me! *I* am your captain now. Follow me!'

Tyler's thousands, standing in silent amaze at the courage of this one boy against so many, lowered their bows and, submissive as sheep, followed where he led out of the market and towards the fields of Clerkenwell.

Heading that army of peasants, Richard drew his sword and flourished it, calling to his retinue, 'Keep back — all of you! Leave this to me alone!'

Only Robert de Vere and the faithful Standish made to go after him, Robert crying. 'Don't be a fool, Richard! You must not —'

'Yes,' he shouted back, 'I must! I want none of you, not Kent nor you, John, neither.' His lip curled in disdain as he leaned forward on his horse's neck to gallop him through that surging crowd who were now his ardent followers, for he saw his two half-brothers had deserted his escort and were making for the safety of the Hackney marshes.

They fought beside my father in France, he told himself, *but cannot fight for these downtrodden wretches who have come to me for help … So help me God, I will!*

And now the mob were at his horse's heels voicing their pride and loyalty to him with yells of, 'The King! Our captain! God save our King! God bless him!'

He could not know this was to be the one great moment of his life…

A few weeks after that day of Corpus Christi in June 1381 Richard, kneeling on the window seat of his mother's apartment at Westminster Palace, had much to occupy his thoughts concerning less of the past than of his future, or more directly of his present.

Sun from a cloudless sky poured down where his mother sat at her tambour frame and burnished her gold hair, undimmed by the passing of forty-odd years. Below, in the gardens of his palace, the parterres of flowers spread a colourful mosaic between the green shaven lawns to dazzle the eye in that hot sunlight. But Richard's thoughts were not of flowers, nor of the roses red and white that stood boldly under his window. He could not know that these roses red and white were to be the symbols of another war which would begin with the end of that hundred years during which he, his father and grandfather had been born.

Always war, he mused. *If not among my own people, then across that narrow strip of sea that divides England, my England, from France…*

His memory went searching to bring again that day of his great triumphant moment. He heard the ringing shouts of the masses that had followed where he led, and as memory revived, a shudder passed through him. 'Yes, God forgive me,' he whispered, 'I led and — misled them!'

He again felt the dark shadow of remorse that had haunted him through the weeks following his victory over the Peasants' Revolt. *How,* he asked himself, *if it were a victory, could I have intended to crush them who had asked me to save them from slavery, taxed to starvation by their overlords who ruled and still rule them — and me!*

Head and shoulders out of the window, he sniffed the warm fragrant air. A lovely scent came to him — *very different,* he recalled, *from the stink of those streets we passed to and from Smithfield. Blood! Dried rusted stinking blood and corpses crawling with blowflies, dogs prowling in the filth thrown from the windows of people who stood to cheer me for having saved those poor wretches who dared plead with me to free them from their 'bondage' ... and I failed them. Hundreds, no! Thousands of years before Our Lord Jesus came to save the world, God's prophet Moses who spoke with but didn't see God, led the Jews from bondage out of Egypt. Moses did not fail them — but I did!*

Yet it wasn't I, was it, God?

He often would speak to God within himself as if he spoke to a friend. He remembered asking his dear old Archbishop Sudbury. (He shuddered again as he recalled that head with its terrible bleeding gash where the axe had felled it from its body, stuck on a pike along with Hales's.) *Yes, I did ask my old confessor what exactly was prayer, and he said, talking to God as if he were your dearest friend — as he is! And Walworth the mayor, he found Wat Tyler dead in that ghastly Smithfield Market and he cut off his head and stuck it on a pike along with other rebels. And he took the heads of my good Archbishop and Hales and all who had been murdered, and he had them buried in sanctity.*

Yes, and I knighted Walworth for having killed — no! He didn't kill him, it was Standish who stabbed him to death, to save Tyler from killing the mayor...

He remembered how when, after that battle at Smithfield he had returned to his mother in the Wardrobe, and how he sent for Walworth and knighted him. *'Kneel,' I said. He knelt and I lifted the sword Standish had brought me and I said, 'Rise, Sir...' What was his name? William. 'Yes, rise, Sir William,' I told him, and although he got up he said, 'I do not deserve this honour. I am only a mere tradesman of the Fishmongers' Guild and I have no right to claim the Chivalrous Order of Knighthood…'*

I thought that fine of him, but I said, 'You are now and for always a knight, my knight,' and I said in Latin as my dear Sir Guichard had taught me, 'fortement et od bone volente…'

'But,' Richard said aloud, 'although he deserved to be knighted, for he risked his life for me, I can't say *I* would have deserved it if I could have knighted myself!'

'What, darling?' His mother glanced up from her tapestry, her needle poised. 'What are you saying about knights?'

'I was thinking of that time last Corpus Christi when I knighted the Mayor of London for saving me from Wat Tyler's dagger. He would most likely have killed me if the mayor hadn't gone for him, but it was Standish who really killed him. I couldn't knight Standish, as he was already a knight, but I did give him my gold locket with our coat of arms on it. Yet what a waste it was — those thousands of rebels all pleading with me to save them from their overlords and … I didn't save them! I wanted to, but…' He shook his head. 'I'm just a name. I can't do a thing of my own free will — at least I can't do what I would *want* to do without Parliament, or Uncle Gaunt, and now 'tis Tom Holland — Buckingham — who always interferes with me. I liked him before I made him an earl. And now they are going to marry me off to a girl I've never seen!'

Joan rose from her seat and went to him. 'It is because you are not yet of age that you have to submit to what Parliament or your uncles decide is best for you and for your country.'

'If I *were* of age,' he argued, 'it would be just the same — I mean with regard to my marriage. I would have no say in the matter. But you did, didn't you? Or rather my father did when he married you. Although you already had a husband and the

Pope allowed you a divorce. Suppose I marry this girl, this Anne of Bohemia, and find I don't like her, would the Pope give *me* a divorce?'

'Richard! You mustn't even think of such a thing! Others have thought for you, and because you *are* king you have to do what is best for your kingdom.'

'Not what is best for myself?' He took her hand that was caressing his hair and kissed it. 'My father, although he wasn't king, he would have been had he lived — *he* did what he knew was best for himself when he married you.'

'If he hadn't married me,' she said, her eyes brightening with tears, 'I would have missed the happiest years of my life, and I should not have had you!'

'It might have been better if you hadn't had me,' he muttered, but this she did not hear, or perhaps feigned not to hear when he followed it up in almost the same breath, 'This girl from Bohemia — what an outlandish country! And how can my marriage to her be of any benefit to me or England?'

'Bohemia is by no means an outlandish country,' replied Joan, 'and the Bohemians are a very cultured race. This Princess Anne is the sister of the King of Bohemia, King Wenceslas — who is an ally of France — and it is through the diplomacy of Sir Simon Burley and your good Sir Michael de la Pole, soon to be your Chancellor, that this marriage has been arranged.'

'I don't even know what she looks like nor how old she is,' grumbled Richard. 'If she's the King of Bohemia's sister she must be years older than I because he — this Bohemian king — he isn't a boy. I am the youngest king in Europe, amn't I?'

'You may be, as far as we know,' his mother answered, 'but King Wenceslas is a young man, although much older than you and his sister. She is just about your age.'

'So she too is being married to me without knowing anything about me more than I am King of England and that I don't care a fiddler's bitch whether I like her or not!'

'Richard!' His shocked mother recoiled. 'Where could you have learned such a vulgar expression?'

'I learned it years ago from my stable boys. My dear Sir Guichard and Sir Simon were always going for me if I ever spoke as other boys of my age would speak. Can't I ever forget I'm a king?'

'It is to be hoped,' Joan said severely, controlling hidden laughter, 'that you will *not* forget you are a king — and that you won't forget you are a husband, when that time comes!'

FIVE

Princess Anne of Bohemia had been escorted on her long journey to England by the stout elderly gentleman who had been presented to her as Sir Simon Burley. With her dear friend and confidante Agnes Lancecrona, her lady-in-waiting, she had been driven from Dover, where after a dreadful crossing on *La Manche* from France, when she and Agnes had suffered agonies of seasickness, they had eventually been deposited at the castle of Sheen by the gentleman from England, Sir Simon Burley. Agnes, who spoke better English than did Anne, had laughed at his name, which she said suited him marvellously, for he has embonpoint comme on dit en Anglais 'burly' and not in the least like the portrait of the King of England brought to the princess by this 'Sir Burly', with, Agnes said, 'the face of an angel, and as handsome as the god Apollo.'

They spoke French together when not speaking their own language, and although Anne spoke fluent French, German and was well schooled in Greek and Latin, she had little English and not until this last month, when she had known she was destined to be Queen of England, had she learned some of the English language.

'How you are lucky,' she told Agnes, 'to be allowed to choose whom you are to marry. Me, I have no choice, I have to marry a man whom I have never seen simply because my brother wished this marriage for affairs of state.'

'I have *not* had the chance to choose whom I wish to marry,' Agnes said, 'because the only men who have wanted to marry me were —' she began counting on her fingers — 'one was the King's gentleman de chambre, le Comte de — I forget his name. He came from the French king as a gift to the King, your brother. Ugly as sin. The next was the ambassador from Austria, fat as a pig. The third was the King's Master of the Horse with a face like a sausage, and the fourth —'

Anne's peal of laughter cut in with, 'Spare me the catalogue! But I have not even the choice of an ambassador fat as a pig nor a sausage-faced Master of the Horse. As for the English king, I don't believe Sir Simon's description nor the picture of him, which is sure to be grossly flattering. Richard of England is more likely to be a hideous oaf with pimples. He is younger than I, isn't he?'

'A very little younger,' agreed Agnes, 'his birthday is in January and yours is in October. He is fourteen and you were fifteen on your last birthday. As for pimples, I expect you are right. I was told that my brother had pimples all over his face at fifteen, but he lost them when he grew up.'

'At any rate, you,' said Anne, 'don't have to marry in order to bring France and England together just because my brother is friendly with France — in fact we are related by marriage to the King of France, because my mother's sister married the Dauphin!'

While this or some such discussion in which confidences were exchanged — or perhaps extracted — between Anne and her lady-in-waiting, the King of England was engaged in a similar discussion with his friend Robert de Vere, expressing in no mean terms his dissatisfaction concerning his forthcoming marriage to Princess Anne.

'It is just a political arrangement because this Bohemian girl's brother, King Wenceslas — or some such impossible name — is an ally of France and as Charles the Sixth of France has loads of money despite he and his country, and all the Kings before him have been at war with us for the past hundred years he this Wenceslas — there's a tongue twister for me to call him with my stutter! — thinks that by marrying his sister to England he can make peace with us and France and get a h-handsome dower for Anne from Wen-what's-his-name. I shan't object to her dower, but I shall certainly object to her! Although if it brings an end to this everlasting goddamn war with France I'd marry myself to a Gadarene sow if there are any of those swines' descendants left since they were pitched into the sea according to the Gospels.'

'You are always quoting the Gospels,' Robert reminded him, 'just because you can read them in Greek. And how do you know they aren't just some old folklore handed out for centuries to make heathens like me beware of hell fire if we don't repent!'

'I mislike your paganism,' Richard told him loftily. 'After all, the greatest intelligence of the Greeks like Aristotle believed in a god as the creator of the universe...'

'A god spelled with a small g? Why shouldn't the gods of the Greeks and Romans — come to that — believe in Olympian deities any more than we so-called Christians believe in a fatherly being sitting on a throne in a heavenly palace with his only begotten son seated on his right hand? But as the Christian God is a spirit, how can he have hands or a corporeal body — *or* a son? Can you tell me that?'

'Suppose we leave theology to those who have studied it and are ordained to teach the truth to heretics like yourself, as I,' Richard said grandly, 'am ordained God's Anointed! But talking of my marriage —'

'Which is unlikely to be made in heaven,' broke in the irrepressible Robert, 'where, as I understand from old wives' tales, the union between man and woman, if blessed by the Holy Church, ought to take place — while my marriage to your cousin Philippa, daughter of your aunt Isabella and handsome as a turnip, is more likely to take place —' he pointed below — 'down there. Another example of *mariage de convenance* is mine, arranged because my Uncle Aubrey de Vere had an eye to the Plantagenet coffers, which are very useful for the Oxford estates. I am now reading an erotic poem especially written for me by your friend Chaucer to do with the raping of a nun. He is a great one for nuns. And only by close attention to Chaucer's graphic description of —'

At that point in this pointless discussion Sir Simon Burley was announced. Richard greeted him warmly. 'I did not know you had returned from Bohemia. I understood you would be here with my —' he flushed — 'my wife-to-be.'

'We had a favourable journey; the roads of Bohemia are well cared for, and although much of the way is mountainous their royal coach is more modern and superior to ours. The princess and her lady-in-waiting, as Sir Michael informed Your Grace, are lodged at Sheen, and in the negotiations of the marriage settlement with His Grace her brother, the King, it was decided to bestow the Palace of Sheen upon your future queen as Her Grace's country residence.'

'She can have Westminster Palace as well, for all I care,' returned Richard sulkily.

'And we, Sir Michael and I,' imperturbably resumed Sir Simon, 'consider it would be a graceful gesture if Your Grace should visit the princess at Sheen. We have already notified the Baroness Lancecrona, Her Grace's Lady-in-Waiting, that if it be at Her Grace's convenience you will call upon her tomorrow.'

'So now I'll know the worst,' Richard told Robert when Simon had left him.

'Which,' said he, 'can't be worse than my first sight of Philippa.'

It was with ill-disguised gloom that Richard submitted to be driven to Sheen accompanied by Sir Simon and Sir Michael de la Pole, soon to be his Chancellor and devoted ally as the King neared manhood. For the present he was still the young King Richard who, since his triumph in proving himself the courageous victor of the Peasants' Revolt, had been returned to his tutelage under the supervision of Sir Simon and, since the death of Sir Guichard, of Sir Michael de la Pole. But his schooling now had less to do with academic scholarship than with affairs of state.

When Richard arrived at Sheen Palace he was conducted to the presence of his future queen. She did not receive him in her state apartment but in the beautiful gardens of Sheen. This at the suggestion of Agnes Lancecrona, who had thought this first meeting between the two young betrothed would be less formal and embarrassing if they were to meet for the first time in a garden.

'As the first couple met in a garden,' Anne agreed, with a dimple appearing as she spoke, 'only *they* didn't have to be married, did they?'

'And got themselves into trouble for disobeying the Lord's instructions,' Agnes reminded her, 'in behaving as if they *were* married — with no clothes on! And we are never told that they *did* marry, at least not according to the Church.'

'There was no Church then,' Anne said, 'so they could live as husband and wife with or without any clothes on — or any tiresome laws to forbid them making love together.'

'There is no law to prevent you and King Richard making love together,' said Agnes, 'so long as you *are* married!'

Anne placed a finger to her lips. 'Sh! Here they come. Which one is which? Not Sir Simon — I know him but — O, God! Not the other one, surely. He's *old*!'

She alluded to Sir Michael, whose portly form had almost entirely obscured the young Richard. He had been dressed for the occasion in a sumptuous tabard, lavishly embroidered with the royal leopards of England and the lilies of France. He had also been provided with a red leather jewel case containing a ring of brilliant diamonds surrounding his own coat of arms in gold. This his mother had given him — her own betrothal ring that was her beloved prince's gift to her when their marriage had been satisfactorily arranged.

We have been given to understand that this first meeting between the King and his future queen proved to be a less formidable encounter than either had foreseen. If Richard were more agreeably surprised when confronted for the first time with his future wife than was Anne at this first sight of her future husband, he had received no description of her, either in portraiture or verbally, as had she on receiving the miniature of a highly flattered god-like being. Robert's dismal allusion to the wife of *his* pre-arranged marriage had left Richard unprepared for the charming young girl who advanced to greet him, kneeling with a curtsy to the ground.

The high conical-shaped head-dress offered a glimpse of satiny dark hair combed back, as was the mediaeval fashion, from a smooth naked forehead that gave no trace of eyebrows, again in the style of the period, in which we may believe fashion dictated that eyebrows be shaved, to judge by what is left to posterity from the beauties of Giotto or Cimabue. But Anne, if not strictly beautiful in the sense that Richard had come to know beauty as exemplified in his lovely, if now a trifle full-blown mother — still extolled by her faithful admirers as 'The Fair Maid of Kent' — this Bohemian princess emanated beauty as an aroma, none the less compelling since no single feature could be judged as beautiful. Yet the ripe red mouth, uptilted at each corner, showed dimples in rounded cheeks when in soft broken English she addressed him.

'I have the *honneur* — the honour — to make welcome the king of England.'

He bowed over her outstretched hand, devoid of rings other than one of heavy gold engraved with the royal Bohemian crest. Raising that hand to his lips, he deeply flushed, as much with relief as with a flutter of his heart to see so delectable a girl whom he was destined to marry, whether he would or would not.

'*V-votre Altesse* does me m-much honour,' he murmured, stammering dreadfully. Then, somewhat recovered from the agreeable shock of this, he said, 'P-pray do not kneel to me, 'tis I should kneel to you as to a —' He stayed himself in time from uttering on the tip of his tongue the absurdity of *goddess.*

Anne's lady-in-waiting, leaning over a bed of roses, her hands full of red, white and saffron blooms, glanced round her shoulder and smiled to herself. And with the roses in her hands she came towards the pair of them who, after their initial introduction, were standing mute! Anne having been adjured not to kneel, it would seem that neither had another word to say.

They can't stand there staring at each other like a couple of stuffed images, Agnes told herself; and to Anne, low-voiced in their native tongue, 'Why not invite the King to your apartment for a cup of wine?'

Before Anne could collect herself to answer that, the Baroness curtsied, kneeling to Richard and saying in French, 'May I, the Lady of the Bedchamber to Her Highness, convey my humble duty to the King of England?'

He did not tell *her* not to kneel to him, although he graciously acknowledged her greeting.

Anne then told Agnes, also in their native tongue, 'I would rather not entertain him in my apartment. Why not stay here? Order wine to be brought to us — over there.' She indicated a rustic arbour surrounded by flowering shrubs.

Agnes went towards the house and clapped her hands for a page hovering on the steps of the terrace. She gave him instructions in English, for he and all the Household staff at Sheen were the King's or his mother's personal servants now, of course, allotted to the princess since the palace at Sheen had been part of her marriage settlement.

Meanwhile Burley and Michael de la Pole had watched from a discreet distance this momentous meeting, and exchanged their opinion that 'so far, so good.'

'Richard always stammers more when he is embarrassed,' said Sir Simon. 'Thank God she is pleasing to the eye. From his gloomy conjecture as to the appearance of this girl, one might have thought he would find her as attractive as Medusa!'

Lackeys carrying small tables were ordered by Agnes to place one to seat two in the arbour and the other to seat two or three outside. *At any rate,* Agnes told herself, *they cannot sit together at a table like a pair of deaf mutes…*

Richard was relieved to find himself *tête-à-tête* with Anne in comparative isolation at that rustic table covered with a cloth of finest damask and gold goblets into which the servants poured the rich red wine of Bohemia. Agnes had arranged that she and the two gentlemen should be seated, if not in earshot, then within sight of their charges.

There was at first no necessity for that polite discretion since the two betrothed seemed still to have no word to utter — until both spoke at once. He, finding his voice, remarked on the excellent vintage of Her Highness's wine. 'I presume you brought it with you from Bohemia?' And she simultaneously, 'I hope, *mon roi,* you will like our Bohemian wine!' Their words trailed off in mutual laughter.

'Our two minds think alike,' said he. 'A good sign, is it not?' He spoke in English and she shook her head, the dimples reappearing.

'I speak so small little English, *mon roi,* I no un'erstan'. I be try learn since I know that —'

'Since you knew,' he supplemented in French to her pause, 'that you are to be Queen of England, *my* Queen?'

More dimples and blushes, and he, leaning closer to her, said, 'Will you permit me to come here every day to t-teach you English?'

'The King of England is too gracious,' she answered him in French. 'It will be my great pleasure to learn English if you, my king, will teach me.'

When Richard returned to Westminster that same evening, Robert was waiting for him to hear the worst, as he fully expected, of Richard's reaction to the first sight of his future bride.

'Well? Is she a fat, bosomy, swarthy gipsy girl? They are all like that, I'm told, from the highest to the lowest, in Bohemia.'

To which Richard deigned no reply beyond, 'I must get me an English lexicon, and one of the Bohemian language, but I doubt if any such exist. I will have to write the words in French and their equivalent in English. I learned Greek and Latin from their lexicons but it would be too much to expect her to learn English from either Greek or Latin, even if she can speak both languages though not so fluently as French. As from what you evidently expected I would see as my future w-wife, I can tell you she is far more attractive than any of my mother's women — they are all fat and bosomy blondes. *She* is dark — at least so much as I could see of her hair, but she was an agreeable surprise after what you suggested she would be.' Richard's approval of Anne gave both his gentlemen and his mother the greatest satisfaction.

'I will drive over to see her at Sheen tomorrow,' Joan told Richard.

The meeting the next day with her future daughter-in-law proved to be highly successful. Anne was charmed by Joan's blonde beauty which she recognised had been inherited by her son, and Joan, thankfully, saw that the girl was eminently suitable to be Richard's Queen Consort. Despite a naturally youthful shyness, Joan saw that this young princess of Bohemia was extremely attractive, not only in her delightful broken English and her easy command of French, German and, surprisingly, Latin with a smattering of Greek, but in her personality. Her creamy skin was the flawless complement to the dark satiny hair that, divested of her head-dress, framed the small delicately featured face. A tall, slender girl, just the right height for Richard since he, rising fifteen and not yet done growing was already near upon six feet and would, Joan surmised, reach the same six feet two inches of his father.

God be thanked, was her inward prayer of gratitude to the Almighty, for giving him this instead of what she had feared would be a resemblance to her dead mother's sister, married to the Dauphin of France. A swarthy, stout, buxom brunette, as she remembered seeing her when she paid a short visit to London, and this close relationship to France by marriage might well bring about the hoped for end to these incessant wars.

France and Bohemia were very friendly. Joan had been told by Simon Burley how the French king Charles VI had manoeuvred the marriage between Anne of Bohemia and Richard of England hoping that the alliance might result in a terminal truce ... *What a mercy,* reflected Joan, *that Anne is as she is! So many European royalties are married without the approval or choice of the two betrothed who may never have seen each other! Although Anne's brother is at least twelve years older than she — there were two stillborn before Anne, and her mother died giving birth to her — he, this Wenceslas — I shall never pronounce it! — I remember seeing him when he came here accompanied by that amusing Frenchman, Froissart* ... The courtly appointed arch-gossip of France, who wrote all he saw and heard, and much that he *didn't* see and hear, about England and the English.

It may well have been he who gave France the idea of promoting this marriage between Bohemia and us, reflected Joan, *even when Anne was only about six and her brother, then the Crown Prince, and the King of Bohemia was already a sick man. The prince was a good-looking boy. I understand there is Austrian blood in them and that the Austrian women, especially the Viennese, are notably handsome, which might account for Anne. And if Richard is not in love with her yet, he soon will be...*

He soon was.

The marriage of this boy and girl took place in the chapel of Westminster Palace on 14 January 1382. Richard was just fifteen and Anne a few months older.

It was evident to all that the young couple were entirely absorbed in each other. The English lessons had served merely as excuse for Richard to spend long hours almost every day with Anne in the palace of Sheen. She was quick to learn and speak in her pretty broken English, but more often they spoke French in which both excelled, and Richard of Bordeaux who seldom stammered in what had been virtually his native tongue, could tell her in French all that he might have been too backward in coming forward to tell her in English.

If the prospective bride and groom were glowingly happy in their brief betrothal, this alliance between England and Bohemia was regarded with the utmost disfavour by the majority of the King's Government and his subjects. In the city's taverns Londoners discussed over their tankards their disapproval of 'this foreigner', as they named the Queen Consort; and other than those who had been politically involved in the union, the contemporary chroniclers deplored the great cost of a queen who could offer their king no dowry as the sister of impoverished Bohemia.

The grumbles of the taxpayer who would be burdened with her upkeep, besides the gift to her from the King of his country palace at Sheen as part of her marriage settlement, was further cause of grievance. The disapproval of his subjects or his Commons or his Uncle Buckingham, later to be self-created Duke of Gloucester, the youngest and most dangerous to the monarchy of the three remaining sons of Edward III, neither affected nor dismayed Richard one iota — even had he known of it, which most likely he did not.

For the first time in his life he knew happiness in its fullest and most youthful sense. Both he and Anne were scarcely out of puberty — they had each been late developers and were singularly innocent and ignorant of sexual intercourse. She, as virginal as was he, shrank from his clumsy experimental and to her rather shocking attempts to assert his manhood in his marital rights. In fact these two were both younger than their teenage years by reason of their cloistered upbringing. She, much junior to her brother, the King, had been kept in almost conventual isolation at the Court of Bohemia. Her one friend and confidant, Agnes Lancecrona, had strict orders from Anne's prudish brother to guard her against contact with the levity and moral laxity of his Court, which he viewed with a somewhat monastic reprehension. Indeed Wenceslas, as Crown Prince, had from his birth hankered after the priesthood, and were it not that his kingdom had been impoverished by the extravagances of his father and grandfather with their mistresses and other excesses against which he conversely rebelled, and since monkhood was denied him, he could have wished his young sister to have taken the veil, except that her wealthy marriage, either to a ruling sovereign or the heir to one, was necessary to replenish his depleted exchequer.

So that Anne and the boy, her husband, were, so Robert de Vere would have had it, 'a pair of sucklings whose ignorance is not *their* bliss!' As he told Tom Mowbray, the second of Richard's closer friends. Tom, having inherited his brother's earldom of Nottingham, had been kept to his tutelage at Nottingham Castle even as had Richard at Berkhamsted, until this last year when he alone had valiantly faced and vanquished the Peasants' Revolt.

Yet if the marriage of Anne and Richard lacked the passion of more adult years, they enjoyed a companionship as between devoted friends. They shared a common interest in literature and art. Anne's strict upbringing had been fostered by her brother who, in his earlier youth, had spent several months in

Florence studying the history of art and the primitive Italian Renaissance.

Anne would tell Richard what she had learned from her brother of the glorious architecture and art of Giotto and Cimabue, and how that the great financier and connoisseur, the first of the Medici, Giovanni had — according to Wenceslas — regarded the English in their remote fogbound island as 'barbarians'.

'Which I have no doubt,' said Richard, 'is also your brother's opinion of us with whom, and the Medici, I entirely agree!'

'Not *you*!' Anne declared. 'You are different from your uncle and your brothers. Their only interest is in war and fighting other countries if not fighting with themselves!'

'You have already seen us — I mean them — as they are. But my father can scarcely be described as a barbarian. He is — or was — the nation's hero, victor of Crécy at sixteen only a few months older than I am now! I must have been as much a disappointment to him as I am to the people of England.'

'If so,' Anne indignantly declared, 'it is they who are barbarians, not you! You are artist. Your mother show me your drawings and paintures and some poems you write when you are a little boy. They are *merveilleux* for one so young.'

'That is because I knew Chaucer when he came to England. He was more often in Italy.'

Anne nodded. 'Yes, my brother he say he meet *le poète* Chaucer when he was in Florence. How different are you from your uncles and brothers.'

'My half-brothers,' he corrected. 'But how — different?'

'*Ton oncle de* Gaunt,' she said, 'he must go always to war. If not in Spain —'

'He has ceased to care about Spain,' Richard interrupted. 'Having made himself King of Castile, he renounces his claim to that province and is now invading Portugal with my uncle Cambridge.'

'It is how I say. Always war with the English. *Non, non,* not you, *mon chéri.* If not war with England against France —'

'It will be Scotland next. Not that my Uncle Edmund is any more use than I was as warmonger.'

'What is it you say? War-monger?'

'Well,' Richard sought to explain. 'We would say a man who is, for instance, a grocer — *un épicier* — and who deals in cheese, we would call him a cheesemonger, so if he deals in war he is a — warmonger.'

'Is war then,' Anne persisted, 'how you say — what is it? trade in England, *comme épicier*?'

'No, not exactly like a grocer,' laughed Richard, 'yet I suppose war is a sort of trade — it is always a matter of finance for gain, the seizing or conquering of some other country in order to possess its lands or kingdom. Just as a grocer sells his goods for money, only 'tis men's lives that are sold in war.'

Anne shook her head. 'That is how I feel of war. I know my brother, he hope that by a *mariage de convenance* between *Bohème et Angleterre* we would be at peace with France.'

'What he hoped,' said Richard dryly, 'is that by marrying us — that is England and Bohemia — he would have enough money to continue the war against France if Charles refuses to p-play.'

'I no understand. How — play at war?'

'A figure of speech, merely I meant that the King of France would not want to go on fighting England if your country — Bohemia — joined up with us, and your brother could have given us enough money to carry on.'

'*Mais!* Why always this talk of money and war?'

'Because war has to be paid for. But when I am of age to be the ruler of my kingdom, I will end *all* wars for and with my country.'

So, at fifteen, he believed; nor did he know himself the first English monarch, ironically, to be a pacifist; he, the son of the Black Prince!

But when after the first two years of marriage no heir appeared to be forthcoming, the disapproval of the people for the 'foreigner', their king's consort, increased as the popularity earned by his courage at Smithfield and Mile End waned. Now more than ever did they see the baronage as tyrants ruthlessly demanding their traditional feudal rights at the expense of the peasants and villeins who had rebelled at the merciless injustice of the barons whose taxes robbed them of their rights to live as men and not beasts of burden. They, the barons, had left a boy of fourteen alone to quell a catastrophic crisis that threatened destruction to the realm and with which they, the overlords, had been unable to cope.

Their young king had pledged his word and delivered to the rebels his royal standards as proof of his bond, proclaiming himself their friend and ally and then, under pressure from the baronage who feared new and devastating forces were at work among the lower strata of society, he had retracted.

The retraction of his pledge had seemed to them, the underdogs, a deliberate breach of faith on the part of the boy to whom they were prepared to devote their lives. And he had failed them! They saw him now no more than the child he was — a tool in the tyrannical might of their enemies, the barons.

Richard's marriage with Anne, when consummated, was for him an absorbing passion to the exclusion of all such trivia as the arguments and quarrels of his elders seeking the governance of him and his kingdom.

Other than his wife Richard's closest friend was still Robert de Vere, but Tom Mowbray whose earldom made him a great baron of vast estates, had little time to give to his boyhood's friend and companion, the King of England.

Moreover, Richard was dismayed to learn that Tom had engaged himself to the daughter of the Earl of Arundel. Arundel, an arrogant, avaricious specimen of mediaeval baronage, had become a self-appointed guardian of the King during Richard's later minority, much to the contention of Simon Burley, Michael de la Pole, and equally to Richard who had taken a wholesome dislike to him. 'I can't *stand* him!' he told Anne. 'How dare he try to lord it over me and put himself above Sir Simon and Michael de la Pole, who both — especially Sir Simon — act as regents until I come of age.'

Richard's dislike of Arundel mounted to positive hatred when Tom Mowbray married Arundel's daughter. 'That's because Tom now is one of the wealthiest barons,' he said, when discussing with Robert de Vere Tom's betrayal, as he called his one-time friend's desertion. 'And that's how you were caught to marry Buckingham's pasty-faced Philippa.'

'Yes!' Robert glumly agreed. 'Because I, like Tom, inherited vast estates, but in my case the fact that I was under age when I was forced into marriage with Philippa could not be irrevocable.'

'I too was — and still am — under age, married to Anne, but as far as I am concerned it *is* irrevocable. That's to say, I would never want my marriage to be broken. I suppose, apart from my mother and father — you know she d-divorced her first husband Sir Thomas Holland, in order to marry my father? They were both madly in love with each other, as I am with Anne — and I think she is with me.'

'You couldn't know it was going to be love,' said Robert, not without some envy, 'when you were not yet fifteen.'

'I did know! I knew the moment I saw her. I was dreading meeting her after what you told me about your marriage to Philippa. But I believe, although our marriage was arranged for diplomatic reasons, that I am the only reigning king who has married for love.'

'At first sight!' scoffed Robert. 'Yet a king — or a boy — young as you were and are, can't possibly know whether it's love — or the other thing.'

'What other thing?' asked Richard, still innocent of the urge of the flesh, though deeply involved with the urge of the heart.

'Oh, well.' Robert's three years' seniority to Richard and a premature puberty had rendered him sexually knowledgeable, while Richard was unaware of his masculine potential. 'To turn to less personal loves and *dis*-loves,' he added, 'I look forward to seeing you and hearing you pitch into Arundel when Parliament opens next month.'

'Yes, at Salisbury where Sir Simon and Michael de la Pole are holding my Court. I like Salisbury better than Westminster — 'tis less formal. I've no axe to grind with my uncle Buckingham, but,' he smiled slyly, 'I'm sharpening one in readiness. This Arundel — my would-be regent, God damn him! — will feel its sharpened edge if I speak in Parliament. Although not until I am king in more than name will I be allowed to speak. Yet, as a peer of the realm, Duke of Cornwall, Earl of — I forget the other peers I represent I believe there's no age limit to a peer from speaking in Parliament so long as he isn't a toothless infant, as a minor is legally defined, or a c-congenital idiot.'

'Many who do speak in Parliament, whether peers or not, are toothless infants and congenital idiots and should be put into a lunatic asylum,' said Robert. 'But you're wrong. An underage peer has no voice any more than you — a king and a minor!'

'Yes,' agreed Richard, 'we should be drowned at birth like my bitch's fifth whelp, the runt of the litter, was put down because he was born with a deformity, poor little beast, so he would have died in any case. Arundel survives *his* whelp, unluckily for me — or, as it may be, for him, if I get the chance to lord it over him who tries to lord it over me!'

That April Parliament of 1384 described Richard's part in it as his 'First Tyranny', doubtless because in the remaining months of his minority and during those early years of his reign he had rebelled against those in authority from expressing any opinion in assertion of his rights. This persistent interference with and suppression of his kingship would infuriate him to sudden explosions of wrath.

On one occasion after a speech delivered by Arundel in a veiled indictment against his friends, de Vere, Simon Burley and Michael de la Pole, Richard's hatred for Arundel burst forth. 'You!' he pointed a ringed index finger at the discomfited Arundel; his voice rang clearly, unhampered by the stammer he now had almost mastered, 'you dare to charge *me* with the extravagance of my Court and my friends — as if I and they are responsible for the bad governance of my country! 'Tis you, and the likes of you whom I charge with the corruption of my government and the persecution of my people who can't speak for themselves. But they *did* speak three years ago when you and others were too cowardly to face them, and left me to deal with them. Yes, and I *did* deal with them! I promised those poor wretches whom you and all of you had drained dry of even the miserable pittance you allowed as their wages, and you poll-taxed them — *you* who should have been *pole-axed*!'

A muffled cheer was heard from where Robert de Vere was seated with his peers, young and old, and from another source the sound of a chuckle — in the direction of Sir Simon Burley, hastily turned into a cough. Richard grinned broadly with the satisfaction of a punster whose pun had gone home.

'Yes, and you made me break my word to them, having promised them their freedom. I meant them to be free, and given a living wage for the work they did for you, the lords of your lands, where they slaved as serfs. And you made me break my word to them. I didn't understand all the p-political jargon you spewed out at me as being illegal, or some such lies to excuse yourselves — but they forgave me, knowing that it wasn't *my* wish to back out of my promise to set them free! And you —' the ringed forefinger closed to his palm in a threatening fist that struck the air as if it were Arundel's face — 'You — you dare to govern me! But you won't. Oh, yes! I and all of us know how you he in your throat with your oily smooth words to accuse me and my friends for the ruin of my kingdom; but in a few months' time you will have to eat your words when I take up the government of my realm. Until then you can go to hell and the devil, where you belong!'

The shocked Parliament sat speechless, while Arundel, equally shocked, sought to find words with which to stem this violent storm of what he was pleased to call insanity as he was unable to find a plausible excuse for the boy's outburst.

Richard was left the victor in the assertion of his sovereignty while still a minor.

The Parliament of 1384 assembled at Salisbury a few months after Richard had assumed premature authority when he vented his wrath upon Arundel, his future Lord Chancellor. Nor did the Salisbury Parliament prove to be more efficient in dealing with its own affairs than with those of the King's subjects. Richard's friend, Robert de Vere and others about the Court, were constantly under hostile surveillance by the Arundel faction, and it may be that a scandalous plot supposed to involve the King's uncle, John of Gaunt if not deliberately implemented by the Arundel contingent headed by Thomas of Woodstock, Earl of Buckingham (Richard's younger uncle) could have been suggested by him.

It seemed that a Carmelite friar, one John Latimer, obtained access to Richard in de Vere's apartment in the castle at Salisbury where Robert was dining with the King. According to the friar, a plot had been contrived by the citizens of London led by Gaunt, Duke of Lancaster, involving treasonable activities against the King. Without judicial inquiry into these serious allegations against John of Gaunt, Richard flew into one of his ungovernable rages and ordered the execution of his uncle!

The horrified priest attempted to persuade the King to investigate the case on which he had loyally embarked on behalf of his sovereign lord. Richard's rageful temper, that rose and was gone within a second and a second, demanded an investigation into the alleged conspiracy that involved his uncle Gaunt. The inquiry brought no conclusive evidence against Gaunt, but although Richard's suspicions alternated between his uncle and the priest, the innocent tool of the infamous conspiracy, he decided that Latimer had invented the whole thing to curry favour and preferment — maybe a bishopric — from the King!

He committed Latimer to the prison of Salisbury Castle in the custody of the King's seneschal, Sir John Montague.

On the road to the castle the seneschal's prisoner and his party were waylaid by Richard's half-brother, Sir John Holland.

He had resented Gaunt's monopoly of young Richard when he, the King's close of kin, had been ignored by Gaunt. Yet, believing the unfortunate friar to be guilty of the plot against the King's uncle, Holland, without giving the friar any chance to vindicate himself, had him seized. His custodian, Sir John Montague, then submitted him to insufferable tortures, including slow roasting, that he might confess to any information of the plot against Gaunt.

The victim of these appalling atrocities of mutilation and burning of the flesh were suffered without uttering a word for or against Gaunt. But the injuries he had received left him a dying man. He lingered a few days, fettered to the walls of that fetid rat-ridden dungeon.

Although the luckless friar consistently declared his innocence as witness or party to the plot, Latimer's agonies ended in merciful death. But his corpse had still to undergo unrightful punishment. It was dragged through the streets of Salisbury until rescued by the friars of his priory for reverential burial.

While neither Gaunt nor the King would have countenanced these horrific tortures, a contemporary chronicler reported that the King was greatly upset and wept copious tears when he heard of the priest's sufferings.

None the less this supposed plot left Richard with a gnawing suspicion of his uncle Gaunt's guilt, doubtless fostered by Gaunt's youngest brother, Thomas, Earl of Buckingham. From his earliest years, Richard had been aware that Thomas disliked him, and with a child's intuition he distrusted his uncle.

Thomas of Woodstock had lived in the hope, scarcely to his inner man admitted, that Gaunt and his other surviving brother, Edmund Langley, Earl of Cambridge (afterwards Duke of York), would die that he and neither of his two surviving brothers should inherit the throne instead of a nurseling of nine years old.

Brooding on what he believed to be a usurpation of his own rights as third in the succession to his late father, the King, and not Richard, the son of his brother, the Black Prince and the original heir, Thomas forced an entry to the young king's apartment in Salisbury Castle and discovered him playing chess with his friend Robert de Vere.

'Years ago,' Richard was saying, 'when I used to play chess with my cousin, Henry Bolingbroke, he always jeered at me for being able to mate me without a queen. But now I am older and have been taught by my good Sir Simon, I can beat Henry even as *I* —' and he took Robert's king with one of his knights, 'can say to *you* — checkmate!'

A frown wrinkled his forehead at the entrance of his uncle Thomas: 'May I ask,' he demanded, 'why I am accorded the p-pleasure of your uninvited company —' irony crept into his pause — 'which is always — welcome?'

'Oh, yes?' drawled Buckingham, 'as welcome, no doubt, as is my sword raised to challenge any —' he glanced from Richard to where the King's ever watchful guardians, Simon Burley and de la Pole, were also playing chess in a far corner — 'I said *any*,' he emphasised, his weapon still raised, 'whom I challenge at sword-point who dares to impeach with treason my brother Gaunt of Lancaster!'

Richard was on his feet; an angry flush mounted to the fringe of blond hair on his forehead, presage of explosive wrath that with an effort he suppressed.

'If there were any man present who would dare impeach my uncle Gaunt with treason —' his voice rose controlling the stammer that invariably accompanied rage — 'or to question my uncle Gaunt's integrity, then —' he drew from his belt a jewelled dagger and in his turn flourished it in the face of Buckingham — 'no sword is this but it has its use as challenge to anyone, whomsoever he may be, if he were the instigator of such an infamous allegation!'

It was the first undercurrent of the tidal wave that in later years would engulf a king, his throne, and a dynasty.

SIX

Although Richard supported his uncle, Duke of Lancaster, against Buckingham's alleged imputations of conspiracy involving his uncle *and* himself, his suspicion as to the duke's integrity was not entirely allayed. This may have been due to the influence of Robert de Vere, who since his earlier days had known of and hated Lancaster's disapproval of 'that obstreperous youngster', as Gaunt regarded this bosom friend and companion of Richard. Gaunt's undisguised antipathy to Robert increased when he realised that de Vere would take every advantage of the King's favour so soon as he became empowered to confer honours on his dearest friend.

But if Gaunt believed Richard's affection for Robert was akin to the first King Richard Plantagenet's amatory friendship with Philip Augustus, King of France, his fear of Richard's devotion to Robert was dissolved when the King married Anne of Bohemia.

After the consummation of the marriage, delayed by reason of his youth, Richard's passionate love for his young wife disproved any homosexual aberrations, prevalent in the Middle Ages as in later centuries. Nevertheless Gaunt may have been dismayed, as were the Lords and Commons, to see honour after honour heaped on Robert de Vere, Earl of Oxford.

No sooner was Richard, at the age of eighteen, king in more than name, and empowered to confer honours without consulting his elders, than he created Robert de Vere Marquis of Dublin, the first marquisate known to the English peerage.

This brought with it a yearly income of 5,000 marks from the Irish revenue paid out of the King's Exchequer.

Such generosity to a peer who already owned vast estates inherited with his earldom, was evident to both the Lords and Commons of reckless extravagant favour and expense from the King's Treasury to Robert de Vere. As far as Richard was concerned he felt not only deep affection for this one friend of his lonely childhood, but gratitude to Robert for his unshaken loyalty in the general opposition to so young a king, not only from his Parliament but from his uncles, excluding John of Gaunt.

Another of Richard's favourites was Nicolas Brembre, a grocer, who succeeded Walworth as Mayor of London. It would seem that this second King Richard was no respecter of persons. He had knighted, it will be remembered, Mayor Walworth of the Fishmongers' Guild for his courage and support of the boy king who alone faced a rebellious multitude in the Peasants' Revolt.

Richard, if not acknowledged as such by his contemporaries, was actually the first democratic sovereign of England who preceded another democratic king five centuries later: King William IV.

With the election to the mayoralty of Brembre, the grocer of the Victuallers' Guild, those of the Drapers' Guild took exception to the King's favour of the grocer.

His fellow tradesmen of the Drapers' Guild considered their calling as purveyors of clothing material some of which was sold to the King's tailor (husband of his childhood's nurse Mundina) as greatly superior to that of a purveyor of cheese, sides of bacon and suchlike lowly edibles to be consumed by the King's servants, never by the King … The fact that

Brembre was also a vintner who supplied the King's cellars with wine, was deliberately ignored.

Led by John of Northampton, the Drapers' Guild looked to their patron, the Duke of Lancaster, for their protection. They knew that Brembre of the Victuallers' and Mayor of London, and many of his Guild were capitalists, men of wealth who helped the King's finances.

'No wonder Brembre the mayor is the King's favourite,' grumbled John of Northampton, 'a tradesman, grocer, victualler!'… John himself had been a former Mayor of Northampton whose 'cheap food policy' supported the poor in the hope of finding favour to vote him Mayor of London again, and also to ruin the Victuallers.

John of Northampton then made it his business to investigate the most disreputable quarter of the City, raided its brothels, seized the prostitutes parading their wares in the gutters and pilloried them. Brembre, the mayor, was one of many who had much property in those slums; even the former Mayor Walworth who drew large rentals from those stews, was not immune from John of Northampton's 'pious mission', as he named his spying upon street walkers and their brothels that they might be saved from sin…

However, the Drapers' Guild was no match for the Victuallers'; and with the election of the grocer Brembre as mayor, the followers of John of Northampton were arrested, imprisoned, exiled and some of them slain.

It was the signal of another revolt within the City, but far less tumultuous than the Peasants' Revolt of four years previously.

Here again Richard took the lead while still a minor with five months yet to go before his eighteenth birthday. His uncle Gaunt was away at his estate in the north of England, and in August of 1384 John of Northampton was arrested and brought to trial in Reading. He at once demanded a postponement of the trial until the return of the Duke of Lancaster, patron and protector of the Drapers' Guild, who he insisted should be present at the hearing over which the King had been appointed to preside. So inflamed was Richard at Northampton's audacity in demanding a postponement of the trial that he burst forth with: 'I'll teach you that *I* am your judge whether my uncle, Duke of Lancaster is here or not. I am the King, which it seems you have forgot!'

And again he demanded: 'Off with his head!' as before, in one of his rages, he had ordered the execution of the friar, Latimer, and his uncle Gaunt, and immediately recovered and revoked the sentence.

A second trial was arranged, this time by Justice Tresilion of the Tower of London, but Richard insisted that John of Northampton be committed to prison.

Richard's partisanship of Brembre of the Victuallers' alienated him from many of the citizens of his capital. It was the first tactless mistake due to his ungovernable temper at the hearing of John of Northampton's trial, even though, after ordering the prisoner's execution, he revoked it.

When John of Gaunt returned to London in March 1385, Richard had attained his majority with little celebration from his government, nor did it deter his uncle from reminding him that he had taken too much upon himself while still a minor, 'just as you did in April of last year when you insulted Lord Arundel, your present Lord Chancellor, and told him,' the Duke cleared his throat, eyeing his nephew severely, 'to go — ahem — to hell.'

'I also told him,' said Richard with a grin, 'to go to the devil.'

'And do you think that is the proper respect due from the sovereign to one of his highest officials?'

'Yes, if he refuses to show proper respect to me.' Richard allowed no opportunity to escape from proving he was now *the King*, not just a name.

'Moreover,' pursued the duke, ignoring this unwonted self-assurance, 'in August of last year you caused considerable dissension among the citizens of London by favouring Brembre, Mayor of London' (disgustedly) 'a grocer, when I was absent attending to my property at Pontefract, and so was prevented from presiding at the trial of John of Northampton. As I am the protector of the Drapers' Guild I, and I only, have the right to uphold them against —'

'Pardon me, Sir,' Richard interrupted, withholding his incoming temper with honey-flavoured words. (He was learning control of himself in these few weeks of his majority as king.) 'I was nominated to preside at the trial in your absence!'

'Not only,' Gaunt proceeded as if Richard had not spoken, 'did you assume the presidency of the trial, but you held conference immediately after the Christmas festivities —'

Again came the cool reply, 'Yes, when I attained my majority in January as the ruling king of my kingdom with the Divine Right of kingship.'

'Which does not entitle you to command a conference after dining with your grocer friend and taking the air in your barge along with him —'

'With the Mayor of London,' came the quick reminder.

'Where you encountered,' proceeded Gaunt with commendable patience, 'the barge of the Archbishop of Canterbury. He had been entertaining your Uncle Thomas in what was called the "Water Conference", and Archbishop

Courtenay warned you against dangerous and unworthy companions, presumably your friend, the grocer, and your other favourite whom you created Marquis of Dublin.'

'Yes, and I was furious with the Archbishop for his interference and accusations against my friends, Robert and Tom Mowbray, who were both supposed to be p-plotting against you my uncle, Duke of Lancaster. The usual pack of lies from all who r-resented me when I was king at nine years old, especially my uncle Thomas. He has always believed that *he* ought to be king! I may be young but I'm no fool, as you all think me to be — and I'm sick — sick —' and, his temper rising with each repetition of the word, he drew from his belt his jewelled dress dagger — *'sick,'* he shouted, 'of this c-continuous interference from you and my Uncle Thomas. But now I am of age and king in my own right, I know what to do without advice from you or anyone!' And his dagger raised, he pointed it straight at the reddening face of the duke. 'Put up your pretty toy!' Gaunt's hot Plantagenet temper was no less hard put to be kept under control than was Richard's. 'And do not dare to threaten me as you threatened the Archbishop when you met him in his barge on the river, accompanied by your Uncle Thomas. Your ungovernable temper will land you in some evil consequence unless you learn to subdue it.'

'Is that what you came to tell me?' As with an effort at impudent irony, Richard sheathed his 'pretty toy' which would have been none the less effective had he used it.

'No, I came to tell you,' and strongly his uncle told it, 'that Charles, King of France, is planning an attack upon England. He has assembled a fleet with intent to invade us together with the Scots.'

'So it would seem,' Richard was calm enough now to reflect upon die seriousness of this latest development, 'that the hoped-for alliance with France and Bohemia by my marriage with Anne has misfired! The good reason of my marriage with Anne was to ally us with Bohemia in the hope of ending war with France. It mattered nothing to you and England that Anne and I had never set eyes on each other. These diplomatic royal marriages usually end in misery or divorce, but in my case,' he flushed and stammered, 'I l-love my wife and she loves me and we can never be grateful enough for this diplomatic marriage, even if it doesn't end war with France.'

'Which has never ended. But,' continued Gaunt, 'we will also be at war with Scotland.' His eyes softened as he looked upon his dead brother's son. 'You will now engage in your first experience of war. It would have joyed your father's heart to know that his son will lead an army against the Scots as I will engage against France. I appoint you General in Chief of your army!'

'Oh no!' exclaimed Anne, when Richard told her that he would lead his army to invade Scotland. 'Not you! You have always said you hate war and the killing — murder you called it — of your fellow men, and for what? To seize lands that belong to some other country and to some other king. I can't bear for you to go!'

He took her in his arms, gazing down into her face, imploringly raised to his. At eighteen, Richard had grown to his late father's height of over six feet, and Anne, although tall for a girl of the Middle Ages, was barely on a level with his shoulder.

'My darling, I must go. How can I refuse to lead my army as if I feared death to myself, but not to them?'

'Death!' she shuddered. 'Yes, that is *le degré suprême* of war with enemies who fight with each other for the supremacy.'

'War,' he said, 'has always brought death to those who fight with each other, long before the coming of Our Lord who bade us love our neighbours — and our enemies — as ourselves. Greed and financial gain from the lords of the lands are the reasons for the merciless massacre of our brothers.'

He spoke with unhesitant emphasis. He never stammered when talking with Anne. This discussion ended with the entrance of a page announcing: 'My Lord Marquis of Dublin, Your Grace, and Sir Ralph Stafford.'

He was a recent newcomer to the Court, son and heir of the Earl of Stafford who had become an instant friend and favourite of Richard, partly because Robert had introduced him as a friend of his, and any friend of Robert's would be a friend of the King.

Anne greeted them with, 'Have you heard the latest news? Richard is to lead an army to Scotland. It is to be war with the Scots!'

'Thanks to the so-called alliance between ourselves and Bohemia!' said Robert bitterly.

Anne flushed. 'It is not my brother's fault that the alliance has failed. Wenceslas had hoped we and France would all be united in peace. He, like Richard,' she took his hand and held it against her heart, 'hates war.'

'As so do all of us,' put in young Stafford, 'but needs must when the devil drives.'

'The devil in this case,' Richard told him, 'is Charles of France. England is only five and twenty miles across the sea from Calais. We are always at each other's throats — that is, if we are near enough for strangulation! This enmity has been going on for — God knows how long, ever since the first King Richard Plantagenet and France became enemies after having been sworn friends and allies in the Third Crusade.'

'England has an army of volunteers, besides your own defence army,' young Stafford reminded him. He was a handsome lad, the same age as Richard. 'And I will volunteer as one of them.'

'And I,' said Robert, 'will enlist to serve under you, Sir,' he saluted, 'as my General.'

Richard held out a hand to each.

'Against my will and inclination, I appoint you both my first and seconds in command, much as I loathe and detest this insensate war with the Scots. We — England — have one foot in the border and the other foot outside of it, here. We ought to be one country,' he continued, 'not two against each other.'

'You must never, *never* go to war in Scotland,' pleaded Anne. 'Let my brother lead his army, he is responsible for the failure of the alliance with Bohemia united with England. I deplore the — how you say — foolhard rush to war in so small provocate.'

'As you say, "so small provocate".' Richard lifted her chin to kiss her, ruefully agreeing. 'And so do I deplore it, but my friends, Robert and Stafford, are determined to go, which I am not — so go I must!'

'You know nothing of war.' Anne was blinking tears from her eyes. 'Why should your uncle Gaunt insist that you go? He has been fighting wars all his life. Why cannot *he* lead your army as general?'

'Because he isn't king — yet,' muttered Richard.

That 'yet' was taken up by Robert, who had invited young Stafford to sup in the apartment Richard had allotted to him as Marquis of Dublin in the Palace of Westminster.

'Gaunt is forcing Richard to go to war and I'll wager that he and that swine Buckingham — he is the worst of them — are hoping that Richard will be killed.'

'God save him!' Young Stafford signed himself. 'Those uncles of his — my father has always mistrusted them and our futile government for what they call and resent "a child king".'

'As he *was* but he is of an age now to speak his mind if anyone will hear him.'

'He must make them hear him,' Stafford said stoutly. 'He'll be as good or better king than his old grandfather.'

Robert grinned. 'Edward the Good, they named him until — as my father told me — he got himself caught by that painted old bitch Alice Perrers who bled him white of all she could grab hold of when he was in his dotage. It was said she stole the rings from his fingers when he lay in state in the chapel of the Abbey. But old Edward, Richard's grandfather, went to war along with his son, who was younger than you are now, only sixteen when he won the Battle of Crécy. 'Tis hard luck on Richard to have to follow the nation's hero. But of course he can't stay behind and let his army go without him…'

In the first week of July, 1385, the whole strength of the King's armies was summoned to Newcastle *en route* for the border. It had been hard going during a prolonged heat wave, armed as they were in readiness for a surprise attack. It was fairly certain that the Scots knew of the English approach, but not until the royal forces led by Richard accompanied by de Vere and Ralph Stafford reached Beverley Minster in Yorkshire, was the army's advance delayed.

Richard, at the head of his Lancers, heard a shout from Robert a length or two behind him. 'Good Lord! Look what's going on outside the Minster!'

The troops had divided to ride two abreast in the narrow streets of Beverley, and while Richard halted to mop the sweat from his brow, he demanded that a fresh horse be brought to him. While he waited for another horse from a relay of mounts at the rear of the cavalry as substitutes if the going got too hard for the chargers in the heat, he saw that which Robert had called to him to see, a mob of townsfolk scattered in a *melee* at the oncoming troops amid clouds of dust, the clatter of hooves and clash of steel where two of Stafford's men were met in a fight. Suddenly he saw a favourite squire of his half-brother, John Holland, rush forward in attempt to intervene in what seemed to have been a trivial scrimmage and developed into mortal combat. That attempt on the part of the young squire to separate the combatants brought him to his death.

Scared for their lives, Stafford's two soldiers — none could tell which had been the killer — ran for sanctuary in the Minster. As Richard rode through the gathering crowds, John Holland, enraged at this wanton murder of his squire, dismounted and tore after them to the doors of the Minster.

'No, John!' Richard shouted, standing in his stirrups. 'You can't break sanctuary — I forbid you!'

John, in a frenzy of passion and grief at his favourite's death, yelled back at him, 'Who are you to forbid me? I'll have his blood for this!' Then, sighting Stafford, he dashed at him, dragged him from the saddle, and ran his sword through to the heart.

Anne was at Sheen with her mother-in-law, Princess Joan, when King's Messenger brought them the news of Stafford's death. Hot and dusty with his ride from London, he was hesitant in telling the queen and princess how Stafford had died.

'They are not yet at the border, are they?' enquired Anne.

'No, Your Grace, they are waiting.' The messenger looked uncommonly hot even for the heat of that July day.

'Waiting — for what?' queried Joan, sensing something that her mother's instinct feared to know … She had two sons in or near the battle front. Her eldest son, Thomas, Earl of Kent, was away with John of Gaunt. The courier evaded direct reply.

'They are waiting for the Duke of Lancaster to join the King's forces, Your Highness. He is on his way from Durham.'

'Is that what you have come from the King to tell me?'

An exhaled breath of relief passed from the mother's lips.

'Y-yes, Madam,' he faltered, 'the King sent a courier to Westminster and I was told to bring the news to the queen.'

'News of what?'

It was Anne's turn to fear the answer now.

Accustomed to bearing news, good or bad at the bidding of authority, he knew what he had to tell would be sorry hearing, less for the queen than for the King's mother since the Earl of Stafford's son was dear to her as one of her own. She had known him all his short life, now so cruelly ended.

He addressed himself deliberately to Anne, that he might lessen the shock he was about to deal to the King's mother. As one of the senior King's Messengers, he must, in his youth, have learned of rumours spread about the Court that the Earl of Stafford had been an ardent admirer of the then 'Fair Maid of Kent', and that he had unsuccessfully wooed her who had obtained a divorce from Sir Thomas Holland after having borne him two sons.

Among her many suitors, before and during her first marriage, was the Prince of Wales who succeeded in winning her for wife where Lord Stafford had failed. And to the Black Prince she bore a third son, the future King of England.

It was her second son, John Holland, who had dealt the death blow to young Stafford and it required all the diplomacy of King's Messenger to convey the shattering news to John's mother.

He hesitated a moment before answering the queen, to come out with suitable woe: 'I greatly regret that the King commands me to inform Your Grace' — he turned to the princess — 'and Your Highness, Madam, that Sir Ralph Stafford has been killed.'

The princess covered her eyes, asking on a sobbing breath: 'Killed in battle — or how?'

After the initial horror of the death of his only son had passed into the agonised desire for revenge on the killer, the grief-stricken Lord Stafford claimed King's Justice against Sir John Holland.

Richard, while loth to bring what he knew would cause the deepest sorrow to his mother as well as to himself, for John had always been dearer to him than his elder half-brother, Thomas, he knew he must deliver judgement on that which the father of his dead friend had condemned as — 'Murder! Cold-blooded murder!'

It was not cold-blooded; Richard, who had witnessed that killing, realised it had been done in a moment of red-hot fury, which even as far back as the early Middle Ages might have been condoned in France as *un crime passionel.* Yet for his mother's sake as well as for his own, Richard could not bring himself to condemn John to the death penalty, and in response to his mother's frantic appeals brought back and forth to him by courier, he refuted the death sentence and committed John to banishment and the confiscation of his property. This, at least, would give their mother some respite from the dreaded loss of life to this second son of hers, and the hope that in

God's good time the King would restore John to her from his exile...

That restoration was not to be. The mother, broken-hearted at the fate of John, went in fear for the lives of her other two sons, Richard and her first-born, Thomas Earl of Kent. Although he had not joined the Scottish expedition, he was in command of the Duke of Lancaster's army, bound for war with Spain.

'Richard is too young,' she told Anne, 'to lead an army at the head of highly trained soldiers. He was not born for war as was his father, God rest him! Richard has never raised a lance or any deadly weapon against a man let alone in warfare. And now Thomas is to set sail any day for another war with Spain by way of Portugal ... Always fighting, always lost in fields of blood if not maimed for life or ... dead. All are lost to me.'

'None is lost to you yet, ma mere.' Anne crossed herself. 'The Blessed Virgin is watching over them. John will be safely back to you again, I know. Richard won't let you be parted for long.'

Striving to comfort the sorrowing mother, Anne noted with a pang how the faded pink of her once lovely skin had shrunken, was too finely stretched across the delicate cheekbones. Her women had brought a day bed to a window of her chamber that she might look across the gardens where the lush green of the grass had yellowed in the heat of August's sun.

'It has been so hot and weary a summer,' she said. 'One can hardly breathe. I think always of my sons, armoured from head to foot, marching in this heat. And my — *your* flowers, my love, for Sheen is yours not mine — are thirsting for rain.'

'Sheen is and ever will be yours, ma mere. I am only the tenant.'

'Sheen is yours,' Joan repeated, 'while I live and when I die…'

'How she has changed in these last few weeks,' sighed Anne, discussing with Agnes Lancecrona her anxiety concerning Joan's health. 'She has never recovered from the shock of John's cruel banishment.'

'How much more cruel if the King had demanded that he pay the full penalty of the law,' Agnes reminded her. 'He has been let off very lightly, considering.'

'As if Richard would have demanded that John should pay the full penalty!' Anne protested. 'Nor can it be called a light punishment to banish him into exile, take all his property and leave him — God knows where — to die.'

'He won't be left to die,' Agnes told her, 'nor will he be gone for long.' She bent lower over her tambour frame; she was embroidering a cushion cover for the queen's day bed. 'This continuous war which is worrying the princess to death will soon bring Sir John back to her for they want every officer available for the war with Scotland.'

'War!' Anne turned on her. 'Ever since I came to England, and in my own country too, it has always been this one, that one, who fights. They are fighting mad, all of them … No, not my brother, he wants only unity between nations, which is why he married me to Richard, God be thanked! But I must know, I *pray* to know, how long it will be before this wicked war with Scotland ends.'

'It has only just begun. I had a letter brought to me.' She bent still lower to her tambour to hide a warm flush.

'From Robert?' Anne asked smiling. 'I know how you watch and wait, as do I, for King's Messenger. Richard's letters are brief but long enough to fill the page with the same word repeated … and I guess,' she said slyly, 'that Robert writes the same, or almost the same words, to you. Both letters are enclosed in the same packet brought by messenger. But such a long way to come and such a long time to wait for their coming…'

It was in the first week of August that the English forces crossed the border, and in celebration of the event, Richard created two dukes and one earl, at the direction of John of Gaunt, who although Richard was no longer a minor, his senior uncle still regarded himself as *in loco parentis.*

Gaunt's brother, the Earl of Cambridge was now Duke of York, and the youngest brother and third surviving son of Edward III was created Duke of Gloucester, while Michael de la Pole was given the earldom of Suffolk.

And now the war with Scotland began in earnest. The English advanced solidly, while the Scots, to evade immediate pitched battle, retreated to the North. The English pushed on to Edinburgh, destroyed the abbeys of Melrose and Newbattle, raided Edinburgh Castle, and ravaged Holyrood, to counter the Scottish invasion of Carlisle and Penrith. Gaunt, returned from Spain, had taken command of the army and also of Richard. He was determined to cross the Forth and cut off the Scots. After the raids on Carlisle and Penrith they were forced to retreat to the Lowlands.

Richard now asserted himself. Rounding on his uncle, where they had encamped for the night near the western coast, he protested against the risk of invasion in so remote and unknown a terrain.

'The Scots will be after us here,' he told Gaunt. 'Our supplies come from the eastern route, so they can intercept them.' His hot temper blazed. 'You and your lords can feed yourselves on the private stores you have brought with you and of which you have a good enough supply to feed my whole army! Would you see my soldiers die of starvation while you and your lords and your brother, my uncles Thomas and Edmund, of Cambridge, are glutted on food and drink — whole barrels of sack — from England!'

Surprisingly, Gaunt replied to this outburst with consummate amenity.

'You are my leader and my king. I must follow where you lead.'

Richard was immediately contrite at his uncle's good grace. They were sharing a tent where they had camped for the night. Leaning across the makeshift trestle where they had been served with Gaunt's 'good enough supply' of food, and a haunch of venison well roasted, brought from Windsor forest, he seized his uncle's hand.

'Forgive me, Sir. I renounce my leadership. You are Commander-in-Chief. I am but a novice in warfare. If what you decide to do is for the best, I will obey.'

'That's my good lad,' was the avuncular concession to this apology. 'But novice though you are, your youthful intuition is better than the knowledge of long experience.'

Reconciliation achieved, and on Gaunt's part with an eye to advantage gained by flattering indulgence to a hot-headed youngster who was beginning to realise his potential as monarch, Richard submitted, 'If you, Sir, approve, I suggest it were best we retire to Berwick and avoid the Scots' advance while we await further supplies and ammunition for the troops.'

So without any spectacular success on either side, the Scottish expedition was brought to an end; but it had served its purpose in that France would have to forego the invasion of

Scotland as a base for further hostilities until the next three-quarters of a century.

Richard's homecoming was met with the news of his mother's ill health that had been held from him during his Scottish expedition. Her death a few days after his arrival at Sheen where she had been staying with Anne, completely shattered him. The loss of a beloved parent, his sole comfort and support throughout the early years of his boyhood's reign, was a deep and bitter sorrow. But after the first shock of it, he turned instinctively to Anne. Her love and selfless devotion and her gentle influence in a hard and brutal age, did much to mould the character of the youthful monarch. Yet his boyhood's triumph during the Peasants' Revolt and his dauntless courage that endeared him to thousands of rebels did not fulfil its promise of a wise and valiant king. His indiscriminate bestowal of honours on unscrupulous favourites in general, and Robert de Vere in particular, sowed seeds of envy and malice among his ministers and others less favoured.

The government's dissatisfaction with the King's suzerainty that gave him the right to distribute honours and wealth to his friends and favourites, not only from his personal coffers but from the Royal Exchequer, caused Parliament to demand that a list of the names to be endowed must be submitted for ministerial approval.

This demand in direct opposition to that which hitherto had been the King's individual privilege, evoked an outraged storm of dissent from Richard.

To a shocked assemblage of Lords and Commons who had dared to defy the traditional rights of the sovereign — 'By God!' he swore, 'there is none but I — *myself* who can dispense honours and gifts from my personal coffers or my ex-

exchequer — A fleck of spittle appeared on his lips which had whitened in this stammering recital — 'without your damned interference and d-disapproval of those whom I choose to honour or —' he pointed a quivering finger at the rows of faces before him — 'or dishonour.'

That furious denunciation of authority resulted in the dismissal of the Commons and further embitterment from the Lords and even from Gaunt whose interests were centred as much in his personal ambitions as in the curbing of arrogant youth who without a firm hand on the reins might take the bit between his teeth and bolt ... Richard's apology to his uncle before the end of the unsuccessful Scottish expedition had been a purposeful gesture on his part having only just attained his majority and with it the consciousness of his royal prerogative.

The amiable relations between the powerful uncle and the youthful monarch induced a sense of relief in all quarters, and from the city's usurers mostly of the Jewish persuasion who had always been ready with financial aid to royalty in order to save their skins and their synagogues.

Richard's sympathetic tolerance of all mankind, whether Jew or Christian, peasant or peer, was extended to any who sought his aid and protection, even to his Uncle Gaunt, to whom, with no demand for repayment, the King loaned thousands of marks from his own coffers to finance the Duke's preparations for war in the Peninsula.

In July 1386 the Duke of Lancaster with his Duchess set sail from Plymouth for the Peninsular Expedition. He was given an uproarious farewell from the Devonian crowds who with cheers, hand-wavings, flag-flyings, watched them go; and from Richard and his queen each a golden coronet. Moreover, although their mother did not live to see the restoration of her son John, Richard took the opportunity to release him from banishment and bring him home to join the expedition.

The tumultuous send-off of Gaunt, and the King's costly endowment towards expenses for the war aided by munificent finances from the Jews, gave Richard hopefully to see himself in the full authority denied him during his minority, submissive now to no man, surrounded by friends of his choice and his own two trusted guardians, Sir Simon Burley and Michael de la Pole, Earl of Suffolk.

Although he was now Supreme Head of his realm with none to criticise or query his prerogative to govern himself and his kingdom — 'As if I should have to ask permission,' he complained to Anne, 'to benefit my friends for faithful service … God knows I need it. I smell enemies in the very air I breathe. They still look upon me as the child I was when I became king instead, as I am now, a man with a will of my own to govern my kingdom!'

When Gloucester's brother, Lancaster, was safely out of the way, he seized the chance to enlist a group of supporters unscrupulous as himself and equally hostile to the young king who now that he had attained his majority, had the right to rule his kingdom beholden to no man for that right.

Gloucester's paramount desire was to form the nucleus of a Commonwealth that not for another three centuries would temporarily usurp the Throne of England with the murder of a king.

This company of Church dignitaries and barons included Richard Fitzalan, Earl of Arundel, one of the King's most powerful enemies, his brother, Thomas Arundel, Bishop of Ely, who was to succeed Courtenay to the Archbishopric of Canterbury. The Earl of Nottingham who as Tom Mowbray had been one of Richard's boyhood friends and the son-in-law of Arundel, had gone over to the side of the angels, as Tom believed the Bishop and Archbishop to be.

All these feudal lords and distinguished churchmen were determined, as was their leader Gloucester, to take unto themselves the power of the King. One who refrained, for reasons of his own, from enlisting with Gloucester's company was his nephew, Gaunt's son, Henry Bolingbroke.

The jibes with which Henry as a boy had teased Richard for his inability and disinterest in sport, jousting, tourneys, falconry, and his ineptitude at chess were now carefully disguised under a façade of friendly cousinship, until such time should come for which Henry had watched and waited — to strike!

SEVEN

With the departure of the Duke of Lancaster, Richard's reign as Absolute Monarch began in earnest; but they were not to be the years of peace he had wishfully envisaged. The undercurrent of hostility and envy of his kingdom from his uncle, Duke of Gloucester, persisted.

Although his elder uncle Lancaster had always held aloof from participation in governmental differences concerning his nephew's sovereign rights, he may have foreseen a disruption of a parliamentary crisis, if not of a dynasty when his son, Henry, should succeed him as heir to the vast possessions with which the late King Edward, Gaunt's father, had endowed him. He was now in his mid-fifties and good for another twenty years. By then Richard should have learned how to rule his kingdom that was continually in a state of civic and parliamentary unrest…

Meanwhile, the fair breezes that had accompanied Gaunt's fleet to the Peninsula changed as they swept across the sea from Spain bringing bitter winds to Westminster barely three months after Gaunt had sailed.

In October 1386 Richard in full regalia, crowned, enthroned, attended the first opening of Parliament since he had attained his majority. Euphemistically styled the Wonderful Parliament, it apprehensively discussed rumours of a planned invasion from the French, an ever-present fear.

Brembre of the Victuallers' Guild and John of Northampton of the Drapers' were both seated in the gallery to hear the debates below on the floor of the Chamber.

The breach between the two guilds had never been healed, and Brembre's mayoralty and the favour of the King had caused a tumult in the City with the arrest of John of Northampton, finally released at the intervention of his patron, the Duke of Lancaster.

The two representatives of these two City's guilds were talking at each other in voices loud enough to be heard above the discussion of the members of Parliament in contumelious controversy. It was Brembre who set sparks flying.

'I see the King has honoured you by wearing the cloth and velvet supplied for His Grace especially for the opening of Parliament. A Wonderful Parliament indeed!' sneered Brembre, conscious of his superiority as ex-Mayor of London and friend of the King to that of a dealer in 'fustian', as he contemptuously regarded the trade of a cloth merchant who had only the remotest connection with royalty through the medium of the King's tailor.

Very far removed from a personal relationship with the King was John of Northampton when only the day before the opening of Parliament Brembre had been honoured to present the King with a barrel containing five dozen flasks of wine brought by the Flemings, and graciously accepted by His Grace in a message delivered by Maudelyn, the King's private secretary.

'I said "Wonderful",' capitalised Brembre, determined to be heard above the row of the debate below in the Commons discussing the threatened invasion of the French. 'Thanks to Parliament's *Wonderful* inefficiency we will all be massacred when the French occupy London — as you will see!'

And as they might have seen had not the Commons ordered a troop of volunteers in addition to the standing army assembled on the Kentish coast in defence of invaders.

This ill-advised state of emergency caused terrified citizens of London to take refuge in their cellars or to escape by barge on the Thames armed with any rude weapons such as pickaxes and shovels they could find. Sir Simon summarily dismissed such unnecessary precautions as 'Rubbish! Why put the fear of God into the Londoners for a pack of frog-eating Frenchmen who have been attempting invasion of England ever since the Duke in Normandy took possession of us at the Battle of Hastings, after killing the last of our Saxon kings? Why can't you go about your business — such as it is — instead of listening to the teetering twaddle of taverns?'

Yet it was not in response to Sir Simon's alliterative advice to whom Parliament hurled its challenge, but to Sir Michael de la Pole, the recently appointed Chancellor who strongly opposed the present administration whose interests were centred as were Gloucester's in gaining complete control of the King and his kingdom.

In order to avoid the storm they knew would burst upon them when they should announce to the King their intent to dispose of the Chancellor, they chose a day when Richard would be in his palace at Eltham to fling down the gauntlet with the dismissal not only of the King's Chancellor, the Earl of Suffolk, but of the King's Treasurer, John Fordham.

Richard was enjoying a sunny October afternoon in the pleasure grounds at Eltham in company with Anne, the ubiquitous Robert de Vere, and Agnes Lancecrona when a courier brought to Richard news of Parliament's disposal of those two high officials of the Ministry.

Having scanned the offending document handed to him on a salver as if it were the head of John the Baptist on a platter, Richard started up from the bench where he had been basking in the autumnal sun, and in a voice stuttering with rage he bade the courier, 'You can tell them who sent you that I would not dismiss one of my scullions at a grubby-mouthed Parliament's command, nor will I attend any one of their sessions until they ap-apologise for —' He paused to find a suitable malediction with which to describe this inexcusable offence to himself, the King. Since the absence of the Duke of Lancaster he had emerged from under the ducal thumb to take full possession of his royal anointed self. 'Apologise for —' he began again, prompted by Robert, *sotto voce:* 'For their bloody-minded presumption', echoed by Richard with a grateful grin of agreement. 'And you can tell them to go to the devil — or to come to me here with a deputation of forty knights when I will deal with them and their — (another sanguinary adjective) — demands. Go on, get out!'

The courier hastily got out, and rode hell for leather to Westminster where he repeated, with reservations, the King's ultimatum.

Richard, still simmering, turned to Robert. 'I'll wager that bastard Gloucester is at the bottom of this. He hates my guts and all I represent — always has, ever since I came into it for my sins. I'll show them they can't dictate to me or get rid of my ministers without I … Yes! I know what I'll do. They are, or Gloucester was, sick as a cat when I made you Marquis of Dublin. He has had his eye on Ireland ever since Gaunt made him, or made *me* make him, Duke of Gloucester. So now,' chuckled Richard, 'he'll have a bellyful of you, my Lord Marquis — *Duke* — of Ireland!'

The day after Richard received Parliament's defiance of his seignorial authority in dismissing two high officials of his Ministry without his permission, he dictated a letter to his secretary Maudelyn to be delivered by King's Messenger to the

Commons.

In this he commanded a deputy of forty knights to be interviewed by him at Eltham. 'I'd rather deal with large numbers,' he told Robert, 'than a couple or two of those sods!'

But instead of the forty knights he had expected, it was his two most dangerous enemies whom Maudelyn, with some misgivings, announced, 'The Duke of Gloucester and the Lord Arundel crave audience with Your Grace.'

'So do they!' flared Richard. 'Then you can tell them *I* crave to have them kicked out since they come here uninvited, blast them! Oh well, I suppose they will have to come in.'

They came in and were met with barely concealed acrimony at sight of this 'couple of sods'.

After the first perfunctory greetings, Gloucester at once expressed his disapproval of 'Your ill-advised distribution of honours to your worthless friends and associates...' ('That's a cut at you for your dukedom,' Richard reported later to Robert, 'which puts you into multiplication.')

Gloucester, having made his first introductory point drove it home deeper. 'And will, I fear, lead you to a similar fate as that of our forbear, King Edward the Second.'

'What about him?'

Gloucester's eyebrows rose up in mild surprise at this ignorance. 'You surely should know that Edward the Second was deposed.'

'Deposed — or disposed of?'

'Edward the Second,' Gloucester sternly pronounced, 'suffered the stigma of deposition for incompetence and irresponsibility as monarch, not only to his subjects but to his government, whom he consistently defied. Take heed, Richard, that you do not follow his disastrous example.'

Richard, who had held himself in, now let himself out. 'Do you d-dare,' he explosively stuttered, 'to-to threaten me?'

'I do not threaten,' replied his uncle, cool as the King was hot, 'I offer advice in that you act according to the statute of Parliament which demands if the King does not attend his Parliament within forty days, and your insolent message to your government states your refusal *ever* to attend a parliamentary session —'

'Unless Parliament or you who back them,' interrupted Richard, 'and apologise to me for their, or *your* goddamn insolence in dismissing my two chief ministers without my permission.'

'And,' continued Gloucester still with that same exasperating cool, 'if you do not attend Parliament within forty days which is your duty as the sovereign, I and Lord Arundel,' he turned to him who was impatiently waiting to edge in his word, 'are come to advise you how to deal with certain inefficient officers of State. We are far more experienced in the administration of your government than are you, who are still in your minority.'

'How old am I?' demanded Richard.

'You are not yet of an age to undertake the responsibilities of —'

'I asked,' came the heated interruption, 'how old am I?'

'You are not yet eighteen.'

At which Richard, red-hot, let forth, 'Damn you to hell for a liar! You know I was nineteen last birthday, and am now in my twentieth year!'

At last Arundel managed to circumvent Gloucester's shocked retaliatory reply. 'For shame, Your Grace! I trust you will ask forgiveness of Almighty God for your blasphemous address to your good uncle.'

Good uncle, my fiddler's bitch! was Richard's regression to his boyhood's vernacular; but this he did not say aloud. What he did say was, 'I merely desired my *good* uncle to rest assured I am now of an age — which he seems to have forgotten — to assume the responsibilities of my kingdom as God's Anointed. I have been crowned and will endeavour with the grace of Our Lord and Saviour Jesus Christ,' he crossed himself, 'to be worthy of that crown.'

'*Dominus Vobiscum,*' intoned Lord Arundel. 'And let us pray it will not be a crown of thorns.'

That meeting at Eltham, having ended in deadlock with Richard's vituperative assertion of his rights as king to take control of his government, left him undecided if he had or had not won the battle between himself and his 'good' uncle.

Gloucester's reminder of the second Edward's deposition and ultimate murder of which Richard had feigned ignorance, did nothing to relieve his anxiety concerning the threatened disposal of himself and his personal followers.

'You see,' he was restlessly pacing the floor of Anne's chamber at Eltham, 'I know Gloucester would have me out and himself in by fair means or foul if he could lay hands or an axe on me!'

Anne was always ready with sympathetic consolation. Taking his arm, she led him to the day bed where she had been resting. She would often rest in the afternoons, as advised by one of the Court physicians, who diagnosed her condition as Hippocratic empyema that he professed to have translated from the original Greek and for which he recommended a draught of powdered poppy seed added to honey and sweet wine, boiled in water and taken frequently during the day.

'That old doctor,' she told Richard, 'is so proud of what he thinks he knows of Greek, that he can only quote bits of what Hippocrates wrote in *de morbis*.'

'You could do better than that,' said he, 'or even I who was taught Greek and Latin by my good Sir Guichard, God rest him … but I don't like that little hard cough of yours. Let us hope your old doctor with his poppy seed and honey and his knowledge of Hippocrates and empty-what's-its-name will get rid of your cough.'

'It is only a tickle in my throat from talking too much.'

'It isn't you who talk too much, 'tis I who have far too much to say, as I said yesterday to Gloucester.'

'Never mind about him. I cannot believe he means to harm you, but he resents that you succeeded to the throne as the late King Edward's grandson and not one of his sons.'

'Himself, of course,' muttered Richard.

'I find it so difficult to understand these envies and jealousies of your uncles and your government against you who are the rightful King of England.'

'I am the wrongful king to them!'

'In my country,' she continued, 'they did never speak against the king. Wenceslas was not much older than were you when he became king. He was too young to carry so much on his shoulder. He had not only his country to care for, but me. He had to be my father, mother and brother while he was still a boy. You know my mother died when I was born. He is loved by all his people and his government. They do never throw — how you say — the logs at his head.'

He laughed and gathered her into his arms. 'Angel! I adore you when you speak in our idiom.' He kissed the tip of her nose. 'Yes, my government and Gloucester are always at loggerheads — as you say — with me, but worse than that 'tis what they did to another king — Edward the Second.'

She laid a finger to his lips. 'Don't say such things, or even think them!'

'I do think them, and I haven't a friend among the whole damn lot of them who is loyal to me, except Simon and de la Pole, and he is to be thrown out for his loyalty.'

'You will always have a friend in Robert,' Anne reminded him. 'But lately,' she smiled, showing dimples in cheeks that were not quite so rounded as they used to be, 'he has been entirely absorbed with Agnes and has no thought even for you and your troubles, my darling.'

'There will be trouble enough for Robert, poor devil, if he gets rid of Philippa. He has been trying for a divorce from her ever since you brought Agnes here with you. It was love at first sight with him, as it was when I first saw you! Robert was forced into marriage with Philippa. He was only a year or two older than I when he came into his father's earldom. Philippa is my cousin — worse luck. Her mother is my aunt, Isabella, and Gloucester's niece. There will be hell to pay if Robert can have a dispensation from the Pope on the grounds of nullity — meaning, as he says, that he'd sooner bed with a sow than with her! But Gloucester will never forgive him if he goes through with it. My "good uncle" hates my "worthless friend" as he calls Robert, now that I've given him the Dukedom of Ireland even more than he hates me.'

'After what Gloucester has told you,' said Anne, 'I mean about Edward the Second, do you think it would be wiser if you do attend the next session at Parliament?'

'As a sign of grace or of weakness? I don't know. Wait! I'll ask Maudelyn.'

When Maudelyn answered Richard's summons he was asked, 'When is the next session of Parliament?'

'Today week, Your Grace. I was about to advise you that it would be to Your Grace's advantage to attend.'

Anne nodded approval. He blew her a kiss.

'So be it! My two oracles have spoken.'

On 23 October Richard braced himself to suffer Parliament's decision, prompted by Gloucester, to secure the immediate dismissal of the most efficient of the King's ministers, Chancellor Michael de la Pole, Earl of Suffolk, impeached on treasonable charges. Moreover, Richard was further humiliated to see Suffolk replaced by his bitter enemy Arundel as Chancellor, and John Fordham succeeded by another of Gloucester's factions as Treasurer and Keeper of the Privy Seal.

Exhausted with the doings of the day, Richard retired early to bed in Westminster Palace and sought the comfort of Anne's arms to complain, 'So much for my authority as king which is of less account to the governors of my kingdom and myself than a fiddler's bitch!'

Despite Anne's sympathy for him in his unsuccessful fight for his two ministers, she bubbled into laughter. 'Wherever did you learn that bizarre expression you so often use?'

'From the village lads at Berkhamsted when I used to sneak out and play with them, if I could get away from Dame Mundina, my dear old nurse. But I'm not going to let Gloucester and the whole hellish lot of them get away with the dismissal of my Chancellor and Treasurer on any of their trumped-up charges — as you will see!'

His vigorous attempts to intervene on Suffolk's behalf against the alleged and wholly fallacious charges of treason and treasonable activities, did at last obtain a retraction of the penalty that would have been certain death to Suffolk. But there was no redress for the Chancellor's imprisonment in the Tower of London or the confiscation of his property.

Richard, in a forthright address from where he sat enthroned in his royal regalia of kingship, confronted rows of faces staring stonily at him — 'like so many gargoyles', he later described them to Anne. 'Where is your proof?' he demanded, 'of the charges with which you dare to impeach my Chancellor who gave thirty years' faithful service to the late king, my grandfather, and loyally serves myself?' He pointed an accusing finger at Gloucester who sat immobile and unflinching among his Lords and Commons. 'I command that you produce witnesses to support your false accusations. I have here evidence of that which you have c-clumsily' — for the first time in his indignation he began to stammer — 'd-devised against those of my esteemed m-ministers and myself!'

He drew from his sleeve a roll of parchment, and with it he smote his chest, on which the velvet robe bore the Plantagenet insignia of golden lions rampant. Gaining confidence from those watching faces that seemed to flinch at his outraged words, and unhampered by hesitation in his speech, 'I have here,' he continued loudly, 'the power that is my Divine Right to condemn the guilty who condemn the innocent, as you dare to condemn *me*!'

A murmurous buzz from those seated rows indicated denial of such infamous intent, but from Gloucester a shake of the head and the movement of his thin sneering lips offered no support to the majority's disclaimer of the charges against the King's ministers and against the King.

Pointedly addressing Gloucester: 'You,' said Richard, 'my dead father's brother, I refuse to allow the impeachment of disloyalty or of any treasonable act or thought to be arraigned against the servants of the Crown, for in such arraignment you impeach the King! I therefore remit the forfeiture of my Lord Chamberlain's properties and I commute his sentence from imprisonment in the Tower of London to my castle at Windsor, there to remain at the King's pleasure — as my guest!'

It was a bold move, and if it did not entirely revoke the forfeiture of Suffolk's property, it sufficed to show the King's determination to defeat Parliament's unauthorised control of the State and of his ministers, who had so ably fulfilled the offices of which they were now deprived. Richard further refuted the more serious charges against Suffolk by inviting him to the Christmas festivities at Windsor. There was dancing, music and a choir of singing boys from the Chapel of St George, and much feasting and toasting of the King and his two condemned officials, who had reason to hope that royal justice would be done and their fate averted...

A hope deferred.

Another vindictive attack as a result of Richard's support of Suffolk and his defiant objection to his Chancellor's imprisonment, was levelled against the King in a Commission headed by Gloucester and Arundel. This hastily devised Commission, that included the newly appointed Minister of the Exchequer and Keeper of the Privy Seal, consisted of fourteen barons, the self-named Lords Appellants, headed by Gloucester and his satellite, Arundel.

The statutes controlling monarchical rights gave Parliament the Commission and custody of all personal goods, jewels and dwellings appertaining to the King and his officers of State with an additional grant of 'exceptional powers' to amend the administration with full authority to enter the King's houses and those of his said officers, and any of the King's Courts and palaces as they willed.

If by these 'exceptional powers' they thought to bring Richard to his knees, submissively agreeing that governmental policy was superior to his own inexperience which would reduce him to a figurehead finally to deprive him of his throne, they were mistaken. Richard was no longer the 'pretty boy' of his mother's idolatry. During his marriage and under Anne's loving influence, he had come to a fuller appreciation of his stature as monarch; nor had he lacked wise and loyal counsellors in Simon Burley, Lord Suffolk (Michael de la Pole) and Maudelyn, his personal secretary. This would ensure, in the event of whatever fate should befall him, that he would not be left undefended to the mercy of those who sought to deprive him of his royal heritage.

When the latest machinations of the Gloucester-Arundel partnership and their Appellants fell as a thunderbolt with intent to deprive Richard of his last vestige of authority, he gathered together his faithful advisers including the ex-Chancellor Suffolk, still retained as a prisoner — at the King's pleasure — in a suite of apartments in Windsor Castle.

In his audience chamber, pacing the floor in long restless strides, he halted to address those he had summoned to hear him.

'I have thought of an alternative to frustrate my "good" uncle and my "very good" Lord Arundel' — he resumed his panther-like stride, head bent, eyeing the floor as he spoke his thoughts aloud — 'that I entirely reject the vindictive and in-incalculable attack on me and my throne! I used to believe my cousin Henry was my enemy, or at least in league with Gloucester, who is also *his* uncle — much good may it do him!' He rounded on those seated at the table with Anne at the head and Simon at the foot. 'But I have reason to think that at present Henry Bolingbroke has no desire to replace me while his father, my uncle Gaunt, is alive. For while Gaunt lives, Henry knows he hasn't a dog's chance in hell to do his damnedest to me along with his uncle, Gloucester. He was the youngest and most ambitious of the late king's sons.

'What I propose to do —' he laid a hand on Robert's shoulder — 'is that you, Duke of Ireland, shall collect a force from my regiments at Chester and the northern counties, and Ireland too, so that you are prepared to fight those who seek to finish me — if not with the axe, although I don't d-doubt they wouldn't stop at regicide! — then with imprisonment and not at *my* pleasure, as they have attempted to do with my Lord Suffolk. So what say you, Robert?'

Robert sprang to his feet, his eyes kindling with excitement. 'I am as ever at the service and command of Your Grace.' He was always punctilious in his respectful address to the King in public, in order to avoid any scandalous interpretation of his intimacy with this friend of their early boyhood.

Then Suffolk, rising from the table, suggested, 'Since the Crown and the higher officials of the government have been deprived of control and if as a last resort, with all respect to Your Grace,' he bowed, 'and to my Lord Oxford, Duke of Ireland, you were to plan an armed force from Cheshire and the northern shires to stand in readiness to defend the King, such an issue might lead to civil war.'

A gasp of dismay from Anne and a murmur of dissenting voices from around the table followed Suffolk's statement.

'But in order,' he raised his voice, 'to avoid any such calamity, I advise Your Grace to seek counsel from the Chief Justices of your kingdom.'

It was Burley who now rose to confirm Lord Suffolk's opinion that: 'The Duke of Ireland's praiseworthy readiness to fight for and defend the King's sovereignty —'

'I would lay down my life for him!' cried Robert.

'Which,' Simon imperturbably continued, 'lacking a sufficient standing army, it were better to wait until regular military forces can be assembled under the Duke of Ireland's command.'

After much discussion for and against Burley's suggestion, both Richard and Robert reluctantly agreed to the advice of their elders. Accordingly, in the new year of 1387, Sir Simon Burley and the Controller of the King's Household, Sir Baldwin Raddington, a nephew of Sir Simon, both competent militarists having served under the Black Prince, accompanied Richard on a tour of Yorkshire, Lancashire and North Wales, ostensibly a ceremonial visit but with intent to gauge the strength of the King's armies. Anne, however, refused to be parted from her husband for what might be 'a year at least,' she told him, 'as the roads will be dreadful in the northern counties during the winter. I insist on going with you!'

Richard caught her up in his arms. 'Dear heart, the roads, if not dreadful for us who are accustomed to travelling in winter, would be impossible for you to venture out. And do you think I would allow you to risk the discomfort of so rough a journey, putting up at whatever bug-ridden hostelries we could find to house you and your suite?'

'Agnes wouldn't mind *les punaises* — what is it — buggers? Nor would I — so long as she could be with Robert and I with you!'

'Well,' Richard doubtfully conceded, 'as you and Agnes have decided that you would sooner endure the miseries of travel — and *bugs,* darling, not buggers, you need have no fear of them!

— than be left behind while Robert and I review our troops in the north at the risk, if not of imprisonment in the Tower of London or else on Tower Hill with our heads in the sand —'

'We are not ostriches,' laughed Robert with his arms round the waist of the girl who had come to his side, while her mistress, the queen, spoke for her.

'I know,' Robert agreed, 'that Richard thinks we can do better in our search for traitors than go to earth here with a pack of hounds at our heels out for our blood!'

'Not your blood,' grinned Richard, 'but mine. Gloucester has been thirsting for it these ten years!'

In the end it was the girls who insisted they would go with their men whatever perils they might encounter on the journey; and neither Richard nor Robert were disposed to be parted from their women for at least a year, especially as Robert had been granted his divorce by a complaisant Pope to enable him to marry the girl with whom he is madly in love.

'As my ex-wife is Gloucester's niece,' he told Agnes, 'it will make him as great an enemy of me as he is of Richard. And he'll have his knife in you too, now you're my wife. So I am not anxious to leave you here without me.'

However, although Anne was persuaded not to travel with Richard, Agnes insisted on accompanying her husband to Chester; yet he sent her back to join Anne, refusing to allow her to go any further with him.

Richard, finding he could well leave Robert to assemble his armies in Cheshire and North Wales with a formidable force of archers and Welsh pikemen, he and Anne returned to Westminster. He thought that with so much hostility against him and his supporters, he must remain within reach of his capital.

So soon as he arrived at his palace he consulted Tresilian, the Chief Justice of the King's Bench, as advised by Suffolk and Burley, concerning his right to contend the Commission of Government. He then summoned Gloucester and Arundel — 'to have them under my eye,' he told Anne, 'for Tresilian says they have no legal right to issue their iniquitous Commission without consulting me. Besides which, they are — or Gloucester is — so enraged at Robert's marriage, not only because she is a foreigner but because of his divorce from Gloucester's niece, which he takes as a personal affront to himself.'

'I, too,' Anne reminded him, 'am a foreigner, and did Gloucester and the people of England object to your marriage with me?'

'You are no foreigner. You are Queen of England,' was Richard's answer to that, 'and my wife.'

He then commanded Gloucester and Arundel to be brought before him, that he might confront them with treason against the sovereign for having issued that iniquitous Commission to include the appropriation of the King's personal properties and free entrance to his houses and palaces. But Gloucester and Arundel both refused to comply with the royal command.

Having in their turn assembled their private armies in defiance of de Vere with his experienced pikemen and archers who had flocked to the King's banners from Cheshire and Wales, the Gloucester-Arundel contingent advanced upon Waltham Cross in Hertfordshire on the borders of Essex where, a few years before, the men of Essex together with the Midlands, Southern and Western counties, had risen in their thousands to revolt against the feudal lords of the lands whose serfs laboured in virtual slavery.

'I have no fear of the men of Essex,' Richard said, 'it was their peasantry and villeins who rebelled against the poll tax that drained them of the miserable wages they earned for their labour. They called on me to help them when I was only a boy, and I *did* help them. They are not likely to forget that and turn against me now.'

'Yes,' Anne nodded. 'I remember when Wenceslas heard of your courage during the revolt of the peasants and how you faced them alone while others much older than you held back and let you speak with them. It must have been about the time when Sir Simon was on his way to Bohemia to ask permission of my brother for our marriage. I think Wenceslas must have heard of your so brave support of the thousands of rebels who were invading London, and that gave him to hope our marriage might bring England in alliance with France and Bohemia to end this so wicked hundred years of war.'

'Which has not ended yet,' said Richard gloomily, 'and it looks as if another war is brewing — here!'

While the Lords Appellants were marching their army towards Waltham Cross, Gloucester had cunningly cloaked his intent to impeach the King's friends and supporters with treason. Among those to be wrongfully accused and subject to imprisonment, if not execution, were Tresilian the Lord Chief Justice, one time Governor of the Tower of London, and Brembre, ex-Mayor of London and the King's personal friend.

Besides this latest devilment of Gloucester and the Appellants, acting without the sanction of the Crown in issuing the Commission, they were also paving their way to be rid of the not so 'Wonderful Parliament' and to replace it in the coming year with a Parliament of their own choice, rightly named 'the Merciless'.

Meantime de Vere was marching his armies to the Severn Valley, but when news was brought to him of Gloucester's army advancing on Waltham Cross led by Henry Bolingbroke, Robert at once turned about to lead his archers and pikemen north-eastwards to meet and challenge Bolingbroke.

Henry had been of two minds whether or not to throw in his lot with his uncle Gloucester or to wait, as he had originally intended, for his father's return from Spain; or better still to wait until his father should be dead. He realised that while Gaunt, Duke of Lancaster, lived there was no chance of his immediate succession to the powerful Duchy of Lancaster with the vast estates of almost half of England bequeathed by the late King Edward to his son. He therefore decided to take sides with Gloucester against Richard.

Henry had now learned that Robert had reached the valley of the Thames and he lost no time in mustering his forces to meet and combat 'that upstart de Vere', for like Gloucester he detested and feared Robert's influence with the King.

Robert had with him an army of near upon four thousand, and Henry doubted if his own troops would outnumber them, even though Gloucester had mustered in addition to his own army some hundreds of volunteers. Robert was greatly relieved to hear that Richard, with the queen and Agnes, were safely lodged in the Tower of London, for he knew there would be fierce fighting between himself and Bolingbroke within easy distance of the capital.

No sooner had Richard been told by King's Messenger that Robert had left Wales and was marching towards the valley of the Thames, then he at once told Maudelyn, 'I leave the Queen and the Duchess safeguarded in the Tower and with my army in the south I will join Robert to support him. He may be outnumbered by Henry with Gloucester's men. You must remain here with my bodyguards in the Tower in charge of the Queen and her Court.'

'Indeed, Your Grace,' objected Maudelyn, 'I strongly advise you to remain in your capital. Should Gloucester and Bolingbroke attempt to invade London, you cannot desert your citizens. The Londoners will look to their king to support them in the event of an attack. If I may venture to remind Your Grace,' firmly pursued Maudelyn, 'you were here in your capital *and* in the Tower during the Peasants' Revolt that you so courageously put down.'

In the end Maudelyn won his point supported by the entreaties of Anne.

'For God's sake, Richard, do not join Robert against Henry and your Uncle Gloucester. You have not enough forces to fight the armies of Gloucester and Henry *et les autres* — how you say — the Appeals?'

It was during the argument between Richard and Maudelyn that King's Messenger again arrived with news that Robert had encountered Bolingbroke at Radcot Bridge near Eynsham on the Thames.

Richard's first thought had been for his friends and allies wrongfully impeached of treason and who stood to pay the penalty of the death sentence; then realising that de Vere and his army were in danger from Bolingbroke's forces at Eynsham 'I agree,' he told Maudelyn. 'I cannot leave my capital and my Londoners at the mercy of those who are after my blood and the blood of my friends. I must make sure they are safely away if there should be an attack on London. But let us not waste time discussing *my* safety. Much as I fear for Robert with that hell-hound Bolingbroke on his track, we must see to it that Suffolk, Tresilian, Brembre, and all who are victimised by my uncle, God damn him, be got away at once.'

He began his restless pacing up and down the room while he spoke his thoughts aloud. 'How am I to save my friends from our savage enemies who dared not take the murder of the King upon themselves? If they are discovered either here or at Windsor or anywhere within distance of London, they will be made to pay for a trumped-up charge of treason either on the gallows or by the axe, if they can't get at me! I don't know how many Gloucester has in mind to dispose of...' He wheeled round to tell Maudelyn, 'Two of my frigates are at anchor in the mouth of the Thames. You must go to Gravesend and command that their captains lay by and wait for the tides — it should be high tide by nightfall to judge by the river I see from these windows, and —' He again resumed his stride. 'It shouldn't take more than five or six hours — the captains will know how soon they can reach France if there is a wind. Although we are still supposed to be at war, I'll send a message to the King of France —' Again he halted to ask Anne, 'did you not tell me that Charles and your brother are good friends?'

'Yes, ever since they were boys. Charles often used to visit us. He has known me all my life.'

'Then I will send a message to Charles and you must add your name to mine. Maudelyn, take this down.' From a bulky packet attached to his belt, Maudelyn produced his tablets. Richard dictated: '*To my dear friend and brother, Charles, King of France. I beg the clemency of Your Grace* — Am I going too fast for you?'

'... fast for you?' repeated Maudelyn, scribbling.

'No, don't write that, you fool! Go on: *Clemency of Your Grace that you will give refuge to my Chancellor, the Earl of Suffolk, my Chief Justice, Tresilian and* ... name them all, Maudelyn. You can remember, I can't. There must be at least a dozen in danger of their lives from those devils, my uncle and my cousin Henry and all their murderous gang just because they are my friends! Tell the captains that they and their crews will be handsomely rewarded if they set sail tonight … where was I?'

'Chief Justice Tresilian, Your Grace.'

'Yes, you name the others … and go on with grateful thanks and God's blessing on Your Highness, *I am as ever, your humbly devoted* … his devoted what? … yes, devoted friend … Your *stylo,* Maudelyn.' After reading the letter, Richard added his signature and told Anne, 'Sign here, my love, below my name.'

Obediently, Anne wrote, *Your Grace's humbly affectionate Anna R.*

'A lot of honeyed slop,' scoffed Richard, 'to the enemy of England! Go then, Maudelyn,' he bade him. 'Take this letter, address it and I will seal it.'

'As Your Grace commands it shall be done.' Maudelyn bowed himself out as the pale queen ran to Richard.

'What — oh, what does it mean? What did King's Messenger say in the report? You read it so quick — and then you order your ships to take your Lord Suffolk and *les autres* to France. I know Charles will receive them, but what does it *mean*?'

'It means,' Richard answered between his teeth, 'that civil war is about to begin.'

EIGHT

The beginning and the end of Richard's fateful prophecy that England was on the brink of civil war was begun and ended in a matter of twelve hours.

Henry Bolingbroke and Tom Mowbray — Earl of Nottingham, friend of Richard's boyhood — were in charge of the Lords Appellants' armies under the command of the Duke of Gloucester, but he backed out of having to fight instead of threatening to fight, and stayed safely housed in the King's Palace at Westminster, which he had taken for himself under the Commission.

As the youngest son of his father Edward III he, unlike his famous brother the Black Prince, had never been called upon nor would he have cared to participate in the war with France. Yet his reason for maintaining his pacific conviction according to the Word of God, 'Thou shalt not kill', was less in fear of disobeying the command of the Almighty, than in fear of death or the maiming of his body. Gloucester's care was ever for his body rather than his soul. He had daydreams, possibly nightdreams, of himself enthroned, in robes of monarchy, crowned and seated in the council chamber of this very palace where he would lay down the laws of the kingdom he intended to possess.

From a safe vantage point in his nephew's Palace of Westminster, and protected by the King's own bodyguards, Gloucester sent his Appellants under the command of another nephew, Henry Bolingbroke, to meet and vanquish the loathly Robert de Vere (Duke of Ireland, forsooth!) who had disgracefully obtained a divorce by a too-indulgent Pope from Gloucester's own niece...

There was much for Gloucester to chew over and regurgitate against de Vere, not only because of his evil influence with the King who had no right to be King of England, where he had not even been born! A native of Bordeaux, he should rightly be named Richard of Bordeaux and leave it at that.

Seated at the table in the dining hall of the King's Palace of Westminster with his guest, the newly appointed Chancellor Lord Arundel, Gloucester liberally savouring the rich red wine supplied to the King by his low friend, the victualler Brembre — also impeached of treason — he said, 'I warned, indeed I besought my nephew Richard — hic (pardon me) not to be led into the cal-hic-calama-hic-tus deposition of King Edward —' He gestured a servant to refill the gold goblet and that of Lord Arundel.

'An excellent wine,' approved his lordship, who too had taken a goodly share of it.

'I was saying — what was I saying?' Gloucester's own share of the excellent wine was proving a little too much for his not very strong head.

'That your nephew, Richard, must not follow the example of—'

'Yes. Against me and my-hic-Lords of Appell ... will you take another slice of this fine ven-hic-son from my forest of Windsor?'

Between mouthfuls of roast venison, Arundel said, 'It is to be feared,' he drained the gold goblet of the excellent wine and beckoned a servant to refill it, 'that your nephew, miscalled hic-king (he belched) is under malicious influ'sence from de Vere who is assembling an army at —'

'The torches flicker,' interrupted Gloucester with a shiver as he bade a servant. 'Draw the curtains.'

Richard had caused heavy curtains of purple leather to be draped across the apertures of the windows of the Norman palace, which were filled with glass from Venice.

'It is a foggy night,' said Arundel, 'a sign of Grace from Almighty God, for fog —' another and more pronounced belch — 'is an en'my of war.'

'War?' bemusedly repeated Gloucester. 'Are we still at — where are we at war?'

On that foggy December night Robert de Vere, determinedly marching from the Cotswolds, had fallen into a trap set by Bolingbroke, Lord Derby, supported by the forces of the Appellants.

Although Robert had his Cheshire and Welsh archers and pikemen led by Sir Thomas Molyneux, Constable of Chester and two other valiant officers, the Appellants had a stronger army than de Vere's men, weary from a long three days' march from the Severn Valley. Nor did the damp freezing fog help the footsore troops against the Appellants and Bolingbroke's men assembled at Eynsham and holding Radcot Bridge across the Thames. There was little bloodshed or loss of life despite the desperate efforts of de Vere and his officers against overwhelming odds. What had looked to be a victory for either side developed into a humiliating defeat for the King's army under de Vere. He was forced to retreat sooner than surrender. Only Captain Molyneux, Chief Constable of Chester, put up a one-man fight against Bolingbroke and met his death from a rain of bow-shots from the Appellants.

Robert, having seen his troops well away, and under the belief that his officers were marshalling their companions in orderly retreat, was unaware of that killing. He made for the river bank and swam his horse across the Thames to the opposite side. Riding all night with scarce an hour's halt to rest his horse since he was loth to leave him behind, he reached the coast. There, he managed to hire a trawler to take him to Calais.

Richard, impatiently awaiting the return of Robert after the defeat of his army at the battle of Radcot Bridge on that raw and foggy December night, did not know of Robert's escape to France.

A dismal contrast was this Christmas from that of the year before when he had entertained his Chancellor, Lord Suffolk, imprisoned 'at the King's pleasure' in Windsor Castle.

The sorry news that Bolingbroke and the Appellants had made a triumphant entry into Oxford was brought to Richard by courier on Christmas Eve. He flew into one of his tempestuous rages that he had partially learned to control since his marriage.

'I'll have those murderous traitors hanged and their entrails flung to the dogs along with the heart and liver of that devil's spawn, my uncle Gloucester!'

He was white and haggard, having passed a sleepless night. Anne had gone to Midnight Mass while he, who would never miss a Mass or Day of Obligation, passed the night on his knees before a crucifix or pacing the floor of his chamber in an agony of fear for his friends.

Some comfort in answer to his prayers came with the arrival of another courier hot haste from the coast to say that a fishing boat had come with a message from the Duke of Ireland that the Duke was safe and well in the care of the King of France. And to Richard, a scribbled note: *All's well. Will return soon as possible.*

Anne endeavoured to implore Agnes to remain with herself and the King, for she was determined to follow her husband. She would not — could not stay, for God alone knew how long away from him…

Hard on that brief note to Richard came further news that Suffolk, who had been shipped to France with others of the King's friends, had taken refuge with his relatives, the de la Poles in Touraine. So all boded well for him and, so far, for Brembre. He, having refused to leave the King, was installed in the Wardrobe, an annexe of the Tower, that had been used by the late Princess of Wales. But Tresilian, who also had refused to leave England in the King's frigate, had taken refuge in the Abbey of Westminster.

According to the Chronicles of Adam of Usk who kept a faithful record of these vicious persecutions, Gloucester when Tresilian was discovered, ordered him to be dragged from sanctuary.

Having run their quarry to earth, and despite his protestations of innocence and the violation of sanctuary, he was drawn on a hurdle to Tyburn Gallows.

Nothing the King could do or say saved his staunch friend and legal adviser, the Lord Chief Justice, from the barbarous death penalty of hanging, quartering, disembowelling and cut down while still alive. The fact that he had counselled the King against the so-called 'Law of the Land', as conceived by the Appellants — a law unknown to any lawyer and least of all to the King's Chief Justice, was sufficient to convict him of treason.

The Appellants and Gloucester, having done to death their first victim, were hot on the scent of a second. Word had come to Gloucester, Master of the Bloodhounds, that the low friend of the King, Brembre, the victualler in wine and groceries, was hidden in the Tower. Bribes had previously been offered for any information as to his whereabouts, but none could be found to betray the ex-Mayor of London and personal friend of the King. Nor would the loyal Guild of Victuallers be coerced into giving evidence against him; and even the rival Guild of Drapers were cautious of implicating him until, or unless, he could be proved guilty.

The Appellants and their Master of the Hunt were not disposed to let another victim escape the 'Law of Parliament', and after a short mock trial Brembre was pronounced guilty of treason and sentenced to death on the block. A more merciful end than the savage hanging suffered by the Lord Chief Justice of England whose only crime was maintaining the right of the sovereign to rule his kingdom.

But the bloodlust of the Appellants was not satisfied with two out of a possible dozen or more to be run to earth — that is to say those loyal subjects and ministers of the King, some of whom might be members of the Parliament due to assemble in the New Year of 1388.

An eye-witness account provided a record of the lawful — or unlawful — proceedings attributed to the notorious *parliamentus sine Misericordia.*

The first assembly of that rightly named 'Merciless Parliament' opened in the White Hall in the Palace of Westminster. The king was on his throne with the Chancellor, Bishop Arundel on the Woolsack below him, while all the great lords and barons were on the left and right of him. The knights and burgesses, wherever they could find room to stand or sit, packed the hall to capacity.

A startling and dramatic entrance was provided by five of the Appellants walking arm in arm and identically clothed in cloth of gold, each separating to make his obeisance to the King, who was hard put to it not to demand if they were a troupe of mummers come to perform for him.

After the tedious preliminaries announced by the Speaker of the Commons, there followed a long document that took two hours to read, and moved the audience either to yawns or a few cheers and hisses from those for or against Gloucester and his Appellants.

For some obscure reason the dreary articles of this document were read in French, of which none but a very few could understand a word, other than Richard who dozed halfway through it and woke to declare, 'I object to the blame you attach to the Archbishop of York and to my Chancellor, Lord Suffolk, to my friend the Duke of Ireland and certain of my ministers for what you call incompetence. If there be any incompetence among you of this M-Merciless Parliament, it is here before me!' He gave a brief nod of his crowned head in the direction of the figure on the Woolsack sumptuously robed in red velvet and ermine. 'And read it in English, can't you, that all may understand your false and infamous ch-charges!'

There was a moment's silence followed by heated controversial arguments concerning the impeachment of the ex-Lord Chancellor Suffolk's integrity. Could the appeal for treason be justified by precedent? queried one of the judges, and the Sergeants-at-Law found it to be illegal by every standard known to them.

Gloucester, despite his own support of his recently-appointed judges, was furious at what appeared to be a *volte-face* on the part of the Appellants' original advocacy. Certain loyal adherents to the King in this first session of the merciless assembly indicated that they would oppose any direct implication against the sovereign's rights.

The debates and arguments concerning the legality of the Appellants' declaration of supremacy as defined by their Law of Parliament went on for a week and left Gloucester and his Appellants the triumphant victors, to organise their next move — or Meet — of the Hunt.

This involved four knights of the Household, intimate supporters of the King, who were to be run to earth. The first named of these four men was Sir Simon Burley, the guardian and much-loved tutor of Richard from his earliest years, together with Sir John Beauchamp, Sir John Salisbury, and Sir James Berners. All these knights were Richard's personal attendants and Gentlemen of his Bedchamber who had known and loved him since his childhood.

When the knights were brought to trial, the Appellants met with considerable opposition from the Lords, including Richard's two half-brothers, Thomas, Earl of Kent and John Holland who had been pardoned by the King on his return from exile after the killing of Stafford at Beverley Minster. He was created Earl of Huntingdon when he witnessed against the illegal convictions demanded by the Appellants.

In vain did Richard humble himself with entreaties to save his friends. The trials and sentences went on for more than a month while the King fought with every effort to delay or overcome the Appellants' decision to convict his beloved Burley and his three other true knights.

On the last day of those four terrible weeks he and Anne together thought out every possible means to save their friends, 'short of hiring assassins to capture and murder Gloucester and the rest of them'... as Richard, in the final stages of despair wildly suggested, and was at once reminded by Anne: 'Not you, but God alone can judge. It is not for us to seek revenge on those who persecute the innocent.'

'I know — I know!' he cried. 'But why should Simon, the friend and comrade-at-arms of my dead father — why should he and others have to suffer martyrdom for me? Why can't they take *me*? It is I they want to destroy, but they daren't, for regicide would be death to them.' He began his restless pacing of the floor. 'I believe that half of their Merciless Parliament, and certainly almost all of the people of England and Ireland still want me for their king, much as I would wish to be free of all to do with kingship. I never wanted to be king. It was the accident of my birth, and apart from my marriage to you, my darling, I wish to God that accident had never been!' He wheeled round to hold her in his arms. 'If only I could take you with me to my old home in Bordeaux where we could live together as husband and wife as we were meant to live, and have, as I have prayed to have, a child or children … I would gladly exchange my throne for the humble dwelling of one of my peasants who rebelled against their unhappy lot, not half so unhappy as that of their king!'

'Dear love,' she whispered, 'I too long for and pray for a child. And how I wish that we *could* live together just as husband and wife were meant to live in peace and for each other. Why, oh why do my prayers for a child — your son — go unanswered?'

'As God wills it, so must it be in his own good time — if ever.' He kissed her closed eyelids, wet with tears unfallen. 'But now,' he said as he released her, 'let us think how best we can save our friends and Simon.' His eyes kindled. 'I will beseech Gloucester — not in person. I'll send Maudelyn to plead for me … No, I'll go myself, if I have to crawl on my knees to that swine who is the head and front of his hellish Appellants, and if he fails me —'

She laid a hand to his lips. 'Then *I* will plead with him. He can't refuse both of us!'

When Richard sought his hated uncle who still lodged an uninvited guest in the King's Palace of Westminster, he was received with scant ceremony. 'What do you want of me?' Gloucester demanded. 'And what is the reason for this, er, welcome visit?'

'Welcome or unwelcome,' Richard replied, withholding his clenched fist from assault upon his uncle's person, 'I am here to enquire why you and your Appellants persistently attempt to deprive me of my regal rights.' His face flushed with the anger that threatened to consume him. 'Do with me your damnedest if you will, but spare my friends and my much-loved guardian and tutor, Sir Simon Burley.' He allowed a second's pause for recovery and continued more calmly. 'Have you forgot the duty you owe to the son of my dead father, your eldest brother? Is it my fault I was heir to this kingdom which should have been his? That you have resented me and my lawful inheritance all these years, you should not seek to revenge yourself for —'

'Stop!' roared Gloucester, his hand raised as if to strike. 'What I do is for your good in order to avert the possible revolution from a vast majority of the people of England who resent your sovereignty and your consort — a foreigner whom you married without my consent or approval and that of your Parliament. In the absence of my brother, John of Gaunt, I have endeavoured to act for you in *loco parentis*. And —'

'I am of full age,' came the heated interruption, 'and in no need of you or your s-satellites as paterfamilias who would destroy me were they not fearful of the penalty that would follow my death! I request — no! — I command, as my sovereign right, that you release Sir Simon Burley and all other of my friends from your bloodthirsty revenge upon me in your thwarted envy of my lawful inheritance!'

'Have a care, Richard!' Gloucester's voice was ominously cool, his steel grey eyes bored like gimlets into the flushed face of his nephew, whose upper lip was drawn tightly against his teeth as he strove to restrain a further volley of wrath. 'I repeat, have a care how you threaten me and those who seek only for the good of the State, which you are not yet competent to govern without the advice of your more experienced elders and myself, your close of kin lest —' his voice rose threateningly — 'lest you risk the loss of your throne.'

'Which would be no loss to me, and less gain,' he retorted, 'to you!' And without another word or backward look he left the room.

During that encounter the five Appellants, who were standing in a recess of the chamber used by the King for private audience and was now monopolised by Gloucester, came forward with unanimous expostulations against the leniency His Grace of Gloucester had shown to his unruly nephew. 'Still less a man than an undisciplined presumptuous boy,' was their verdict.

'Wait!' Gloucester told them. 'I have not done with him yet. My brother Gaunt is unlikely to be back in England before next year, and by that time —' His pause left unsaid what the menace of 'that time' might portend.

Richard returned to Anne, undefeated. 'I'll have at him yet,' he told her. 'He can't get away with his bluster and threats of a risk to my throne. If any risk there is it will be when I condemn him for treason to me!'

'My darling,' Anne took his hand and held it to her heart. 'With all the will in the world and all the right of your kingship, to fight against Gloucester and his insane obsession against you and your sovereignty is like hitting your head at a brick wall! Let *me* go to him. He dare not be so *hautain* — as you say high — with me!'

'And bash your head against him too!'

'My head is strong,' she kissed him. '*Vois-tu,* I go.'

She went, attended by Agnes who, as they drove up to Westminster Palace, drew from a capacious reticule a thin steel stiletto. 'I take this with me and will have no scruple about using it on the King's villainous uncle, should he dare insult *you,* my precious!'

'I would be only too glad if you did,' Anne ruefully replied, 'only that you too would be condemned for treason against the King's uncle.'

'If so, may the devil take him to himself where he belongs!'

As the queen, with Agnes behind her, entered the chamber, Gloucester, seated in a throne-like chair — the chair reserved for Richard when receiving intimate guests — rose effusively to greet her with a wide show of unpleasantly discoloured teeth.

'Welcome, Your Grace, my dear niece and queen, wife of my beloved nephew, the King.'

At which Agnes murmured under her breath the equivalent, if inelegant, remark in her native tongue of, 'Here's mud in your eye from Her Grace, the queen, your dear niece — you green-toothed rat!'

'And what can I do for you, my dear?' Gloucester winningly enquired.

'Better ask *me* what should be done to *you*!' came another murmur from Agnes.

Anne, between striving to control her repugnance for the persecutor of her beloved Richard and her amused approval of her attendant's muted chorus which had not escaped her ears, replied, 'I'm here to ask — no, to plead with you — for the life of Sir Simon Burley.' She was down on her knees, her hands clasped in prayer to him who sat in chilly silence in the King's chair. 'Sir, I swear as God is my witness that Sir Simon, the much-loved guardian of my husband's youth, is innocent of any treasonable thought or deed against the King's Government or yourself.' She struggled with rising tears. 'Sir, I pray you of your mercy in the name of our Saviour, Lord Jesus Christ, that you will spare the life of this good and worthy man…' Sobs choked her words.

'Get up!' was the harsh command from him whose hand pointed to the door, where stood two of his guards in readiness to seize and eject her. 'Save your prayers for yourself and that husband of yours, who has been corrupted since his childhood by him for whom you demand mercy. There is no mercy for one who endangers not only the throne but the life of your husband — the King!'

When Burley and the King's three other knights, Beauchamp, Berners and Salisbury, were brought for trial, a number of the Lords and Commons opposed the charges of treason against the accused as unproven.

The insult to which the queen had been subjected by Gloucester for interceding on behalf of Sir Simon Burley was met with strong counteraction from all loyal subjects of the King. They regarded as a treasonable charge the contempt of the Queen Consort's intercession to save the life of Burley, the monarch's guardian and tutor since his early youth. All to no purpose were the demands of those who besought Gloucester that their own lives should be exchanged for the lives of the unjustly accused.

Baldwin Raddington, Burley's nephew, was on his knees pleading for the life of his uncle. 'Take my life,' he cried, baring his chest in readiness for the sword, to be contemptuously dismissed as was the queen.

The Duke of York openly defied in Parliament his brother for illegal charges brought against 'these worthy knights and gentlemen of the King's Household'.

Gloucester, confident of a secure majority in the Merciless Parliament, refused to consider their pleas for mercy and pursued the hunt of his quarry to the kill.

One concession only was granted to Sir Simon, the old comrade-at-arms of the Black Prince. He did not have to undergo the barbarous penalty of hanging, quartering and disembowelling suffered by the King's three other knights. He was privileged to die by execution on the block as accorded to a nobleman.

Gloucester and his accomplices, having done to death or exiled all the closest friends and allies of the King, it remained only to ensure themselves against any repercussions that might arise from the murders of the King's faithful adherents.

They therefore granted the sum of £20,000 each to the loyal Appellants for the enormous expense which they had incurred in the good cause of the monarchy. We may be sure that Gloucester saw to it that he should be well subsidised not only to the tune of £20,000, but an annuity of another £160,000 for life as the lion's share of his exertions on behalf of the King, 'his beloved nephew's rights'. He knew that had his brother John been in England during the persecutions of the King and his loyal knights, the charges of treason would have redounded from them to himself. However, there was yet another year to go before the return of Gaunt from Spain, and Gloucester and the Merciless Parliament made the best use of their time.

Although they were left to the uninterrupted enjoyment of their spoils robbed from the King's Exchequer, Richard would not submit to their villainies unchallenged.

Soberly and with none to advise and console him save his queen, who in her turn had been grossly insulted by Gloucester when she pleaded for the lives of Richard's friends, he laid his plans for revenge upon those who in the last few years had made his life a living hell.

Richard knew that his uncle Gaunt, soon to return from Spain, would support him to keep Gloucester at bay; he knew too that the only man his uncle feared was his brother, John of Gaunt.

Although his Spanish expedition had brought him no spectacular success, Gaunt, who had been Lord of Spain, renounced his title for the vast sum of six hundred thousand gold francs as his agreement to the marriage of his two daughters to kings: the one to the King of Portugal, the other to Henry of Castile. He therefore came back a far richer man than when he went out, irrespective of the wealth with which his father had endowed him of almost half the shires of England.

Richard realised that he would require financial aid in his offensive against Gloucester and his Appellants should they counterattack, in which case he would have Gaunt's unlimited wealth to assist him in the fight for his kingdom.

Before Gaunt's official return from Spain, he paid a hurried visit to Richard in the Tower en route for Aquitaine as King's Lieutenant, an appointment that Richard, anticipating Gaunt's arrival in England, had conferred upon him; this at the advice of the late Sir Simon who had told him that his uncle Gloucester intended taking the Lieutenancy of Aquitaine for himself.

The reunion between uncle and nephew was, on Richard's part, so effusively joyful even after an absence of three years, it confirmed Gaunt's suspicion arising from rumours in England that all was not well with the King.

Gaunt had always mistrusted Gloucester, the youngest of his brothers, even as he mistrusted his son, Henry. *They are of a pair,* he told himself, *both intent on the same end, which they hope to be the end of Richard — but not in my time, please God!*

To his nephew's affectionate greeting: 'No words can tell how thankful I am to see you, my good uncle. I have sadly missed you.'

'As I can well believe, but now that I am here, and will be with you permanently within a few more weeks, your difficulties — and I can guess how many — may be peacefully resolved. I was grieved to hear of the death of your good Sir Simon and others of your faithful knights.'

'The murders, you mean, of my friends!'

'Careful.' Gaunt glanced cautiously around the oak panelling of the King's room. 'Walls have ears, and these walls, although well guarded, are not entirely deaf! And why are you here and not at Westminster?'

'Because Gloucester has — but that,' he hastily finished, 'is too long a story to tell.'

'No story is too long for me to hear,' Gaunt said, stroking back a fallen lock of fair hair from the boy's forehead, 'having heard but the barest half of it during my travels abroad. I suggest you make instant arrangements to take up residence in your Westminster Palace and that you hold a meeting of your council in Westminster Hall.'

'I had already determined,' Richard told him, 'to do just that, but I waited until you were here to support me. I have been too long alone.'

'I shall not be here to support you when you preside over your council, for thanks to my Lieutenancy of Aquitaine I must go at once to Bordeaux, but I will be with you in spirit, and I have here' — he produced a document of scribbled notes — 'the gist of what you can use in your address to the council. But you must speak in your own words, and do not spare your words,' he significantly added. 'I applaud the courage with which you have stood up to your —' he substituted the word *offenders* for *enemies* — 'and will continue to stand up to them with or without my support. And remember that in future I will always be with you when you send for me. You are no longer alone.'

Braced by the strong support of his uncle Gaunt, whom Richard knew could subdue and intimidate Gloucester, he assembled a meeting in the council chamber of Westminster Hall in the spring of 1389.

Acting on Gaunt's advice he sent Maudelyn with his request, more in the nature of a royal command signed and sealed, that the Duke of Gloucester must relinquish his temporary residence in the King's Palace of Westminster, where his uncle had been permitted temporarily to lodge at the King's convenience. But now that the King desired to take up residence in his royal palace with his suite and the Gentlemen of his Household, the Duke of Gloucester must prepare to vacate his lodgings forthwith.

'Not that there are more of my knights or gentlemen-in-waiting left to me than I can count on the fingers of one hand,' he gloomily told Maudelyn.

'Not so, Sire,' was Maudelyn's prompt reply. 'May I remind Your Grace that, besides the knights and Gentlemen of your Household still remaining in your service, there is always your personal attendant — my humble self, at your command.'

'Yes, always, Maudelyn,' Richard heartily replied. 'What would I have done without you through all these difficult times, for which I am constantly grateful. See here...' He produced a crumpled parchment. 'My uncle Gaunt made a few suggestions for a speech when I address Council.' He handed him the document. 'If you can read my scrawl just look over it and make any alterations you suggest. You are much better at speechifying than I, and you aren't cursed with a st-stutter as I am, and never know if my tongue is going to dry me up!'

When crowned and ceremonially robed he entered the council hall and took his seat on the throne facing that vast assemblage of Lords and Commons, he astonished them by his first peremptory demand: 'What is my age?'

This was the same question he had put to Gloucester in a previous encounter with his uncle. On this occasion of his first public defiance of his aggressors in open court, he was prepared for the unanimous reply.

'Your Grace is not yet of an age to govern your kingdom with the competence and experience of your present ministers.'

Richard held a moment's ominous silence before he flared out with, 'You lie! You all know my age was twenty-two in January of this year and that I attained my majority four years ago! Therefore, I am of full age to govern myself, my people, and my realm.' He paused to glance at the document he had unfolded and on which he had scrawled his rough notes.

'During the last few years of my reign,' he continued, 'I have been ruled by others and treated with less —' a slight stammer preceded the words — 'con-consideration and respect than I would accord to the poorest and most oppressed of my subjects. Eight years ago when I was only fourteen, I stood alone and unsupported by any one of you to speak — at the request of those who had rebelled in their thousands against the grievous taxes and above all the merciless poll tax you imposed upon them. They called for my protection as their king, and I promised to do all I could to help them and gave them my written word and my seal that I would endeavour to regain their rights to live as men and not as b-beasts of burden. They dispersed thankful and relieved that I would keep my promised word…' His voice faltered, but he continued, 'I failed them. Yes, I f-failed them because they who governed me were too cowardly to face those rebellious thousands who besieged my capital and ravaged the houses of their oppressors and set fire to half the city. They, my ministers, whom you say are more competent to govern my country than I, they — to my shame — governed me, and although I displayed my banners in their villages I was returned to my schoolroom as a — a child who had no word, no right to protect my downtrodden people!' His voice rose threateningly. 'Not now, and never more, will I be governed by any other than *myself,* your king by rightful heritage! I declare,' again he glanced at his notes, 'and I swear here before my God and before all of you who have taken unlawful command of me and my kingdom, that from now and henceforth I remove from my council all those men who, in their rapacious greed, have allowed me to do nothing to protect my people and to save the lives of my faithful knights and friends from their deaths by murder … I hereby declare and will sign and seal my declaration that from this day I, the King, will undertake the governance of my kingdom. This being so, I will in future select the ministers I choose to promote as governors of my realm — with my approval. Therefore I now dismiss my Chancellor, Thomas Arundel, Bishop of Ely and replace him with my Lord Suffolk, my late Chancellor now in exile. And I command,' his voice rang through the hall, 'that Thomas Arundel surrenders to me my Great Seal and the keys he holds in my name. He is dismissed from office by order of — the King!'

NINE

The years following the overthrow of Gloucester and his Appellants gave to Richard a belated self-confidence in his monarchical statecraft. They who supported the Lancastrian faction with whom Henry Bolingbroke held a watching brief, were confronted by the royalists ranged on the side of the King whose courage in upholding his dynastic rights they described as a 'touch of genius'.

Contemporary records influenced by Lancastrian prejudice ridiculed any such fulsome praise from the King's party; but future historians have agreed to it. Yet the youthful king was neither genius nor a 'dictatorial tyrant' as the feudal barons described him for his determined support of the wretched conditions imposed upon the peasantry and serfs.

The dismissal of the Chancellor Thomas Arundel and the surrender of the King's Great Seal gave additional security to Richard's attack against a belligerent offensive.

None the less he felt a lurking apprehension that the seemingly peaceful submission resultant on his hold assertion of the sovereign's rights, might well be a cunning device of his enemies to call his bluff while they assembled their forces for a renewed and more dangerous assault.

Although Gaunt had returned he was not yet enabled to support the King against his aggressors. The Lieutenancy of Aquitaine claimed his immediate attention, and the brief unofficial visit he paid to Richard on his arrival from Spain was prompted by concern for the governmental difficulties that beset his nephew.

Richard uneasily believed that Gloucester would take full advantage of his brother's absence, unaware that Gaunt had already left Spain and was less than twenty-four hours' journey by land and cross-Channel to England.

'I'll see that young devil axed on Tower Hill!' raged Gloucester to his accomplice Arundel, who was even more fearful than Gloucester as to what dire consequence Richard might have in mind to wreak upon the pair of them for their assumption of authority claiming his sovereign rights.

The king had been exceptionally generous to the Appellants in allowing them to retain the self-allotted £20,000 in return for 'good service rendered to the King'. They persistently maintained that they had acted solely in the interest of the sovereign and his State with which he was incompetent to deal, by reason of his youthful inexperience. Needless to say Richard was unimpressed by their thoughtful altruism in his interest; nor was he deterred from his policy of ultimate vengeance.

Meanwhile, he presented a façade of grace and favour to the Merciless Parliament and his enemies who had fought, so far unsuccessfully, for his downfall.

Gaunt, from his temporary residence in Bordeaux, heard approvingly that Richard played a tolerant if cunning hand with Gloucester and his Appellants while he awaited the ripening of time for the destruction of those who sought to destroy him.

As for Gloucester, he fretted himself sick wondering whether or not to take advantage of Gaunt's absence to demand the instant deposition of the King or to submit without immediate reprisal to 'that wretched boy's' dismissal of his Chancellor Arundel.

'God alone knows what further mischief he has in mind — his demented mind!' fumed Gloucester, whose latest machination was to suggest that the King was suffering from incipient insanity.

'Which is the reason,' he gave out to all and sundry, 'why I endeavoured to guide and advise the King in his incompetence as ruling monarch.'

He took himself and his anxieties to Arundel, his ex-Chancellor. 'This Christ-like forgiveness of his that I may retain my Lieutenancy of Ireland which has always been my right along with Ireland's dukedom which he has given to his worser half, the rascally de Vere, is a sure symptom of insanity as also is his exaggerated devotion to the Faith and his attendance twice, sometimes thrice, daily at Mass! Such intense orthodoxy in a boy of his age, who has no leaning towards the priesthood, is indicative of religious mania! He will, of course, recall that villainous de Vere from exile unless he gets himself conveniently killed in Touraine. Richard has already made you give up the Great Seal, but if he were in his right senses he would never have dared offer such an insult to his Lord Chancellor and Bishop. What more hellish mischief has he in mind — his demented mind — to do to you and me?'

'Have no fear,' was Arundel's unconvincing advice. 'The Lord cares for his own. Your nephew, the King, is, alas, possessed, but God the Father — our Father, not his, poor lost soul — will see that neither you nor I will be sacrificed by the follies of misguided youth.'

'There has been far too much talk of his youth!' snarled Gloucester. 'There was nothing youthful in the torrent of abuse he poured on his Parliament and myself, and on you. He has the devil's own age-old iniquity!'

Poor comfort for either of them was Gloucester's opinion of Richard's sudden assumption of authority. Still more alarming to Gloucester was the unexpected arrival of Gaunt several weeks before his return had been officially announced. Gloucester knew nothing of his brother's earlier visit to Richard prior to the King's rageful outburst publicly addressed to his council and the hostile members of his Merciless Parliament. Gloucester realised that Richard, with Gaunt beside him, would be powerless to strike. He guessed that those who had submitted to the King's sovereignty would rise against him with a stronger force than ever, supported by the Duke of Lancaster.

A tumultuous welcome greeted Gaunt when he arrived at Plymouth in the autumn of 1389. Flags were flying, crowds cheering, and the King, as if conducting an orchestra, stood with his queen beside him, a hand beating the air in time to the loud-voiced cheers and shouts of, 'Welcome home, our Duke of Lancaster!'

Soon after the Duke's return Richard held a banquet in the Great Hall of Westminster Palace in honour of his uncle Gaunt, to which only a few of his intimates and officers of State were invited, including Arundel and Gloucester.

'More heaping coals of fire on our heads,' muttered Gloucester as their names were stentoriously announced to their host who offered each a hand in warm greeting. Richard had arranged that both should have a place of honour near to Gaunt who sat on his left with the queen on his right at the head of the banqueting hall.

Toasts were drunk and a speech from the King to 'my good uncle, Duke of Lancaster and a second father to me since the lamented death of my own heroic father…' Which caused Gloucester still more anxious speculation as to where 'the wretched boy's malevolent intent might lead' nothing lessened by his 'Christ-like' forgiveness towards himself and his worthy ex-Chancellor Arundel, Bishop of Ely.

The first Parliament to replace its unpopular predecessor met on 6 February 1390, approximately the day of the King's twenty-third birthday. No question now of an immature incompetent youth to whom hymns of praise and thanksgivings were sung in celebration of the thirteenth year of his succession to the throne.

Gaunt, speaking for the King, conveyed to the council that all officers of State should be reappointed with the exception of the Chancellor and Treasurer neither of whom, it was tactfully suggested, should bear any resentment to the readjustment since both were reinstated as Lords of the King's Council.

This final assumption of the King's full power with the counterweight of Gaunt's support, was a clever move on Richard's part to screen himself from opposition in his interchange of ministers. They dared not cavil at his choice; nor accuse him of royal favour to the worthless.

With Gloucester and Arundel restored to the council, and although Richard had sent his secret summons to de Vere for his return, there had been no response as yet to his indication that his friend should reclaim the Dukedom of Ireland. But the King's message to Suffolk for his recall was answered with the sorrowing news that his good old friend and guardian of his youth, Michael de la Pole, had died of fever in Paris where, after his visit to relatives in Touraine, he was temporarily residing while he waited to return to England in the service of the King.

A still greater sorrow than the death of Lord Suffolk, friend and comrade-at-arms of his father, came with the news that Robert de Vere had been killed in a boar hunt at Touraine.

'So that is why I had no reply to my letter calling him back.' Richard rubbed a hand across his eyes, a childish trick to which he often reverted when hiding tears.

Anne took the weeping Agnes in her arms to comfort her. 'I had a premonition,' sobbed Agnes, 'that he would never return when he went into exile without me.'

'I begged you to join him,' Anne said, equally tearful, 'but you refused to leave me.'

'I would never leave you, my darling, whatever should befall my husband, even if never to see him again in this world.'

'We will see him again,' Richard said chokingly, 'when our time comes to follow him. But he will always be with us,' he told Agnes, his arm around her shoulders. 'Neither you nor I are for ever parted from those who go before us to the kingdom that belongs to him and all who live in the Grace of God … I will make arrangements that he be brought here to lie in his family vault at Earl's Colne.'

According to the chroniclers who wrote of de Vere's interment, Richard had ordered a magnificent funeral. The ceremony was performed with great solemnity attended by the Archbishop and many of the higher clergy. All, it would seem, thought it polite to mourn with the King in his grief for the loss of his much-loved friend.

Notable absentees were Gloucester, Arundel and Henry Bolingbroke, all known to have hated de Vere as the King's prime favourite.

Before the lid of the coffin was placed over the body of de Vere, the King fell on his knees beside the grave gazing on the embalmed face, and taking a ring from his finger he placed it on the hand of his beloved friend, saying, 'With this ring I swear to avenge you and myself, who have suffered from the injustice of our enemies. Rest in peace.'

From that day forth Richard was secretly planning retribution for the death of his friend and all who had 'been murdered' by the hanging and execution of those who were loyal to the King.

Although Richard was now established as the ruling monarch, Gloucester and Arundel restored to the council with the careful reservation, as dictated by Gaunt, that such concession on the part of the King was not to be regarded as a precedent, since the monarch had the right to remove or appoint any one of his ministers without dispute or question.

Further to celebrate Gaunt's return to England Richard ordered a service of thanksgiving to be held in Westminster Abbey to which Gaunt returned the compliment with lavish entertainment in his semi-royal palace at Leicester.

Again, if we may substantiate the reports of contemporary chroniclers who were the precursors of the daily press six hundred years later, 'Rejoicing was heaped on rejoicing,' which should have assured Richard of Gaunt's popularity and that of the King who, since his accession to the throne, had been little more than a name to his subjects.

Yet while he took an active and enjoyable part in the festivities he kept a wary eye on his erstwhile tormentors, Gloucester, with Arundel beside him, beaming kindly avuncular affection for the still 'youthful' king.

Both, Richard mentally soliloquised, *are to be trusted as much as the serpent who caused a mort of trouble in a garden, to bring the wrath of God upon the first man and woman for whose sin we are paying in our life on earth until His Kingdom come! I hope we'll be forgiven and admitted by Peter to the Almighty presence, unless we are cast down below to roast in everlasting — along with Gloucester and that old sinner, his brother Thomas, Bishop of Ely. Confound them and their sweet smiles, about as charmful as the grin of a skull!*

So much for Richard's opinion of the amiable advances of his uncle and Arundel, while he laughed and clapped hands with his queen beside him. She seemed to enjoy the dancing and jollification as much as any, with a bright colour in her cheeks — too bright a colour, he anxiously noted, for unlike the women of her time Anne trusted to nature rather than to art and used neither paint nor powdered chalk on her fair transparent skin.

To Agnes, a sad little figure in her mourning purple, Richard whispered doubtfully, 'I don't like the queen's high colour. She looks to be painted. Is she painted?'

'Only a touch of the hare's foot, Your Grace.'

'The hare's foot — what on earth —?'

'The foot of a hare, Your Grace, dipped in a pink powder and used by the silversmiths to brighten and polish their silverware, called rouge. It was first used by the French ladies to tint their faces with colour and now 'tis the fashion here, as you may see that the Duke's Lady Swynford,' Agnes added with smiling spite, 'is à la mode.'

For the whole Court knew and gossiped of Gaunt's infatuation with the beautiful Lady Swynford. Gaunt's second marriage to Constanzia of Castile had been a marriage of convenience, since one of his daughters had married Constanzia's brother, the King of Castile. The duke's first wife, Blanche, of whom Chaucer wrote a poem lamenting her death, was succeeded by Constanzia; and when she eventually died Gaunt married his mistress, Catharine Swynford who had already borne him four children.

Although neither Richard nor Agnes were in any mood for junketing, both in sorrow for the loss of de Vere, they joined the young men and girls in a gay cotillion, the precursor of the galliard of two centuries later.

Richard led Anne in the dance, holding her close. *How light she is,* he thought, *too slender for her height.* A tall girl was Anne, taller than the average woman of her time… 'Just as high as my heart,' he would say, whose six feet two inches towered above her.

That night, when they loved each other and, as he achingly remembered in the years to come, she murmured in the aftermath of their mutual climax, 'This time, dear love, our child will — must be — conceived.'

Conceived, yes, and for twelve weeks they rejoiced together to know her pregnant, but the child they had longed for passed from her. 'As God has willed it,' he comforted her, his tears mingling with hers. 'Our child will live and grow with others who were taken to heaven before they lived on earth.'

'I wonder,' she sobbed, 'I have often wondered if the cherubim we see painted surrounding our Lady are the children born too good for this world.'

That was in July 1390 and in the following October Gaunt arranged a splendid tournament at Smithfield as a hopeful preliminary to peace negotiations with France. He was determined that the people, especially the Londoners and countryfolk from the city's outskirts, should see and know their king no longer as a name. He knew that Gloucester and his allies would convey with significant inuendoes that the King had no sense of kingship and, as many were induced to believe that, he was not quite… 'Not quite … right?' would be the hushed query, answered with meaningful nods and pursing of lips. And in taverns of the city and beyond in the nearby villages of Hampstead and Highgate or south of the river on the Surrey side, 'The late king, his grandfather, was…' Foreheads were tapped with mutters of 'Pity there be none other unless 'tis Lord Gaunt's son, Lord Derby, to follow this one's grandfather.'

But some of their elders who could remember 'this one's grandfather' were quick to tell them, 'A great king and a great soldier was Edward the Third, even before his son, the Black Prince, won his spurs when barely sixteen.'

'But this one,' they demurred, 'has never fought in a war nor never rode in a tourney until he came of age as king.'

'He will ride in the tourney at Smithfield,' was the hot retort from those who had known and loved his famous father. 'And as to being what you call "not right", he is more right than any of you who lecher after women other than your wives. This king has no woman in his life but the queen, God bless her!'

'None blessed her when he married her,' said one of the Gloucester clan. 'A foreigner! Who wants a foreign queen?'

'We all want her!' This from another of the King's loyalists. 'Good Queen Anne, as she is called and rightly so. Did any other queen visit the sick in person and bring them nourishing foods and broths who are too poor to pay for their needs?'

So went divided opinion, as has been for all time to the advantage or disadvantage of royalty.

At the international tourney at Smithfield Gaunt manoeuvred that Richard should lead in the chief events to impress the crowds of Londoners and countryfolk who had come from miles beyond the city to watch the King and see him awarded the honours of the day. Gaunt saw to that, of course, presenting him rather in the nature of a public relations officer or press agent of centuries later. Loud cheers from the multitude of onlookers greeted the King when he won against the Comte St Pol representing France, who gracefully allowed the King of England, nothing like so accomplished in a tilting match as the Frenchman, to carry off the prize of a golden goblet.

Richard held it aloft shouting for all near enough to hear him, 'I offer my prize as a gift to the Mayor of London and the citizens of my capital as a token of respect to my distinguished opponent, the Comte St Pol, who more richly deserves to win than I!'

A gallant gesture, as much to rejoice the public as to flatter the Ambassador of France and other foreign visitors, many of whom were participants in the contest. We may presume that with peace looming on the horizon Gaunt had staged this tournament to end with a chorus of, 'God save our King and God save the King of France!'

Thus ended in jubilant cheers that day, as on another day when a boy of fourteen had stood alone and unafraid to face Wat Tyler and the thousands of bloodthirsty rebels, again to win for King Richard II the hearts of his people.

During the years following the overthrow of Gloucester and his Lords Appellants who had humiliated and deprived the King of all his intimate friends and advisers, Richard for the first time in his reign enjoyed full power.

The ensuing seven years, known as the 'Quiet Years', were anything but quiet. If the promise of peace with France brought a certain tranquillity to the war-harassed people of England, trouble in the North shadowed the optimistic hope of a truce to end the seemingly endless war with France. But while Gaunt at Calais and his ambassadorial delegates including his son, Lord Derby, were engaged in diplomatic negotiations, their proceedings were temporarily halted.

First by a rising in Cheshire possibly instigated by Gloucester in vengeance on Richard for having countermanded his appointment as Justice of Chester, although the King had reappointed him a Lord of the Council. Therefore Gaunt found himself stranded between disturbances in Cheshire and the deep sea of the English Channel. A more serious delay of a hopeful peace came when a message from Paris announced that the King had gone mad!

This sixth Charles of France had, like Richard, inherited his throne when a young boy and was in the care of a regency until of an age to marry.

His wife, Isabeau, Princess of Bavaria, with whom Charles had been deeply in love, probably contributed to the king's breakdown by her notorious promiscuity with any man of her fancy within or without the Court, which could in later generations have been ascribed to nymphomania. That Charles knew himself to be the cuckold of half his courtiers and many other men who were horizontally intimate with his wife, might have deranged stronger sensibilities than those of the weak-minded Charles.

The pronouncement of the Court physicians that the King of France, if not incurably insane, was temporarily *non compos mentis*, could scarcely have motivated negotiations for a permanent end to war. When the disturbances in Cheshire had subsided and Gaunt was enabled to resume his ambassadorial procedures with a regency appointed to partake in an agreement of a truce with France, Richard could now divide his leisure time with Anne at Sheen and his attendance to parliamentary sessions at Westminster.

Here again he met with difficulties from his government, although they were more merciful than its Merciless predecessor. 'They are always wrangling over this, that or the other,' he complained to Anne. 'They are now questioning the "luxurious extravagance", as they call it, of my Court, and demand a loan from the Londoners of one thousand pounds paid to the Exchequer for expenses incurred — by *me,* I presume!' Restlessly pacing the room, 'How dare they,' he cried, 'come down on the citizens of London for the expenses of my Court and my Household and me! It is they who are wasting the money of the Crown with their besotted mismanagement. But the Jews supplied ready cash to the Crown in the time of the first Richard who showed his gratitude and favour to the so-called "despised race". Not so the Londoners who persecute the Jews today. Yes!' he veered round to tell Anne ragefully, 'do you know what they did to the Jews who helped Richard, the Lion Heart, in his Crusade? They broke into the synagogues, set fire to their homes and left their bodies roasting in the gutters!' He resumed his restless pacing while Anne inhaled a breath of horror that ended in a short dry cough. He halted. 'You still have that cough.'

'It is only a tickle in my throat. How horrible to think that human beings — the citizens of London — could so dreadfully persecute innocent men and women. And children too!'

'And on the very day of Richard *Coeur de Lion*'s coronation, as I have read in records of the earlier Plantagenets, they performed their horrific persecutions during the coronation banquet. But the King gave orders that the perpetrators of these horrors should be punished. I've no wish to ask Jewish moneylenders for financial aid, either for myself or for defence of the realm, although Jews are always ready to help with their money of which they have so much — due to their brains, I suppose. They have accumulated wealth since the time of Moses when driven into exile.'

Again he started his restless to-ing and fro-ing, talking more to himself than to her.

'I admire the Jews as I admire and support all downtrodden peoples who have worked and slaved for independence, and are taxed to their last shilling, poor devils. As for my Parliament or Council or whoever attempts to govern me — I'll let them know who is the sovereign in command of my kingdom or else — God damn them! — they'll pay for it! Their time is not yet come, but when it does —' He clenched his fists at his side, his face reddening with fury — 'when it does they'll pay for it as Gloucester and all his murderous gang have made others pay for their loyalty to me. Yes! They'll pay with the last drop of their blood for their massacres of innocents!'

The storm that had brewed in Anne's room at Sheen broke out when Richard faced the rows of Lords and Commons in the council chamber.

'I demand as my right,' he shouted, his face flushed with the tide of his rage, 'that you render me a list of expenses you say are incurred by me or the extravagance of my Court, and are far less than you spend on one week's entertainment in your mansions or that the Londoners spend on the expenses of their guilds. They, the Londoners, and others,' he added pointedly, 'are self-seeking money-grubbers who care for nothing but to fill their coffers with their ill-gotten gains,' he began to stammer as indignation poured from him, 'which are b-bled from those who labour for a pittance — a starvation wage, while the King's lawful and regal expenses are begrudged!'

There was no mistaking now to whom his vituperative address was directed.

'Can you sit there smug, and self-satisfied and raise not a voice, if you have a voice to speak, against these Londoners who have refused one penny piece from the wealth of their coffers or their guilds to pay for what you say is the King's personal extravagance and as you, my council, well know is for the defence of my kingdom in an ultimate truce with France. And that should come from the King's Exchequer and not from the coffers of the Londoners!'

At this, one of the Commons, a squat, paunchy fellow who Richard recognised as Sir Edward Dalingridge and knew him to be an ardent loyalist, rose up firmly to address the King.

'Sire, I regret to inform Your Grace that not only has Your Grace's Exchequer been refused the loan of one thousand pounds to meet the expenses of the peace negotiations with France, but a merchant, a Jew from the Lombard area, has generously come forward with the necessary sum required, for which he specifically states he will not demand repayment. And for his loyal generosity he has been assaulted by the citizens, dragged from his house into the street, severely maltreated and left to lie bleeding from his wounds in the —'

'Stop!' roared Richard. 'If what you say is true, and since none of my council seems able to deal with my kingdom's finances or to obtain the necessary funds for negotiation of peace with France, then *I* will!'

Thereupon without let or hindrance, he flung aside the robe of state he was compelled to wear when in attendance on his council or his Parliament, and which, at the attempt of a page to catch the heavy folds of velvet, the boy fell flat on his back, while the council uprisen to a man uttered exclamations of protest.

'Pray, Your Grace, do not venture on so dangerous a sortie alone.' This from Dalingridge.'Allow me to accompany your—'

'No! I want no one with me.'

From another member of the council, 'I beg Your Grace at least to call out your bodyguard to —'

'Shut your mouth!' inexcusably shouted the King, and unheedful of objections that with the one exception of Dalingridge were not very convincing since none was prepared to expose himself to an infuriated mob, Richard strode from the council chamber and was driven straight to the Tower of London.

Word had been sent to his bodyguard to stand by in readiness for the King's arrival, and forthwith the citizens of London led by the mayor and corporation assembled to hear the address from the King.

As reported by the indefatigable chroniclers, we can picture the tall, slender young man who stood in the main gateway of the Tower, his fair hair bereft of headgear, wind-blown by a breeze, while a rapidly swelling crowd of citizens gathered behind the mayor, his aldermen and sheriffs. They had come with evident purpose to counter any charge against the Londoners whom they represented.

Once before this same young man when a mere boy had stood to address a similar but even more hostile multitude, and had won their respect and affection for his courage to hail him, 'the Londoners' King'. Yet on this day, some several years later, it was no boy but a stern-faced man who now addressed a rebellious populace.

'You, in your greed and arrogance, you refuse the request of your king to assist in the heavy expenses to obtain peace with our enemies who for the last hundred years have threatened this England — your England and mine! Your forbears fought and died in the defence of our country but you — you worthless, cowardly scum! —' He raised a gauntleted fist as if to strike the crowding faces agape with alarm and astonishment at such condemnatory insults from the King. If uttered by one of their own kind, these would have received an equally insulting response, yet coming from the King, although inexcusable, they were left with no alternative, however reluctantly, to accede to their sovereign's demand.

Nemesis!

Not only did Richard condemn those who had assaulted a generous Jewish merchant, dragged him from his house and beaten him up for having supplied the money demanded by the Exchequer which the citizens of London had refused, but they should pay as penalty within the week a fine of ten thousand pounds, and a further fine of thirteen hundred pounds to the Exchequer, besides the sequestration of recalcitrant citizens' property.

Richard ignored the advice of Anne and Maudelyn that such drastic punishment, although well deserved, would increase the Londoners' antagonism. 'Because,' Anne pleaded, 'you run the risk of a rebellion that could be as bad or worse than the Peasants' Revolt.'

'I entirely agree with Her Grace,' said Maudelyn. 'It is of paramount importance that you keep on friendly terms with the citizens of London who, until these unhappy circumstances, regarded Your Grace with reverence and affection. They are repentant now and have accepted their penalties, but there is the possibility they will bear you a lasting resentment unless Your Grace should mitigate their sentences for a shorter interim.'

'They have persecuted an honourable citizen who has paid the Exchequer without reservation the money refused by these Londoners. I will not,' Richard obstinately persisted, 'tolerate injustice or persecution either to Jew or Christian!'

His next move was to depose the mayor from office and nominate a warden to govern the city. He named Sir Edward Dalingridge, who had proved himself loyal to the King. He then removed the Court to York, possibly anticipating the warning of Maudelyn and Anne of a general uprising from the Londoners as reprisal for the justly deserved punishment. The mayor, his sheriffs and aldermen were summoned to hear the King's sentence of imprisonment and all liberties of the Londoners forfeited. But just before Christmas again the conciliatory influence of Anne, succeeded in lifting the ban, and the King's pardon was issued to all offenders and prisoners.

If the King had lost the friendship of the Londoners, his queen was hailed as their saviour, 'our good Queen Anne', who had obtained for them the freedom of the King's capital city at a price.

But not all the queen's goodwill could save the mutinous offenders from the fine of ten thousand pounds for their pardon and the additional thirteen hundred for their mutiny against the King's Exchequer and the Crown's lawful expenses.

Yet despite the financial cost of reconciliation, peace and goodwill prevailed among the Londoners at Christmas with penitential gifts presented to the King and queen, who spent the festive season at Anne's country palace at Sheen.

Among other presents sent to the King and queen were a greyhound puppy that immediately attached himself to Anne, and for the King — of all things — a camel! Whether intended as a joke from one of the younger Londoners who, seeking excitement and adventure, had been a voluntary participant in the recent war between the Ottoman Turks and Hungary, in which Anne's brother Wenceslas had been involved, was a matter for conjecture. But when this singular arrival appeared at the gates of Sheen with a turbanned rider, the porter on duty at sight of it almost passed out with fright.

Its appearance occasioned Richard less fright than amused diversion from recent wearisome anxieties concerning the King's confrontation with his citizens. 'What on earth are we going to do with the damned thing?' he demanded of Maudelyn.

But Anne, who had seen occasional caravans pass through Bohemia during the war between the Ottoman Turks and Hungary, was delighted with it. 'I used to see camels pass in caravans from the Middle East and I longed to ride on one. We must put him out to grass in the paddock with the horses, and his groom — or whatever they call him — can live over one of the stables with some of the stablemen.'

'Who will welcome him as much as do our horses at grass,' replied Richard with ironic amusement, 'especially my favourite brood mare who is in foal. Let us hope she won't miscarry with shock at the sight of this unusual visitor.'

So with a general reconciliation the festive season was celebrated, while village boys sang carols of goodwill and thanksgiving in the grounds of Sheen and the New Year dawned more hopefully than the old year had ended.

Yet all was not to be entirely free from disturbances, especially at York after the Court returned to Westminster. This time the chief grievances in that winter of discontent had been against Gaunt who, with his son, Lord Derby, was still engaged in peace negotiations with France.

Gloucester and his partner Arundel had been ominously quiet since Richard's assertion of authority left the pair of them to nurse their resentment against the King in a simmering cauldron of hate which now was coming to the boil with a rising in Yorkshire. Rumour had it, however improbable, that the insurgents were planning the murder of both Gaunt and his son, Lord Derby. On every church door and on those houses known to be at enmity with Gaunt, were displayed libellous condemnations against Lancaster, the most respected elder statesman and uncle of the King, doubtless inspired by Gloucester in the attempt to denigrate the official status of Gaunt.

Early in the year Richard, after discussing the situation with Maudelyn and Sir Edward Dalingridge, was advised to issue a proclamation in protest against these wild and infamous rumours implying that he, the King, intended to destroy the powerful authority of his uncle, the greatest politician in the realm.

This served *pro tem* to subdue the more active insurgents while Richard sent word to Gaunt in France to suspend the agreement of the truce and come at once to England.

Gaunt was unwilling to leave France at this critical time before the preliminary negotiations were agreed, but on receiving Richard's urgent message that he return without delay, as he had heard something of the difficulties that were harassing the King, he guessed his brother Gloucester to be at the root of the trouble.

'Your uncle Thomas,' he told his son Henry, 'is anxious to be rid of both myself and you, and although young Mortimer, Earl of March, has a claim through his mother to the throne of England, you and I are possible heir presumptives of England should Richard remain childless.'

'Would my uncle Gloucester stoop to murder?' asked Henry who had surmised that Gloucester would be equally desirous as was himself to be King of England, which had been his secret hope since boyhood.

'I regret to say,' his father replied, 'that my brother Gloucester is a cunning, unscrupulous fool, and as ambitious as he is lacking in sense. My father, and your grandfather, King Edward, warned me against him when you were a child, the same age or a few months younger than Richard. "Watch that son of yours," said my father, "lest he inherit that same streak of malicious envy" — an unfortunate Plantagenet failing, for example, John, who from his early youth determined by hook or by crook to seize the throne of the first King Richard. He, although a valiant Crusader, neglected his kingdom and spent almost all the years of his reign fighting the Saracens during his Third Crusade and got himself imprisoned by Leopold of Austria, and gave John the chance to hand out to England that the King was dead. Luckily he was rescued from prison in time to save his kingdom from the clutches of John who did, ultimately and legitimately, succeed him.

'But your grandfather,' Gaunt continued, 'was a very able king, a great ruler and an equally great soldier until in his senile dotage he came under the greedy influence of that trollop Alice Perrers. As for Richard, if given his chance he should prove himself to be almost as great a king as was your grandfather. Had your uncle Edward lived, I doubt he would have gone down to history as one of the great Plantagenet kings other than the victor of Crécy who won his spurs at the age of sixteen.' Then, embracing his son, he said, 'I leave the final negotiations of the truce agreement with you until my return. Fare well, and — fare rightly.'

By the time of Gaunt's arrival in England the difficulties with which Richard had to contend unaided were in part overcome by his proclamation in Parliament denying, in forcible language, the accusation that he had participated in the inflammatory libels against his uncle, the Duke of Lancaster.

Gaunt was agreeably surprised to find that Richard had indeed proved himself well on the way to be a king of whom his grandfather might have been proud. From his journey to Chester Gaunt went on to York, and found that the main cause of the disturbance was not political but economic.

'It appears,' he reported to Richard when back at Westminster, 'that the chief grievances are from the unemployed and unemployable soldiers returned from the war.'

'Yes, I have recruited twenty thousand of them. They are kicking their heels in camp waiting to be called up again.'

'Pay them off and let them go. There is no need for an army to quell a rising for there is no rising and — we hope — no war. The disputes in the north are settled by your proclamation in Parliament that has regained you the good faith of the northerners, although you have lost every friend you had among the Londoners, despite the gift of hounds and camels!'

'In the singular,' laughed Richard, 'not the plural, but Anne is infatuated with the greyhound. As for the camel, having terrified the stable boys into fits and brought on the premature birth of a colt to my best brood mare when we put the camel out to graze in the paddock, I am attempting to rear her foal on cow's milk, as she refuses to suckle while this strange beast roams around, yet I doubt he will eat grass, used — as I suppose he is — to whatever grows in desert sand. But I appreciate this attempt of the Londoners to patch up our quarrel.'

'Neither a camel nor greyhound nor patchwork will mend it, I fear,' Gaunt said. 'And now that you have replaced Gloucester with Mowbray of Nottingham as Justice of Chester, the breach between you and your uncle Thomas will likely widen to a chasm.'

'Tom Mowbray is one of my oldest friends,' Richard told him. 'We had a thumping great row about his marriage to Arundel's daughter, but the fact I have given him Chester should patch up my quarrel with him.'

'Yet it will remain a sore point with your uncle Gloucester,' Gaunt told him.

While Richard endeavoured to maintain a façade of amicable relations with Gloucester and Arundel, he was biding his time to avenge the suffering and humiliation he had endured under the Arundel-Gloucester partnership.

And now the winter of *his* discontent had passed and spring danced again in the gardens at Sheen where, discarding troublous disturbances and disagreements in and out of Parliament, Richard spent the next few months in relaxation with Anne. He loved to watch her tending her flowers, gathering roses just coming into bloom. Those golden days in that year's spring and summer he was to remember all his life as a glimpse of heaven granted to him before the bleak and bitter years of darkness fell.

The greyhound puppy, fast growing to a lovely slender youngster, was Anne's especial pet. He would stand on his hind legs and embrace her knees with his soft paws or jump on her lap and lick her face with kisses as adoring of her as she of him. She named him Matt, short for Matthew Secundus, after Richard's first greyhound, dead of old age.

Richard pretended to be jealous. 'You love him more than you love me!'

'You need never be jealous of my love for Matt. There is only one love in my life, and that is you!' While she knelt over a bed of roses, plucked one and held it to her lips, a sudden fit of coughing caused her to drop the bloom.

'That cough of yours,' he said worriedly, 'seems worse in these summer months than in winter.'

'Yes,' she replied equably, 'it is the pollen from the flowers that tickles my throat. Just see how the bees are drinking the flower dust, which is the pollen from which they make the honey.'

Then, on a wisp of lawn taken from her wide sleeve with which to wipe her lips, he saw a small red stain.

'You are bleeding!' he cried. 'Did that rose thorn prick you?'

'No.' She smiled round at him as she stooped to retrieve the fallen rose. 'It is only that tickle in my throat which does sometimes bleed when I cough. 'Tis nothing.'

Abruptly Richard left her with her roses and the dog, who looked up at her with anxious, questioning eyes. He sent for the Court physician. A younger man was he than his father, now retired, who had originally diagnosed Anne's case as empyema.

'What,' Richard asked fearfully, 'is this b-blood which she says comes from her throat? She has only just told me of it.'

'I have regularly examined Her Grace, and —' for a moment he hesitated to tell him — 'the bleeding of which the queen complains is not from her throat.' He laid a gentle hand on the shoulder of the King, whose face whitened as he heard the grave medical opinion. 'The blood is from her lungs.'

'Her lungs?' echoed Richard, aghast. 'What does th-that signify? And why was I not told?'

'Sire, Her Grace forbade me to tell you what I feared to be her case. The queen did not wish you to be harassed by further anxieties during the disturbances in London.'

When the physician's medical colleagues, whom Richard insisted should be consulted, confirmed the dreaded truth of his beloved wife's condition, she persuaded him that the doctors were mistaken.

'You know that your good old doctor gave an entirely different opinion. I prefer to take the advice of his father who had much more medical experience than the modern, younger men. I am not ill. I have told you all along of this tickle in my throat that makes me cough. My brother Wenceslas has had it too, and his doctors didn't say it was anything serious.'

He thankfully inclined to agree with her, for all through that glorious summer, save that she became more easily fatigued, she appeared to be her normal, happy self. The doctor had ordered a pavilion to be erected in the grounds where she could rest on a day-bed and bask in the sun and the pure fresh air. She would tell Richard, 'I knew those doctors were mistaken. I am so much better and I hardly ever cough now.'

But as the weeks slid by she looked to be more frail; her shell-like transparent skin was flushed at eventide as if with fever, while each day the ruthless enemy advanced to destroy her.

She passed peacefully in her sleep on a sun-blest morning of blue and gold amid the scent of flowers and the fragrance from her garden of roses. Richard had gone to gather some of her favourites and returned with an armful of creamy white and pale golden blooms.

So still, so silently sleeping she lay, he could not believe that which the dog at her side had known when, lifting his head, he uttered a long mournful howl.

In his agony of grief he cried voicelessly, desperately to God: 'You have broken my life! You have taken from me all that made life bearable and have left me lost, alone, for ever burdened by a hateful crown … a crown of thorns.'

TEN

It was generally reported by the Lancastrian chroniclers that the King's excessive grief during his wife's burial service at Westminster Abbey was so uncontrollable as to give credulity to Gloucester's implication that the bereaved husband was mentally deranged.

Further evidence adding insult to injury was provided by Gloucester's partner, Arundel, to increase the antagonism they had deliberately manoeuvred among the King's subjects and the Londoners in particular, hoping to bring about more dissatisfaction with the monarchy than were the disturbances he had recently subdued.

After the embalmed body of the queen had been taken from Sheen to lie in state at St Paul's, the casket was removed to Westminster Abbey for the burial service.

A vast congregation of mourners for the Requiem Mass included the Duke of Gloucester, shaken with well-simulated sobs for all to hear above the chanting of the priests and the sweet clear voices of the choirboys.

Suddenly, and with no regard for the solemnity of the occasion and the grief of the bereaved young husband, Arundel — who had been noticeably absent from St Paul's — arrived at the service very late. As he took his seat while the Archbishop was preparing to give Holy Communion, he remarked, 'I have been delayed on a private and more urgent business than this.'

At such inexcusable and irreverent interruption to the sacred Mass, Richard rose from his knees and, to the consternation of all present and the shock to the Archbishop about to administer the Host, the King seized a wand from the hand of a nearby verger and struck the face of Lord Arundel with such force that he lost his balance, toppled over, and fell with blood dripping over his chin.

During the King's happy marriage and the gentle influence of Anne, he had managed to keep in check his hot Plantagenet temper; but at that moment when wracked with emotion it was excusable if he lost all power of control. Yet, for Arundel's sacrilegious and callous behaviour, there is no pardon or excuse.

Later Richard, calmer but no less grief-stricken, conveyed to his uncle Gaunt a tearful apology.

'I don't know what came over me to do what I did. God knows why. Hysteria, I suppose, brought to b-breaking point by Arundel's irreverence and lack of sympathy for me in my irrep-parable loss. I am wretchedly ashamed.'

To which Gaunt replied, 'None blames you for what was a natural reaction to an unpardonable sacrilege and inhumanity. He deserves that you should banish him.'

'I am in no state to dwell upon the injuries I have suffered from Arundel and my uncle Gloucester,' Richard said blinking back his tears. 'But,' he continued in a firmer voice with a hint of his rare humour, 'I have collected hordes of nails that may be of use if required for certain coffins!'

The Arundel-Gloucester contingent had decided to defer immediate action against the King for his assault on Lord Arundel while the prayerful mourners at the foot of the altar were preparing to receive the Holy Sacrament. The final annihilation of the King's authority as ruler of his kingdom and his government must wait for the time when it would be expedient to strike.

During the next few months they stood apart and watched for opportunity to enlarge upon Gloucester's rumour that the forlorn widower suffered from temporary if not permanent insanity. A further symptom was provided by his enemies when Richard ordered the destruction of Queen Anne's country palace at Sheen. He could not endure to leave it standing there devoid of her beloved presence, inhabited only by caretakers and the few servants left to tend the late queen's apartments. Two or three gardeners were insufficient to save the grounds from falling into neglect.

On the one occasion when he could bring himself to visit the house where he had passed the happiest years of his life, he had wandered through the deserted rooms with the dog Matt the second, a dejected tail down and enquiring eyes raised to his. He could not bear the torment of his loss manifest in every dear reminder of his marriage.

Shortly after that last visit workmen were engaged on razing to the ground his wedding gift to her. This wanton destruction offered Gloucester more seemingly anxious concern for his nephew's disturbed mentality.

The diplomatic negotiations for a truce with France that had been delayed by Gaunt's return to England on the death of the queen, were resumed by him and other English delegates in Paris. In order to secure a permanent end to the war with France, it was suggested that the daughter of the King of France should marry the King of England.

Because the Princess Isabelle was a child of seven years old when the union had been approved by both the French and English, Richard, realising the marriage could not be consummated for many years to come agreed, albeit reluctantly, to take for wife another Queen of England.

However, the fact that this child would be entitled to occupy Anne's country palace at Sheen and that his dear love's private apartments would be given over to nurseries and playrooms finally decided him to destroy every stone and brick of the house that stood to remind him of his loss. The future Queen of England would be given another of his houses as a wedding gift.

A temporary truce was signed and sealed by Richard along with the signature of Charles VI of France, now separated from his wife whose wanton infidelities had been the cause of his temporary insanity.

When Gaunt presented the document for the King's signature and seal he perceived, despite Richard's effort to overcome his irreparable loss, that he was on the verge of a serious breakdown. Consultation with the Court physician who had correctly diagnosed Anne's case as described by Hippocrates as tuberculosis (later known as consumption of the lungs) he prescribed a complete change of scene and occupation.

It was therefore decided that the King should take an expeditionary force to Ireland. No English monarch since Henry II had ever visited the island, and successive Plantagenet kings had shown little interest in it other than their title of *Seigneur d'Irlande.*

Gaunt resolved that the distraction from Richard's grief in new surroundings, and the presence of the King of England would eliminate the state of unrest and potential anarchy among the 'Lordships of Ireland', as the nobles called themselves; in particular one MacMurrough, self-named 'King of Leinster', an inveterate troublemaker. He was a relic of the semi-barbaric chieftains of the Norman-Plantagenet conquest of the island.

With a strong expeditionary force Richard sailed from Haverfordwest on the Welsh coast in the autumn of the year of Anne's death. He found some solace in the enchantment of the lovely island, where the meadows were so rich a green, and the mountains, when not draped in mist, shouldered a sky as vivid a blue as he remembered were his childhood's native skies of Bordeaux.

Only one of Richard's uncles accompanied him and he, surprisingly at the King's invitation, was the Duke of Gloucester. This may have been a strategic gesture on the part of Richard presumably to maintain an amiable relationship with his most dangerous enemy. 'I have drawn his fangs,' he told Maudelyn, who had come with him to Dublin before returning to England, 'or at least the sharper canine teeth before they maul me!'

His uncle Edmund, Duke of York, had been left behind in charge of affairs in England when Gaunt was on his way back to France to finalise the marriage settlement with the child Princess Isabelle. Among others of Richard's barons and squires was the nineteen-year-old Earl of March, a great Irish landowner in his own right and heir presumptive to the throne of England prior to the claim of John of Gaunt and his son, Lord Derby, the future Duke of Lancaster. The claim of John Mortimer, Lord March, after the death of the present king should he die without issue, was to cause much dissension between the rival heirs to England, since Mortimer, Earl of March, was said to have the lesser claim. The main argument being that his mother, the granddaughter of Edward III, and Henry, Lord Derby, the grandson of that king, a female successor, so went the Lancastrian verdict, had prior right to the crown than a woman … Thus seeds of dissension were soon to reap a disastrous harvest.

It cannot be said that the Irish expedition proved to be of much significance other than to keep the King's forces prepared to quell any guerrilla warfare led by the belligerent 'King of Leinster' MacMurrough and his rough and ready followers; but there is no evidence of any pitched battle or hand-to-hand fighting on either side. Richard's barons and squires were far more interested in the beauty of the Irish girls with their inviting smiles, than in the beautiful scenery that served to divert the King from brooding over his loss.

It also gained him confidence in dealing with his leadership as 'Lord of Ireland' without the supervision of his uncle Gaunt, and impressed even the arrogant and hot-blooded MacMurrough. Another of Richard's tactful gestures was to invest him and several of the self-named kings of their provinces with the Chivalrous Order of Knighthood. As they knelt to receive the accolade from the King, the unruly and undisciplined Lords of the Land, as reported by one of the accompanying English chroniclers, were completely subservient to 'the great *puissance* of the King of England who favoured the well-paid and abashed Irishmen'.

It was the well-paid favours that most impressed the 'abashed Irishmen', and noticeably MacMurrough, when Richard raised his standard on all ships of merchandise that were forbidden to cross the Irish sea to buy or sell their products, in England. This won universal approval and helped to lessen the appalling poverty of the serfs and nobles of the 'Emerald Island', so Richard poetically named it; possibly the first inception of that name by which throughout the centuries it has been known.

In the following year, 1395, Richard's return to England saw him reinstated and recognised as the harbinger of peace to the feuds between the clans of the Irish who were ever at enmity with each other as were the clans of the Scots.

Richard had appointed the squire of the Earl of Ormond, one Henry Christed, as tutor and instructor to the Irish nobles and lords of their lands in the mode and manners of English life. Having been in the service of the Governor, the Earl of Ormond for several years, Christed was conversant with the Irish-Celtic dialect and at great pains to teach the nobles not to tear at their food with their teeth or their fingers. They had not the use of knives and forks as had the higher classes of mediaeval England. Christed also supplied each with drinking goblets and cups of silver, and made them discard the kilt as worn by the Scots who, to this day, proudly retain the tartan of their clan; and he induced the Irish to wear cross gartered hosen and trunks, a small detail but sufficient to instil in them a sense of their unity with England and the King; nor were they unwilling to regard themselves as the 'Puissant King's' subjects.

Now that Richard was established and recognised as the ruler of his kingdom, a sense of relief pervaded the whole country and especially the citizens of London. That his enemies of the Gloucester-Arundel faction were noticeably inactive, Richard guessed to be a tacit understanding that they were marking time for a renewal of hostilities.

If the King were not the idol of the Londoners as was their boy king of ten years before, they were, so he told Maudelyn, 'ready to bury their hatchets, if not in my person, in the ground under my feet!'

'Doubtless with intent,' Maudelyn cryptically replied, 'that in their good — or bad — time, the hatchets will explode as in a thunderbolt!'

'I have no fear of their thunder, nor any threat of explosions. I had half the country's peasantry rampaging through the streets of London — a mighty explosion that was! — but I managed to subdue it when I was a boy. So let them try it on, now I'm a man!'

'None has forgotten, Sire, even those who warn you of foul weather to come, that because of your courage you became the Londoners' hero.'

And as the skies cleared there looked to be a forecast of fair weather during the remainder of those not-so-'Quiet Years' of Richard's reign. The peace with France was about to be ratified with the marriage of Richard, King of England and the Princess Isabelle of France.

It was also about this time that Froissart decided to pay his second visit to England in the past five and twenty years. Himself a member of the French aristocracy, he was unknown to the younger generation of Richard's Court. Gaunt, who could have known him from his previous visit was in France finalising the Treaty of Bordeaux that would bring to an end almost a century of war. His brother Gloucester was absent on his own affairs, but the Duke of York who attended his nephew, in the council chamber, appointed one of the King's Council to conduct Froissart to Leeds Castle in Kent where he was welcomed by the Duke; he also remembered him.

Froissart had brought with him letters of introduction to the King who, of course, could never have known him since he was a toddler of barely two years old in his nursery at Bordeaux when Froissart first came to England.

Yet the elderly chronicler was disappointed to learn that his presentation to the King had to be postponed. 'His Grace,' he tells us, 'was sore busied in the council chamber with great and mighty matters.'

'The great and mighty matters' were the meetings of the delegates of France with the English delegates at Leeds Castle engaged in the endless discussions concerning the marriage of the King to his seven-year-old bride. Besides the introductory letters, Froissart had brought with him a gift for Richard, its presentation also had to be postponed until the King could receive it.

Once finished with the 'great and mighty matters', Richard went to his palace at Eltham where Froissart was at last presented to the King. When he humbly offered his gift, a book, on his knees, the old gentleman had some difficulty in rising, and was helped up by Richard who warmly thanked him for this 'very beautiful book'. *It was covered in crimson velvet and embossed,* Froissart tells us, *with roses of gold and gold clasps, richly wrought.*

Turning over the beautifully illuminated pages, Richard asked of what it treated, and Froissart told him: 'It treats of love, Sire,' which greatly pleased the King, as Froissart was gratified to know.

Froissart spent several weeks in England as Richard's guest at his various residences, Eltham, Leeds Castle and Windsor. He learned much from Court gossip and kept his ears wide open to hear what he was not meant to hear regarding the Duke of Gloucester whom he gathered was in great disfavour with the King's loyal courtiers. *His absence, he reported, they applaud since no man dared speak before him.* He learned too that this uncle of the young king was like some greedy spider spinning its web to ensnare and devour the unwary who favoured the King.

But that of which the King's subjects both in and out of the Court chiefly spoke, was of Richard's marriage to the Princess of France. 'So does he mourn his wife's death,' went the adverse criticism of Gloucester's satellites, 'that he marries again within a year…' And from the King's loyal adherents, 'It is a political marriage of convenience to bring about an assured peace treaty. The Princess of France is only seven years old. She is no rival to the late queen of blessed memory.'

The child princess, married by proxy but not yet crowned or acknowledged Queen Consort, arrived at the Palace of Westminster in the care of her nurse and a governess, Lady Coucy. Her husband was the son of the Earl of Bedford. He had renounced his heritage when Robert de Vere divorced his wife Philippa, daughter of Bedford and his wife, the Princess Isabella, favourite daughter of Edward III and therefore Richard's aunt. It was because of this distant connection, although no blood relationship, that Richard appointed Lady Coucy to take charge of the Princess Isabelle of France, and instruct her in the language she must learn to speak as Queen Consort to the English king.

We may believe the little girl to have been kept in ignorance of the high position to which she had been called, and that the tall handsome gentleman who received her in his Palace of Westminster was her husband to whom she had been married a few months before while playing in her nursery.

Charles, King of France, when recovered of his reason and divorced from his faithless wife, had been the child's sole parent and had the foresight to withhold from her at so tender an age, her future royal destiny. After the rough crossing from France to Dover in one of her father's galleys, bumped and jolted along the muddy, rough-hewn lanes of Kent in her husband's coach, she arrived half dazed and thoroughly bewildered at the Palace of Westminster.

Very different was this great castle from her father's country château in the village of Versailles where Isabelle had passed most of her childhood, and which, in a later century, would be built on its site the magnificent palace of another king of France.

Richard had purposely chosen to wear informal dress rather than the Court dress required for the reception of his bride were she of bridal age. She was a pretty child, her dark hair cut short and curled under in the fashion of a mediaeval page, as worn by children both of France and England. Her large velvety brown eyes were raised to his where he towered above her, that he must lift her in his arms to say in French, with a welcoming kiss, 'You shall be my little daughter and I your second father.'

To which the lisped answer came through the loss of two milk teeth in her upper gum: 'I have already a papa. He came very soon to *Angleterre* to see me.' Then, sighting the dog Matt beside his master, '*Ah! j'aime beaucoup les chiens!* I have a dog. Her name is Félicité, she is very big — like this.' Richard having set her down, her hand measured the height almost level with herself. 'She stand up,' she told him, 'and she put her paws on my shoulders and kiss me. She goes to chase the stags with my papa in the *Bois*. There are many dogs who chase the stags but they live in the kennels and Félicité she lives with me. I have had her since she was very small…' Her lips trembled. 'I am sad to leave her in France *toute seule…*'

'Her Highness,' explained Lady Coucy, 'is very distressed at leaving her dog, but we thought that as Your Grace has a dog, a bitch might prove to be difficult at certain times. She is always with the princess.'

'We will have the dog brought to her at once,' he said, and to Isabelle: '*Voilà, ma petite*. You shall have your Félicité with you here. My dog Matt will be happy to have another dog for friend.' And aside in English to Lady Coucy, 'no difficulty, I assure you. They will be kept apart when necessary but,' he added laughingly, 'I think Matt is no womaniser. He seems to prefer boys to girls.'

'Grand merci! Merci M'sieu!' ecstatically exclaimed Isabelle. 'I do love my Félicité. My papa gave her to me on my last birthday when I had seven years. Félicité, she will have had one year when I have eight years.'

Richard swallowed an ache in his throat as he listened to the child's chatter. She had lost her first shyness, and he thought, *Just such a one as this might have been Anne's and mine...*

It was apparent to all his associates that in the coming of this little one he had found some consolation for his loneliness and loss.

In October of the year 1396 the initial celebrations to honour the agreement of peace between England and France, and the marriage by proxy of the King of England to the Princess Isabelle that had taken place in the previous year, were celebrated on a magnificent scale.

The venue selected for the entertainment of the French and English was a few miles from Calais, and gave Richard ample opportunity to indulge in his sartorial extravagance. Gloucester would always criticise Richard's taste for beautiful clothes and jewels as effeminate, another symptom of mental derangement. Nor was he slow to remind the King's many detractors of the propensities attributed to the first King Richard, *Coeur de Lion*, who had been generally accepted to be a lover of man rather than of woman. This, as Gloucester suggested, was evident by Richard's favouritism for the late Robert de Vere on whom he had bestowed the dukedom of Ireland, greatly to Gloucester's disgust who had seen himself the rightful possessor of that duchy.

Since Richard by his own achievements was now in full power of his sovereignty, Gloucester and his adherents enlarged upon any possible symptom of the King's supposed insanity. The chroniclers of France and England gave accounts of how the King had chosen to be dressed for the opening ceremony of the celebrations in a robe of crimson velvet studded with precious stones, and a head-dress sparkling with jewels presented to him by Charles of France. More gifts from the gratified Charles included a gold goblet gemmed with diamonds, rubies and emeralds to express his satisfaction at the union between France and England. Finally, he added a picture of the Trinity purloined from one of his own châteaux; but that which caused a general raising of eyebrows was Richard's own gift to himself; a gold necklace strung with pearls that he had given to his late wife.

Vast crowds came to watch the celebrations attended by country folk from far and near, besides the barons and knights of the French and English Courts. Before the end of that triumphant day, there were emotional speeches from both kings in French, translated into English by Richard for the benefit of those from his Court who did not speak French. There followed a great banquet provided by Richard and held in an enormous marquee to seat more than two hundred guests.

Of course Gloucester and his faction were full of abuse for what they called Richard's 'wanton extravagance and reckless expense of the nation's money to enhance his own importance'... But none of this prevented Richard from thoroughly enjoying the lavish food and wine provided by his Exchequer for the entertainment of *'mon cher frère'* as he toasted Charles.

The two were a trifle hazy and Richard, whose head was spinning, stammered quite dreadfully when he recovered from the ardent embrace of Charles with kisses on both his cheeks to tell him in French that, 'We, the English, do not embrace men, only the ladies,' amid cheers from all and torrents of kisses blown from the fingertips of the French king's court.

Gloucester must have been a veritable skeleton at that feast, and at great pains to remind his own crowd, and later the Londoners how they had been drained of £10,000 plus another £3,000 as the price of the King's pardon to go towards the cost of the peace treaty with France.

This reminder by Gloucester of the quarrel between the King and his Londoners was deliberately manoeuvred at a time when Richard's heedless spending of money gave his detractors more excuse to damn him.

'All this farrago,' Gloucester complained to his party, 'is costing a cool £200,000 plus the dowry of the Princess of France. You may wager your shirt on it that Charles would be thankful to give her to Richard with nothing but her shift!'

'And he won't want to strip her of that,' chortled another of his cronies, 'for the next eight or ten years to come, if then!'

In the following November, Isabelle made her state entry into London as the bride, not yet crowned, of King Richard. The usual multitude of onlookers were assembled in full force, and many were the criticisms of those who found fault with this choice of the King's consort prompted by Gloucester and Henry Lord Derby and his dissenters. 'Ridiculous for the King to marry a coddling who is cutting her teeth before she is cutting her capers!'

Henry was quick to seize on that. 'Her mother, the consort of Charles, would partner her capers with this one or that in her bed!'

'Yes,' Gloucester agreed with a grin, 'and she sent the French king off his head when he found her capering with any man in his shift — save himself!'

None the less, the majority of those who had tramped through the night to see the child who was their king's queen, saw her as the living emblem of peace to end war for all time between the two countries, when many of their fathers, husbands, sons, had died on the bloodstained fields of France.

As for Isabelle, she was deafened by the cheering, shouting and yelling of the crowds to hit the sky, knowing no reason why they should shout so loud, and every now and then she heard her own name roared. Why? And why was she all alone in this coach drawn by six horses that rocked and rattled over the cobbled stones of the streets to make every bone in her body ache and her stomach turn that she felt to be sick in this heavy great velvet cloak lined with fur, so she must whisper an *Ave Maria* to her Blessed Lady that she be not sick all over the gold and silver trappings of the seat when her head was bumped to the gilded roof of the coach ... *And what a cold, miserable day with this brouillard they call 'fog' — ugh! pour me faire doulereuse dans le nez et la bouche!* How ugly was this great city of wooden houses and how hideous these people who resembled one huge mouth wide open to swallow her!

She gulped down a sob while one little hand strayed to find her rosary but she could not tell her beads in all this noise and oh, how thankful was she when this long drive ended, to be lifted from the coach by a lackey and embraced by her bonne who waited for her at the *Grand Château* of *le Roi d'Angleterre*...

Relieved of her cloak and robe of velvet, she was put to bed and her fog-bedevilled throat and nose soothed by a hot posset; and was just about to sleep off this dismal drive through this so-ugly Londres when the king, her *papa le deuxième*, as she called him, came to her bedside, stroked back a fallen lock of hair and told her, '*Voilà, ma chérie, prends-tu les bonbons.* You have been so good a little one bravely to respond to the Londoners who greet you, *ma petite reine.*' He kissed her, and opened a silver box filled with marchpane and candies.

'Ooh!' she squealed delightedly, '*les marrons glaces! J'aime bien les marrons glaces…*'

He popped one in her mouth. 'You shall eat a dozen for being such a good little girl, *ma petite.*'

And Isabelle, her mouth full, asked, '*Ma Félicité*, is she not yet come from France? You have promised her to me, *mon roi papa.*'

'She arrives today and you will see her when you wake … *Au 'voir, ma chérie.*' He kissed her again and left her curled up in her bed and, still munching the last of the candied chestnuts, she fell happily to sleep.

On 6 January 1397 Richard saw Isabelle, now just eight years old, crowned in Westminster Abbey. He insisted on a simple coronation for his child queen, knowing that her first state entrance into London had thoroughly upset her. As he watched the Archbishop place on her small head the bejewelled gold fillet, substituted for the much too large and heavy crown worn by previous king's consorts, he may have felt pardonably self-satisfied in the knowledge that in these last seven years he had seen the end of war between England and her hereditary enemy, France; had married the heiress to the Kingdom of France and now, coincidentally on his thirtieth birthday he realised that against all opposition he had proved himself to be the indisputable monarch of his realm.

As for Isabelle, seated in solitary grandeur on the high gilded throne in the Abbey of Westminster, despite that her *deuxième papa*, as she called him, had promised she would never again have to suffer another of these *bouleversements* as the centre of attention for all of England, but would be allowed to live in a house in the country, Berkhamsted, Richard's wedding gift to her. He had refurnished and converted a suite of rooms into day and night nurseries, playrooms and a schoolroom, where her upbringing would in no way differ from that of any English child, with no frightening state ceremonies to disturb her.

Whatever time he could spare from his monarchical duties, he was teaching her chess and found her an apt pupil, quicker to learn than he had been at her age. He also took the opportunity of instructing her when a pawn on the chequer board was taken by the queen, that she too could become a queen, '*parce que la vie d'une reine ou du roi est comme le jeu de l'echecs.* Now repeat that in English, and always speak English with Lady Coucy, for you are now the queen of England as well as the queen of the chessboard...'

It was more agreeable, Isabelle decided, to be a pawn on the chessboard of life, 'and perhaps,' she told Lady Coucy, '*mon deuxième papa, le roi,* he tell me I can say — how is it? — "sheekmeat" to the king, who is the colour white in the game, and me, and I am the colour red, yes?'

'Yes, but you must say *"checkmate"* if your queen or your knight takes —'

'*Pardon, Madame,*' Isabelle interrupted; she was always ready to learn this so-difficult English. 'What is this word — "niet"?'

'*Un chevalier,*' replied her governess, 'so if your queen or your knight — your *chevalier* — takes the King, you must say "checkmate"...'

Checkmate, silently said Richard as he confronted Gloucester at the banquet he held in Westminster Palace for many of the garrison officers returned from the captured fortresses of Cherbourg and Brest, pledged to England with the loan of £20,000 for the duration of the twenty-eight years' truce with France.

Richard had successfully ruled without a Parliament for the past two years while he secretly planned for the retribution due to his two most deadly enemies, Gloucester and Arundel who, since his accession to the throne as a child, had made his life a living hell. But now...

He raised his cup to Gloucester and Arundel in turn. 'Good cheer, my lords, and good appetite for the feast I have prepared for you, my uncle, and my good Lord Arundel.'

'Sire,' returned Gloucester glowering. 'You should first give good cheer to the soldiers from the fortresses of Cherbourg and Brest who complain of their niggardly pay while you, the King, squander that which should be their reward for long service on the extravagance of your Court and your own self-indulgence.'

'Repeat that remark —' with commendable cool Richard screened white-hot heat — 'for if I am self-indulgent I indulge myself now to command that you leave my presence at this board and retire to your castle in Essex, where you and I can discuss in private to more purpose that which words cannot settle here. Sirs,' to his guards who stood watchfully at the door of the Great Hall, 'escort the Duke of Gloucester with his entourage to his castle in Essex. It is full moon tonight. They should be there by dawn.'

It was the beginning of the end — of whom? Of Gloucester and his satellite Arundel and others who had despised and denigrated him since he had been crowned as a child of ten, even as his child queen had been crowned in this Abbey of his Westminster Palace. The game, so long and viciously played against him, was now in his hands. He held at bay those who had so ruthlessly attacked him and murdered his own loyal knights. One of them — Tom Mowbray, Earl of Nottingham — had defected from the King's enemies and the Appellants. But he could now repay the pardon accorded him, for Richard could never harbour rancour against a friend.

Nottingham, while dining at the castle of his father-in-law, Lord Arundel's near St Albans, had learned of a plot conspired by Gloucester, the Earls of Arundel and Warwick, members of the Appellants of whom Tom Mowbray had been one. At dinner in the Great Hall of the castle he heard Gloucester urge them all to swear that the Dukes of Lancaster and York, Gloucester's brothers, should be imprisoned for life with the King and that all of the King's Council, known to be loyal to the monarchy, should be executed.

'Swear to it before God that the King shall reign no more, save in a dungeon in the Tower of London. The nation must be saved. Swear!'

All seated round that table stood, and with them Henry Bolingbroke swore to the imprisonment of his own father, the Duke of Lancaster. With them stood Tom Mowbray, Earl of Nottingham, whose inner man prayed, *God forgive me that I take false oath against my friend, the King … Holy Mary, Mother of God, help me!* And 'I swear!' rang out the voice of Tom Mowbray.

All through the night he rode hell for leather, attended only by one servant to arrive dust-dishevelled and breathless at the mansion of the King's half-brother, the Earl of Huntingdon. Scarcely waiting for the King's assent to his request for immediate audience, he was ushered into the dining hall, and craved of Huntingdon private audience with the King who was seated at the table enjoying a breakfast of fried chicken, tearing with his fingers at the flesh of a plump leg.

'Nothing is private here, Tom, in the presence of my brother John and Maudelyn, my Secretary of State,' said Richard. 'But why this mighty hurry at so early an hour? Sit you down.' Richard gestured a servant to fill a cup of wine. 'Drink and break your fast, and then say what you have to say.'

Tom sat but did not drink the brimming cup of the good red wine of France, nor did he take of the proffered dish. And still out of breath with his hard ride to London he said, 'There is treachery around Your Grace. Take heed, Richard,' reverting to the familiar use of his name as when they were boys together. 'I beg you be prepared. Assemble your bodyguard, your men-at-arms and your archers. The fight is on and I am with you heart and soul, though I die for it! Gloucester is bent on your downfall — there is no time to lose!'

Up from his seat sprang Richard, and in a triumphant clarion voice he cried, 'It has come, the day of reckoning! I have waited ten years for this.' And to Huntingdon, 'John, come with me — and Maudelyn, have the buglers call my men-at-arms!' To the guards at the door, 'Call out my bodyguards. My good friend here,' he leaned across the table to lay a hand on Tom's wrist as he was about to lift the cup of wine to his lips, 'my good friend,' he repeated, tears of emotion filling his eyes, and stammering as whenever moved by emotion or anger, 'h-henceforth, for his loyalty to me, he is Tom Mowbray, Earl of Nottingham and D-Duke of — Norfolk!'

The inn at Pleshey on the Duke of Gloucester's estate, and in London's taverns, talk brought by journeymen and waggoners, was all of how the King with his armed forces had invaded the duke's castle, 'and found him sick in bed,' as reported over tankards.

'Sick me arse!' jeered one of Gloucester's servants of whom only a few had known him as a boy before the birth of his nephew, King Richard. 'Sick for fear of what's comin' to 'un, for Nottin'um did tell the King of 'ow his uncle Gloucester be plottin' to prison the King — or worse.'

'When this 'un's gran'feyther were fightin' the French along o' the Black Prince, this 'un's feyther,' quavered an old fellow between toothless gums, 'the Duke o' Gloucester, wor no more'n Tom Woodstock, allus a bad 'un. I mind me as I see 'un hang a litter o' pups on a horse post for the larf of it, an' 'e robbed me one apple tree of its bit o' fruit in me yard. Yeh! a reet bad 'un 'e be wot the King, 'is own nephew, made 'im a Duke...'

'An' this 'un,' stoutly remarked a young forester wearing the white hart of the King's livery on his tunic, 'a reet good 'un 'e be, good King Richard.'

Murmurs of assent were capped by, '*Good* King Richard, God blast 'im!' from one who spat into the rushes at his feet. 'Good to 'imself, with his jools an' his Court and the brat wot 'e's made "is queen so's to give 'im half o' France along of a fortune from 'er feyther, the mad French King!'

'Not so mad neether is Charles o' France,' broke in a down-at-heel and out-at-elbow one-armed soldier, 'and glad is 'e to be quit o' the loikes o' me wot's left me arm on a field in Normandy. We's bin fighting France for a 'undred years and now — no more!'

Talk in the taverns of London and in the Pleshey Inn, divided for or against Gloucester, did not affect Richard nor deter him from his long-awaited chance of retribution for the wrongs he had suffered in the past. But on arriving with his brother Huntingdon, his men-at-arms and his archers to force entrance into Gloucester's castle, he was told that the duke was ill in bed and must not be disturbed.

'The king demands that the duke,' Maudelyn insisted, '*shall* be disturbed. It is of vital importance that the King's command is obeyed. He must speak with the duke.'

The pale duchess, Gloucester's wife, was on her knees to Richard. 'For God's sake spare him! I know why you are here. Word has been brought to him that he is betrayed … Whatever treasonable lies have been told, do not believe that the duke, your own father's brother, wishes you ill. But if you believe the mischief of Gloucester's enemies that you bring your armed men to capture him — I beg you to know him innocent — I swear to it before Christ's image!' She indicated a large crucifix on the stone wall. 'For the love of God who died for him and you — and all of us, I implore you,' she was frenziedly sobbing, 'spare him! He has always been hasty, impulsive. Pray, Richard, let not the sun go down upon your anger.'

Richard raised her, and because he was never proof against a woman's tears, he soothed her, stammering, 'Have no fear, good aunt. I wish no injury to my uncle. I d-desire only that he withdraw from me and my government that he can be saved from f-false or what may be false witness against him. It were best he leave England for a while. He shall sail to Calais in the care of my trusted officers until further investigation into the truth of these c-calumnies of treason shall be proved.'

'Richard!' John of Huntingdon seized his arm as the duchess, hysterical with thanksgiving, was led away by her women. 'Are you out of your mind? Such tolerance to him who is plotting for your throne, if not your life, is indeed a symptom of the lunacy with which Gloucester persistently damns you! Exile him and take time, if you must, to consider your verdict.'

'I have considered it,' Richard said quietly. 'I remember how my beloved Anne, God rest her soul, would remind me when I was determined to revenge myself on the wrongs I have endured from Gloucester and Arundel, that vengeance is God's, not mine.' And to Maudelyn: 'See to it that the Duke of Gloucester be taken from his sickbed, if,' with a touch of malice, 'his sickness be not of his stomach but of his mind in fear and trembling. Have him escorted to Dover and shipped in one of my frigates for Calais, there to be lodged in my fortress.'

'Coals of fire!' muttered Huntingdon furiously. 'They will rebound on your own head, mark me. You'll regret your leniency to him who deserves all he intends for you!'

'The only coals of fire that will fall upon him when he has earned God's vengeance is,' Richard pointed a finger downwards, 'there — below. But this I swear: that when Gloucester leaves England for France this night, he will never return while I am king!'

ELEVEN

Richard kept to his decision for Gloucester's exile by imprisonment, despite Huntingdon's warning that he would regret his leniency.

'You might as well capture a man-eating tiger,' he told him, 'for whether or not he is guarded he'll escape. He has powerful allies waiting to maul you, as he will do sooner or later!'

'I also have allies,' replied Richard. 'I send Gloucester in care of my good friend Tom Mowbray who saved me from prison or death at the risk of his life.'

'To save his own life,' retorted Huntingdon, 'for had he not turned king's evidence against his fellow traitors he would have met with their fate!'

The other conspirators, Arundel and Warwick, were arrested at Arundel Castle by the Earl of Kent, Richard's nephew, the son of his half-brother Thomas, deceased, and his cousin Rutland, son of his uncle Duke of York. Both Arundel and Warwick were seized by a strong force under the command of the two young earls, and imprisoned in the Tower of London to await their trial. Derby, had Richard known it, was a more deadly enemy than the other three conspirators, but, as the son of his uncle Gaunt, Richard spared him the immediate penalty. Henry's time, he told himself, would come.

There remained only the judicial trial of the two prisoners in London on a charge of treason — and attempted regicide.

Richard was well aware that his former popularity had decreased in the last year, thanks to Gloucester's insinuations regarding the King's inefficiency as monarch due to his (supposed) mental derangement and, above all since his marriage to the child Princess of France, whose coronation had cost £200,000. This provided more dissatisfaction among the citizens of the King's capital for after a bitter fight they had been forced to subsidise £10,000 towards the peace negotiations. If Richard had shown tolerance to Gloucester and Derby, he was adamant in his determination to punish those others guilty of a treasonable plot; yet they would be judged in trial.

The autumn Parliament of 1397 met in a packed hall — not Westminster Hall, which was undergoing structural repair, but in a temporary makeshift building open at the sides to let in gusts of wind and rain, to cause further complaint from Gloucester's allies and the Londoners. It was obvious, went the general opinion in the taverns of the city, that the King intended the worst possible discomfort in 'this miserable barn of his — to give them all perishin' colds!'

Richard realised that he might have been too ready to accept Nottingham's betrayal of the conspiracy at Arundel Castle 'to save his own skin', as Huntingdon reminded him, 'and to gain a dukedom into the bargain! You are always too ready with your dukedoms...'

It may have been that John Huntingdon, Richard's half-brother and his closest of kin since the death of Thomas, Earl of Kent, had hoped for something more than a mere earldom. He had never approved of the King's favour to his late, much-loved friend, de Vere, first created Marquis of Dublin, and then Duke of Ireland, forsooth!

Before Parliament assembled, Richard sent one of the King's Justices, Sir William Rickhill, to obtain a confession of guilt from Gloucester in the prison at Calais. He brought no decisive confession, for Gloucester insisted that if he were presumed to have conspired against his 'beloved nephew King Richard', it was a series of wicked lies invented by the King's allies and his, Gloucester's, enemies. If the King chose to believe these lies against the King's uncle he must plead mercy for the penalty he would have deserved. 'He ended,' Sir William reported, 'on his knees clutching at my legs, grovelling and hysterically weeping, in a panic as to what his penalty would be.'

'If the King believes me a traitor,' Gloucester had blubbered, 'he will have me brought to trial. As you can see, I am already at death's door. I was dragged from my sickbed when my misguided nephew stormed my castle with a force of armed men and I was brought here to this noisome rat-infested cell to die … I implore you, as King's Justice, to tell the King that I am a prisoner in a filthy cell as if I were any common felon, starved and watched by rough gaolers — not,' wailed Gloucester, 'in the state apartments where I understood the King, my nephew, had ordered me. Alas, he is sick himself, not in body but in mind … Do you wish for a mad king like Charles of France? Can you, as a Justice of Law, believe the King to be in his right mind?'

'A well-rehearsed performance,' Sir William added drily. 'I have here an unconvincing, jangled confession.'

'Which can be used,' Richard reminded him, 'if he returns while I am King.'

He did not return, for when Parliament met news came that Gloucester was dead. Whether he died from the sickness of which he was supposed to be suffering when arrested in his castle and imprisoned in the fortress at Calais, or whether he had been deliberately done to death on Richard's instructions either by Nottingham or Rutland — both having had him in custody — is a moot point. Richard had never been told of the general suspicion that he was directly or indirectly responsible for Gloucester's death. That he had been guiltless of vengeance for his uncle's treachery was the more likely conclusion, since he had intended Gloucester to be exiled and imprisoned for life, unless Richard should die before him. Yet even had the King been guilty of murder, he would still have carried a cleaner record than that of his former or contemporary Plantagenets, unless it were the first Richard, the Lion Heart, who would kill only for his cause — his Third Crusade.

Parliament opened with an address from the Chancellor Sir Edmund Stafford, Bishop of Exeter. It was unfortunate that the draughty makeshift 'barn' of a place had given the Chancellor, in common with many of the members, both Lords and Commons, a tendency to sneezing and coughing as preliminary to a worse condition. In the case of the Chancellor it had developed into a streaming cold in the head that greatly interfered with his well-prepared speech. He chose to deliver it in the form of a sermon based on the text from Ezekiel, 'One King shall be King to them all', which evidently signified that anyone who plotted against the King must pay the full penalty of the law.

'It is the fashiod of this Parliabent,' began the Chancellor, unsuccessfully halting a sneeze, 'to investigate any one person who has endeavoured to plot against His Grace the King. It is therefore necessary that I (A'chew! Pardon be) do request that the Speaker call upod the Archbishop Arundel in defence of his brother, the Earl of Arundel...'

This was a bad beginning, for not only was the Chancellor's speech almost unintelligible owing to his cold, but also the Commons raised the objection that the Archbishop could not defend his brother without equally condemning himself as a traitor conniving at treason. When the Archbishop rose forcibly to deny any such condemnation, Richard, from his throne that must have been shakily insecure on the rough-hewn boards, commanded the Archbishop, 'Be silent! I compel you to withdraw from this session!'

Further interruption came from those of Gloucester's faction and from some of the Londoners who had managed to squeeze themselves into the packed 'barn', huddled in corners and seated on bare boards. From the report of the chroniclers who witnessed the hearing, *There seemed to be some bustle, and the archers at the back of the hall did draw their arrows to the great terror of them all. But the King did quiet them…* Of course, the Lancastrians made much of Richard's attempt to restore peace and order as evident example of his 'tyranny' in that, as the Gloucester faction would have it, he had insulted the Archbishop by compelling him to withdraw.

Arundel, in his peer's robes, was the first to be tried, and Gaunt who had obviously taken over the prosecution for the Crown, ordered him to remove his belt and hood. Whereupon Arundel, pointing a finger at Gaunt, shouted, 'If a charge of treason is in question you, Duke of Lancaster, are more guilty of such a charge than am I.'

Before Richard could again call for 'Silence', Henry (Lord Derby), in support of his father, took upon himself the King's prerogative to command the withdrawal of Lord Arundel and, emboldened by the knowledge that he was exempt — at present — from any accusation, reminded Arundel of a discussion between them concerning the capture of the King and his imprisonment, to which Derby maintained he had strongly objected.

Then Richard, white with anger, rose from his throne and in a voice hoarse with passion cried, 'I deny the in-inf-famous allegations made by Lord Derby against Lord Arundel. He l-lies in his throat! If he believes his lies will further my belief in Lord Arundel's treason he is mistaken! I command that you, Henry B-Bolingbroke, withdraw your infamous allegations or face arrest!'

Henry, red as Richard was white, offered a mumbled, 'I withdraw.' At which Richard, scarcely heeding his apology, proceeded.

'I must remind Lord Arundel of how he said to me when we met in the b-bath at the back of the White Hall,' which occasioned laughter among some of the younger members to which, Richard, frowning round at them repeated, 'In the b-bath. Yes! We do bath ourselves, if you don't! I must remind my Lord Arundel how you,' he had recovered his speech and his temper, 'told me that my dear friend and tutor and guardian of my youth, Sir Simon Burley, was worthy of death and that you and my uncle Gloucester wickedly did slay him against my pleas for his pardon when he had done no wrong as you — the vassal of Gloucester — well know. And how Gloucester spurned my beloved wife who was on her knees to him, pleading for his life…' His voice broke, tears filling his eyes at that memory. 'And you and Gloucester now — God be thanked, dead — insulted her!' He sat down and under his breath muttered, 'May Gloucester burn eternally in hell with *you*!'

No answer was given from the assemblage, suddenly silent: some were emotionally stirred at the young widower's revival of that incident in which his Anne had been so cruelly insulted.

Arundel, pale with the realisation of what his sentence must be, clutched with both hands at the table before which he stood, and heard Gaunt, as Seneschal of England, pronounce his doom.

'You are sentenced to death as a traitor. All your properties entailed and unentailed are forfeit to the Crown.'

Amid a buzz of horror from his own party, mingled with shouts of applause from the King's loyalists, Arundel was seized and hustled to the place of execution. In regard for his noble birth, Richard excused him the penalty of hanging, drawing and quartering. He was beheaded on the block at Tower Hill in the presence of Nottingham who, having got himself a dukedom in betrayal of his father-in-law, performed an act of contrition by bandaging his eyes.

With Arundel disposed of there remained only Warwick to be tried. Contrary to Arundel's resigned acceptance of his death, Warwick showed himself a pitiful coward. An eye-witness described him as 'wailing and whining like a wretched old woman…'

When the King asked him who had induced him to be a party to treason he replied, almost inarticulate with fright and sobs, that it was the Duke of Gloucester and the Abbot of St Albans who had made him swear to —

'Enough!' Richard interrupted, and a chronicler reported, *'By St John the Baptist,' he cried, 'Thomas of Warwick your confession bears out the truth of Gloucester and Arundel's treachery and is of more value to me than the forfeit of all your lands!'*

But although Warwick had confessed he had been 'tempted', as he said, to be a party to the conspiracy, there was no positive proof of his treason so he did not have to undergo the supreme penalty. His lands and properties were confiscated and he was banished into exile under the Lord of the Isle of Man.

Since Gloucester was dead before his trial, his confession, read by Sir William Rickhill, that gave Parliament a full account of his guilt, made sorry reading; nor did Sir William spare the details of Gloucester's grovelling pleas for mercy. It is not certain if he died of the 'sickness' that had kept him to his bed at the time Richard invaded the castle of Pleshey or, as was generally assumed, he had been deliberately murdered either by suffocation or poison at the instigation of the King. If so it is highly improbable that Richard would deliberately have killed his dead father's brother, no matter how much suffering his detested uncle had caused him. Richard's punishment for the treachery and treason of his relatives and associates was far less ruthless than many of the murderous acts of the Merciless Parliament, and was more lenient than they actually deserved in an age when many a treasonable word, let alone an act against the sovereignty of the monarch, was barbarously punished.

In the disgraceful appropriation of public funds exacted by the Duke of Gloucester and Parliament during the Londoners' revolt, the King offered no financial reward to those whom he knew to be loyal, but gave them instead honours and titles. He created five new dukedoms; that of Nottingham, given verbally as reward for his betrayal of the conspiracy at St Albans, was now formally honoured with the other favoured four.

His brother John, whose earldom of Huntingdon had been recreated from that of Richard's good friend and tutor, Sir Guichard d'Angle, now became the Duke of Exeter; Richard's nephew, having succeeded to his other half-brother's earldom of Kent, was made Duke of Surrey, and his cousin Rutland, the Duke of York's son, was created Duke of Albemarle. As for Derby, Richard had no intention of letting him off his well-deserved punishment, but while waiting and watching as in a game of cat-and-mouse, he was given the dukedom of Hereford. His uncle, John of Gaunt, was further honoured by the recognition of his eldest illegitimate son John Beaufort, born of his mistress Catherine Swynford; he created him Marquis of Dorset.

None loyal to him was forgotten. Earldoms and baronials abounded. As for the five new dukes, the chroniclers moved to sarcasm referred to *strawberry leaves sprouting from five coronets of the 'duketies'*. The name stuck.

Nor did the King forget himself. He took the title of His Grace, the Prince of Chester.

There were some theatrical scenes devised by the King in token of his triumph over his enemies. He arranged a review of the armed forces of Londoners and rode with Gaunt through the shouting streets. Flags were flying, mobs cheering and at the end of the day he held a great banquet in Westminster Palace attended by the five new dukes and earls, the bishops and clergy and all. There was much drinking and gaiety, dancing and music, and when Richard, never very strong in the head after copious libations and the answering of loyal toasts, finally retired to bed, he slept the clock round and woke with a heavy hangover.

By the Christmas of that year in which he had vanquished his enemies and the third and most dangerous of them being dead, if not directly by his instruction but as he believed and probably rightly, by the judgement of God, he could look forward to a long and prosperous reign.

The Parliament of January 1398 met at Shrewsbury and occasioned much discussion as to why the King had chosen so obscure a location for the first Parliament of the New Year. The reason apparently was because of its proximity to Cheshire, the seat of Richard's famous Archers. Moreover the cost of sustaining his luxurious Court had been a source of continuous disapproval and discontent to his Parliaments and his successive Treasurers.

That the citizens of Shrewsbury were greatly honoured by the presence of the King, caused some dismay when the cost of sustaining his splendid Court was counted. But there were more immediate concerns to cause his government anxiety; this was to do with two of the King's newly created dukes.

Tom Mowbray, Duke of Norfolk, and Henry Bolingbroke, Duke of Hereford, were involved in a mighty quarrel that began with a trifling conversation while the two were riding to London from Tom's Nottingham seat. As one of the Appellants of the Merciless Parliament, Tom had been loyal to Richard by betraying the St Albans' conspiracy for the imprisonment or life of the King. Nor had Richard forgotten how Tom Mowbray was second only to Robert de Vere in his affections until he married Arundel's daughter and turned from friend into foe. But Tom had atoned for that by his staunch support of the King and also in the capture and imprisonment of Gloucester and, as was suspected, had been instrumental on behalf of the King in Gloucester's death.

As for Henry (now Duke of Hereford), Richard still had an axe to grind with him, for however much he may have protested that judgement was not his, he knew, sooner or later, that Henry would be charged with the treason he had nurtured against him all their young lives.

The story of this famous quarrel was brought to Richard before the Shrewsbury Parliament met. Norfolk had asked Henry if he had any idea how near to the fate of Arundel, his wife's father, they both had been. Hereford demanded to know what on earth he meant, to which Norfolk replied that they were the only two survivors of the Appellants from the Merciless Parliament.

'Even though we have both been pardoned,' Norfolk said, 'I, at least, have remained faithful to the King, and it was I who let him know that Gloucester and Arundel were out for his blood. I knew for a fact,' Norfolk persisted, 'that some of Richard's friends, including his and your cousin Rutland, York's son, were urging Richard to get rid of you — and me!' And circumventing Henry's indignant denial of any such treasonable charge, Norfolk piling on the agony continued: 'They are also naming your father as one of the traitors, and that his loyalty to Richard is all a bluff. He is marked for the block as are you — but not *me* because I turned king's evidence against the plotters at the St Albans' conspiracy.'

The row between these two, as reported to Richard, gave it that Henry called Norfolk a bloody liar and strongly denied that his father, the Duke of Lancaster, the most powerful and honoured statesman in the kingdom, would ever have been a party to Norfolk's damnable accusations. He ended by swearing he would go straight to the King with a full account of Norfolk's attempt to endanger not only Henry's life but that of his father, Richard's uncle Gaunt, and the guardian of his youth.

That Henry did go to Richard with a hotch-potch of this conversation between the two Knights of the Order of Chivalry (forerunner of the Knights of the Garter in later centuries) is doubtful; but that the narrative did reach the ear of Richard either directly or indirectly is certain.

Richard's first reaction was to demand the truth of this 'heap of garbage'. But while Norfolk stayed silent, Henry, bent on pursuing his attack on Norfolk to save himself from any suspicion, stated he would put in writing his charge accusing Tom Mowbray of lies 'against my honoured father'!

It was evident that Henry Bolingbroke in deliberately breaking the Knightly code of Chivalry, intended to supplant Norfolk in royal favour that would have given Henry a firm hold on the King, eventually to bring about his downfall. However, he had miscalculated. Far from replacing Norfolk in Henry's favour, Richard dismissed the pair of them:

'I can't be bothered with their piddling rows,' he told Maudelyn. 'Let Parliament deal with them!' And he ordered that the disputants should be placed under arrest until Parliament *had* 'dealt' with them.

Henry (Hereford) obtained bail from his father, but Norfolk found no bail and was committed to Windsor Castle, yet because of his loyalty in betraying the St Albans' plot, thus saving the King from imprisonment or death, Norfolk was given the command of the fortress of Calais. So if Norfolk were at Calais he would be unable to attend the trial of Parliament's Committee, which was just as well for Henry, Duke of Hereford. Thinking, in the absence of Norfolk, there could be no disclaimer against his charges, he added to his original accusation of Norfolk's treachery, that not only had he been responsible for the murder of Gloucester, uncle of both him and the King, but that he had robbed the funds entrusted to him as captain of the garrison at Calais.

Henry had again miscalculated. Norfolk was not in command of the fortress at Calais, for when the Committee of Parliament demanded that Henry substantiate his serious charges, he was unable to offer conclusive proof, and the whole question would have to be postponed until decided by combat.

Before the publicity given to the Norfolk-Hereford dispute, Richard attempted to effect a reconciliation between the two who were determined to fight their duel to its bitter end. Only when he realised that he could not appease the disputants did he let them get on with it.

'And good riddance to one or the other,' he told Maudelyn.

'They have brought me nothing but trouble since both joined up with the Appellants. And the fact that Norfolk purported to have saved my life at the risk of his own by betraying that pack of traitors of whom he was one of them and got himself a dukedom for his pains, does not vindicate him from what he was, and probably still is. How can I trust anyone who professes loyalty to me — except you — Maudelyn, my good friend.'

'Always, now and for ever,' replied Maudelyn. 'But Your Grace has more friends and devoted servants than I in your service.'

'Then let them show themselves to me,' returned Richard. 'As for this senseless row between Henry and Tom Mowbray, both new dukes, though God knows why I gave Henry a dukedom! I gave it to Nottingham when he came to me with his tale of treason from the St Albans' pack of bloodhounds! However, I'll get some amusement out of their duel and give the countryside a day's holiday!'

Not only the countryside in the neighbourhood of Coventry where the final arrangements for the duel were held but, according to the ubiquitous chroniclers: 'A number of foreigners from over the sea, and a Scottish knight, one of the Stuarts, gathered to watch the lavish ceremonial prepared for the entertainment of the King, his peers and the 'foreigners' including the Duke of Milan and other royalties or semi-royalties, besides hosts of country folk.

It must have been a brilliant scene on that sun-filled September day. The brightly coloured gowns of the women who, with their husbands in Court regalia, surrounded the King enthroned on a dais, presented an eye-dazzling spectacle. Chroniclers vied one with the other to give enthusiastic reports of the two challengers and their escorts.

Hereford was the first to enter the lists, *Mounted on a white courser* as an eye-witness tells us, *banded* (we presume the saddle cloth) *with green and blue velvet sumptuously embroidered in swans and antelopes.* Norfolk followed him, *his horse … banded in crimson velvet with silver lions and mulberry trees.*

The whole vast assembly excitedly watched the Earl Marshal examine the mounts of the duellists, measure their lances and see to it that their armour and shields were faultless. While this was done the two combatants dismounted and took their seats at opposite ends of the lists. Then the Earl Marshal having ordered the grooms to examine the horses' hooves, and run expert hands over their legs and hocks, he pronounced the condition of the chargers satisfactory. The king's herald sounded a loud trumpet call, the duellists remounted and the fight began…

But did it?

Another trumpet, on a louder and more warning note, was heard at the command of the King. The duellists, their lances poised at the ready, halted their impatient steeds. The sun shot fiery rays from their shields and armour; Norfolk lifted his vizor, Hereford did the same, and from that huge concourse of spectators came a confused buzz as of a gigantic hive. The amazed onlookers saw the King on his dais cast down his staff and beckon the Earl Marshal to him. A short conference ensued and, to the wonder of that multitude, the duellists were commanded to dismount and return to their seats. The horses were led from the lists and the duel was ended before it had begun!

Why?

Amid a hubbub of disappointment, speculation and rumour, Richard held a counsel with the most important of his peers, among them his uncle, Duke of Lancaster. He may have been relieved that the combat was delayed or not to be fought at all for, although Norfolk stood a poor chance of winning against Henry, a famous duellist, the unlikely might happen, a chink in the armour could have led to Henry's death. After a long and private talk between the peers and Gaunt in evident agreement with the King, it was decided that Henry, Duke of Hereford, should be sentenced to exile for ten years.

A tremendous uproar greeted this announcement, boos and hisses intermingled with shouts of applause from Richard's loyalists near enough to have heard the proclamation of Hereford's penalty.

The Duke of Norfolk, however, was to be exiled for life and his property and lands confiscated; so much for risking *his* life to save his king from imprisonment — or death! Again this produced a roar of disapproval amid cheers from Hereford's allies. It was noticed by some eye-witnesses that the King showed signs of doubt and uneasiness at the lifelong sentence of exile passed upon Norfolk. After all he had been loyal to the King in betraying the plot to imprison or kill him!

There were, of course, the usual rumours from the Gloucester-Lancastrian partisans that the King's reckless and unreasonable sentences passed on the two dukes, one his first cousin exiled for ten years, the other for life, was further evidence of the King's mental instability. But Richard, having consulted with his uncle Gaunt and other reliable and unbiased peers, decided that if the battle with the duellists had ended with the death of one, he would still be left with the other dangerous Appellant.

Despite that Norfolk had turned King's Evidence to betray the dastardly St Albans' plot even to bring about the death of Arundel, his own father-in-law, Norfolk had looked to his own advantage which had gained him a dukedom.

Richard decided that to be rid of both, at least with Henry for ten years and Norfolk for life, or on second thoughts, to return them with a king's pardon after a few years; maybe it was better to have the two survivors of the Trial by Battle back again under his eye and well guarded against further mischief.

However, Norfolk came in for the same disappointed blood-lust as the multitude who were done out of what looked to have been the greatest fight to the death of one or other combatant within living memory!

During the next twelve months and with the last two Appellants out of harm's way, Richard could be assured of a reign of prosperity unless either one or the other, or both, should manage to get at him again.

With the worst of his enemies, Gloucester and Arundel, done for, Richard's return to power may have given rise to the accusation of 'tyranny' promulgated by Gloucester and the Lancastrians and first and foremost by Henry, Duke of Hereford. He, in exile — at present — was working slowly and surely for the end of him who from his early boyhood he had hated and coveted the Crown that he, Henry, determined should have been his after the death of his father.

But if Richard's recently achieved power as sovereign did not prove him a tyrant, it did require and demand much money to pay for his collection of valuable treasures, besides the great expense of building a magnificent roof to the hall of Westminster Palace. Yet there were two charges against him of inexcusable misjudgement, if not folly, that brought a disastrous result.

Richard's reckless expenditure throughout the later years of his majority, caused to his harassed Exchequer the necessity of forcing loans on the already overburdened tax payers. Besides this, Richard was charged with the unpleasant fact of issuing crooked pardons, blank cheques, and a final and crowning act of folly, the sequestration of the exiled Hereford's future Lancastrian estates ... Whether or not Richard were directly responsible for his Exchequer's desperate means of raising money, certain it is that the King's extravagance and reckless disregard for the expenses of a monarchy, had brought his Treasurer and Exchequer near to bankruptcy. Furthermore, while endeavouring to cope with their financial difficulties, seventeen counties were submitted to a fine of £1000 each for their disloyalty in supporting the treacherous Appellants in the past, while the rest of the country did submissively accede to their king's, or his Exchequer's, demands.

'They are paying,' Maudelyn warned him, 'for Your Grace's pleasure and interest in the arts and — if I may suggest — your lavish expenditure on your own and Your Grace's Court. It is not for me, Sire, to question Your Grace's indulgence in —'

'It is not for you —' interrupted Richard, a red flush of anger rising to his forehead, where a lock of the fair hair had strayed when he vexedly rumpled it — 'not for you,' he repeated, 'nor any one of you to question what I should or should not do with my money even for my pleasure and that of my Court. D-do you or does any one of you who are s-supposed to advise me, and you especially as my personal secretary, know how I care for the poor of my village at Berkhamsted where I used to play with the boys of my own age, who are now men with wives and children to keep alive on a pittance that is not enough to feed a pig! I have always seen to it that they are comfortably housed and fed wherever there is evidence of their wretched lives for which my government demands that they should pay *them* for their miserable conditions! I tell you' — he thumped the arm of his chair — 'that it is I, their king, who bitterly oppose the bleeding of the poor to fill the coffers of the rich!'

Then, as Maudelyn opened his mouth for further admonishment which he felt bound to offer in his capacity as adviser and personal secretary, Richard forestalled him.

'There's no need for you or my Exchequer to carp at me as responsible for the mistakes of my inefficient government. I am off to Ireland and I will leave you and the rest of you to deal with your difficulties here. I have enough of my own over there where I am urgently wanted. You know, or you should know, that a courier arrived yesterday with a message from young Mortimer, Earl of March, successor to his father's Lieutenancy, informing me that Ireland is involved in the threat of another revolt from MacMurrough who is for ever causing trouble over there. Mortimer came here to attend that famous — or infamous — dispute between my two new dukes, Tom Mowbray and Bolingbroke, and returned to Dublin having found MacMurrough had broken faith with me after my first Irish expedition. Mortimer sent for me to come over and decide what to do with him. So you see, I am thought to be of some use in my Irish province, even if I am known here as an infernal nuisance!' He gave Maudelyn his boyish grin that was no less irresistible to the secretary than to any of his ministers, whether for or against him. 'You can bid me good hunting with my pack and if you want to hunt with me in my land of bogs and fine women — they are worth a rough seasick passage across the Irish Channel, I'll warrant you! — the meet will be held at Westminster this day week.'

The second Irish expeditionary force was led by Richard and accompanied by the most trusted knights and barons of his Court.

As he already had experience of fighting his rebellious Irish, Richard was thankful for the excuse to leave Westminster and the continuous complaints and criticism of his government concerning his extravagance.

The preparations for departure went on apace, but before he left he made his will, desiring that on his death his body should lie beside that of his first wife, Anne.

Richard, having learned from Isabelle's personal physician that his child queen under the guardianship of her governess, Lady Coucy, was not receiving the correct diet for one of her tender years and had been given the rich foods provided by the lady for her guests — chiefly her male guests —politely dismissed Lady Coucy and replaced her with the widow of Roger Mortimer, who had been killed in the battle of Kelliston, County Kelly. This was indicative of the King's belief that the Mortimers were the rightful heirs presumptive to the throne by descent from Henry III.

He paid a final visit to Isabelle, then at Windsor Castle with her governess, Lady Coucy, who was lavishly entertaining at Isabelle's Court. The child, relegated to her nursery, greeted him with cries of delight, and as he kissed her he said, 'I am going away for a short time and will be back again soon —'

She begged to be allowed to go with him. 'I see you not many times, *mon cher Papa*. You are always in London or at Westminster.'

He promised she would come to him on his return, 'and we will ride together here in Windsor Park.' He had bought her a pony and had been teaching her to ride.

He made a point of telling Maudelyn, who accompanied him to Windsor, 'If by any chance I do not return —'

'Say not so, Sire!' protested Maudelyn, shocked.

'If I don't come back,' Richard continued, 'you must see to it that Isabelle is taken to her father in Paris. I can trust you?'

'With my life and honour, Sire.'

On 29 May 1399 Richard, and the main body of his army, set sail to land at Waterford after two days' rough passage.

His uncle, Duke of York, was to act as regent during his absence; not too happy a choice for York of all the late king's sons was the least responsible and had but two loves in his life, the chase of the stag and of women.

With Richard went five young volunteer recruits. Henry, the son of Lord Derby; the young son of the late Duke of Gloucester and the son of the executed Earl of Arundel. Henry Beaufort, younger brother of the Marquis of Dorset, was Richard's cousin by the marriage of his uncle Gaunt to Catherine Swynford; and another cousin, the Duke of Albemarle, son of the Duke of York.

The Percys of the great house of Northumberland, were summoned to the mobilisation of the King's army, but as allies of Gaunt, Duke of Lancaster, they had been shocked at the banishment of his son and much to Richard's annoyance made excuses not to accompany the King to Ireland.

Among those of his followers was the esquire of one of the French knights in attendance on Queen Isabelle. He, Jean Cretan, wrote love lyrics and set them to music during the crossing to Ireland for the entertainment of the King and his army, if not too seasick to enjoy them.

Cretan's eye-witness account of the expedition is of equal value to historians as are the incomparable Chronicles of

Froissart on his few visits to England. From Waterford the army led by Richard marched through the wild and desolate Black Mountains to wait for the recently created Duke of Albemarle, York's son. It seems he deliberately delayed the advance for a week in bringing up necessary supplies for Richard's forces.

Ironically, the young son of the exiled Hereford joined the King's expedition to Ireland and, according to Cretan, was knighted for valour in the fight against the rebellious MacMurrough. It is doubtful that Richard knew who this young boy could have been since he asked his name and was told, 'Henry Bolingbroke, Sire.'

Whereupon Richard drew his sword and bade him, 'Kneel!'

The lad was no more than fourteen but looked older being tall for his age; he must have added two or three years when he escaped from his grandfather's castle at Pontefract to join up with the King as a recruit.

He may have feared the King would use his sword to deadly purpose on the son of his greatest enemy, yet if aware of his anticipated death, Henry courageously obeyed; and as the King touched his shoulder with the sword he said, 'Rise, Sir Henry Bolingbroke, King's knight!'

Nor did he know that the lad he knighted would be the hero of Agincourt and the future King Henry V.

Meanwhile Hereford, since his banishment, had lived in Paris where he was given a chilly reception by the King of France. Charles could hardly have welcomed his son-in-law's exiled enemy, yet he gave him reluctant permission to set up his establishment at L'Hôtel de Cluny, where he entertained a number of the French aristocracy. In fact, his exile was scarcely a punishment; it would seem he had been let off too lightly from the death he deserved for treason, with the prospect of shortening the sentence of ten years' exile to an enjoyable two or three years in Paris.

His return to England came not in a wishful two or three years but in a joyful two or three months.

A few weeks after his arrival in Paris, Hereford received a visit from the ex-Archbishop Arundel who had managed to escape the custody of the Duke of Exeter, Richard's surviving half-brother John, late Earl of Huntingdon. Thomas Arundel told Henry that his father, the Duke of Lancaster, was not expected to live. He had been ailing during the whole of the past year. Henry heard this news with eager expectation.

Within a few days Arundel paid him another visit. He had found shelter with some French relatives in Paris and could not be recaptured while under their roof. He brought Henry the news that his father, the Duke of Lancaster, was dead.

Henry learned of his father's death with a triumphant shout: 'At last!'

TWELVE

At the end of June in that fateful year of 1399 Richard and the royal party in Ireland were struggling against fearful odds for want of food and ammunition. His advance had been deliberately delayed by Albemarle for reasons best known to himself.

From Cretan we hear how the King shared the hardships and semi-starvation imposed upon his troops for lack of the promised supplies. Richard sent envoys to approach MacMurrough with the offer of pardon if he would surrender and so bring to an end this rebellion of the King's colonial islanders.

MacMurrough hotly refused to surrender and, defiantly ignoring Richard's appeal, ordered every village to refuse sustenance to the King and his armies, but they must continue to serve and sustain their own lords of the lands. MacMurrough having dismissed Richard's envoys chosen from his loyal Welshmen and his Cheshire archers we learn, again from Cretan, how the King fought his way towards Dublin where every shrub and bush in this hostile country harboured a skulking enemy. His losses were great, as much from the hardships endured on that long and weary march as from the arrows of MacMurrough's bowmen. His Parliament who condemned this sybarite of luxury and wanton extravagance for wasting the Exchequer's money, might have been disappointed to know that the object of their scorn and contempt, fostered by the King's enemies, scarcely halted for a night's rest to sleep on the sun-baked ground in that dry season of drought. Many fell by the wayside divested of their armour in that unbearable heat, as also was Richard who limped barefoot, his shoes discarded in holes. He insisted on rationing everyone including himself, the scanty water in their leathern bottles, if any could be found in the dried-up springs to quench their raging thirst.

Cretan gives his eye-witness account of how six men shared one loaf between them for six days. The king, in similar plight, refused to take more than his share of whatever food there was in their sadly diminished supplies. When almost nothing had been left fit to eat, much of it gone to waste rotting in the heatwave of that summer, they fell to digging up the roots of carrots or the dried remains of cabbages. In that impoverished land potatoes, the abundant source of food for the Irish peasantry in the future, were not known until the reign of the First Elizabeth when discovered by Sir Francis Drake.

Albemarle having, as he thought, done his damnedest in delaying the much-needed supplies and equipment to hold up the King's advance, had arrived in Dublin with stores enough to feed the famished troops. He met the ships from England at Waterford sent by his father York, the Regent.

Richard realised Albemarle's treacherous intent, and feigned a trust in this latest enemy, his own cousin, that he was above suspicion.

'I'll set a watch on him,' he told Sir William Bagot, an able lawyer who had come over from support of the Appellants to advise and aid the King in his Irish expedition. 'For I would as soon trust Albemarle as I would trust the devil if he came to me in the guise of the Archangel Gabriel…' And he swore one of his favourite oaths: 'By St John the Baptist! I will take MacMurrough dead or alive and all with him who treacherously oppose me!'

For the next six weeks he and his army remained in Dublin cut off from direct communication with England since, at the end of that hot summer, equinoctial gales held up those mediaeval ships from risking a stormy passage across the Irish sea.

Before the worst of the gales had taken toll of ships back and forth from Ireland, Sir William Bagot sailed in the last vessel that could with safety brave the storm. He managed to get back to Ireland before the hurricane had swept other intrepid ships to their doom.

He brought Richard the devastating news that Henry, now Duke of Lancaster, had left France accompanied by the traitor ex-Archbishop Arundel and a number of barons and knights who had joined Henry in his exile. All staunch Lancastrians, buoyed up with hope of future favours, they willingly followed him giving ample support to his mission that he declared was solely to regain his forfeited heritage left to him by the death of his father.

Henry, now Duke of Lancaster, was careful to lend no suspicion to his ultimate motive which was to claim not only his heritage, but the Crown and Throne of England. Yet he would scatter careless hints of a bar sinister in the King's royal escutcheon with a reminder of Richard's mother, the 'Fair Maid of Kent', the desired of all men who had captured the heart of the Prince of Wales, the Black Prince when, after their marriage so much of his time was passed in the war with France. He would tell them that the King's mother — 'Richard's mother,' he meaningfully corrected himself — 'obtained a dispensation from the Pope for a divorce from her husband Sir Thomas Holland, afterwards Earl of Kent. The earldom succeeded to her eldest son, Richard's half-brother, now deceased. 'The king — Richard I mean — has, or had, a habit of creating dukes but he didn't have to create *my* dukedom which is my legal right as is my entire heritage of almost half of England.' And he added silently: *The whole of it before this year is out!*

Lancaster planned his campaign with information from various agents sent to spy on the movements of Richard. He learned that the King having left Ireland had landed at Milford Haven and sailed up the western coast making for Pontefract Castle, the northern stronghold of the Dukes of Lancaster. But Richard was foiled in his attempt to meet and engage Henry's forces against his own troops depleted of adequate supplies, besides that the spread of disease in Ireland had struck down many of his followers during the heatwave and hardships of the expedition.

It was at Pontefract that Henry began undermining the northern and midland shires as he moved south, with cunning allusions to Richard's intent to raise money to pay for the Irish expedition that had lamentably failed. He gave out to the villeins and peasantry that they would be kept in greater bondage even than before the Peasants' Revolt.

As Lancaster halted his troops on village greens he would loudly proclaim, 'I must remind you, if any of you are too young to remember, that King Richard —' he sneered at the title — 'did promise you or your fathers when they, or you, rebelled against the slavery forced upon you by the King himself to deprive you of the miserable pittance you earned at less than a living wage to toil on the lands of your lords and the King's lands … Yes! We know he was only a boy when he promised you his pardon and the restoration of your right to live as men and not as beasts … And he sent you back to your villages as it might be here —' he gestured to the huddle of cottages from where many had come to hear him on the village green — 'Yes, he sent you back to your miserable hovels with fair promises —'

'Promises,' came the roar from some of them. 'Promises he never meant to keep!'

'Yes!' vociferated Henry. 'And I am come to right your wrongs and see that he who is your king shall *keep* his promises!'

'No!' Again came angered howls. 'We'll 'ave no king what promises lies!'

Realising his tactics worked well to his advantage, Henry went further as he journeyed south, to warn them of a dangerous plot which he said he had verified. They swallowed his lies whole.

'A wicked plot that seeks to murder any who strives to lessen the heavy burden of taxation they have already suffered, should they refuse the King's demand for still higher taxes to pay for his personal extravagance and his luxurious Court.'

All this went down with yells of 'Betrayed! The king betrays us with his false promises and bleeds us dry with his taxes that we have to dig up roots for food — or starve!'

To Northumberland who had joined him when he moved on southwards from Pontefract, Henry swore that he had only come from exile to claim his Lancastrian heritage, and that the King must reign until the end of his life when the heir to the succession would be decided if Richard had no issue.

Having assured Northumberland and the Percys that his return from banishment was solely in the interest of himself and the heirs to his inheritance, Henry moved west making for Bristol. He had learned from his scouts that Richard with his sadly diminished army was also bound for Bristol.

The king, who had made every effort to get back to England, landed at Milford Haven, and was met with disheartening news. Henry, with a still stronger force augmented by the Percys whose consciences were satisfied by Lancaster's insistence that he had no intention of raising a rebellion against the King, was advancing to meet Richard on his journey to North Wales. Realising how Lancaster had gulled not only Northumberland but the people in all the shires he had passed on his way from Pontefract, Richard took the only course open to him if he wished to save himself and his throne.

With what was left of his weakened army he covered the hundred and sixty miles to Conway. There he was faced with a situation that might have daunted a more hardened campaigner, yet Richard stood up to it with inherent Plantagenet courage.

He still held his strongly fortified castles of Beaumaris and Carnarvon besides Castle Conway; and with the remainder of his army he had his half-brother, John, Duke of Exeter and his nephew, Duke of Surrey, son of his deceased half-brother, Thomas, Earl of Kent.

He despatched both as envoys to Henry with the offer of more lands and titles if he would cease his rebellion. John made it vehemently clear that the King would never render up his royal heritage to anyone who dared usurp the King's throne until his death when, if no issue, the rightful heir to the succession would be decided by Parliament.

To which John added a threatening finale: 'The king bids me inform you, Lancaster, that if you persist in your rebellion against His Grace he will fight for his throne to the last drop of his blood!'

Strong words that gave Henry to realise he had no snivelling nincompoop to deal with as he gave out to his Lancastrians but a combatant who would fight for his royal rights even to his death — or Henry's!

Lancaster's reply to the King's defiance was to hold Richard's envoys as hostages. He despatched Northumberland's eldest son Henry (later to win his spurs and fall at the battle of Shrewsbury as Henry Hotspur) with an ultimatum that the King must surrender peaceably to the Duke of Lancaster — or if not, by force!

Richard's retort to that, contrary to the cowardly poltroon of the Lancastrian version on his knees begging for mercy, was to demand the immediate release of Lancaster's hostages, the Dukes of Exeter and Surrey.

The Bishop of Carlisle, always in staunch support of the King — as was Maudelyn, who had hastened to his side as soon as he heard of Richard's arrival in England — offered his advice and counsel. 'Since Henry intends, Sire, to force you to abandon your throne, I have drawn up a draft for Your Grace in which to state your terms of the Duke's surrender to Your Grace, which I myself will deliver.'

A council of the King's supporters met at Conway attended by Northumberland. He dramatically swore on oath before the Host that the Duke of Lancaster and himself, the Duke's deputy, did solemnly agree there was no treasonable intent towards His Grace the King. To which Maudelyn offered not one single word for or against this histrionic declaration, but politely escorted Northumberland to the door of the castle where his retinue awaited him.

After Northumberland's attempt at compromise on behalf of Henry, so certainly rebuffed, Richard and his friends rode off to Chester where he could be sure of loyalist support, not by armed force but by stern ministerial decision. However, as they neared the outskirts of Chester, they caught a glimpse of armour through the trees, heard the clink of steel and sound of hooves. Then Richard urged his troops to ride hard in the direction of Flint, where the King could be sure of welcome from his Welshmen. Henry's army followed to surround and waylay him fore and aft.

Northumberland's oath in the Name of the Host had proved him not only a perjurer but a blasphemer…

As before, the Lancastrians' chroniclers gave their own version as to how the King, with cowardly submission, allowed himself to be seized and strictly guarded as any thief or murderer.

Less prejudiced sources told that the King, riding to London as Lancaster's prisoner, was lodged in the Tower, but on passing through Coventry a valiant if vain attempt to rescue the King was made by the men of Cheshire and Wales. On arriving at the Tower of London he was met by the faithful Maudelyn who had come across country by a shorter route than that of Henry and his triumphant cavalcade.

Richard, far from meekly submitting to capture, greeted Maudelyn with the words, 'Thank God you are come! I have no servants here I can trust to take my orders. Go you to Lancaster so soon as he arrives — if ever — for my Welsh and Cheshire archers are on his track and with any luck they will have caught up with him. But when, or if, he comes I command that Henry be brought to me at once. Go!'

Henry, receiving the order peremptorily delivered by Maudelyn in the King's name, indignantly refused to obey. To which Richard haughtily replied, 'Tell Lancaster I, as his king, insist he obey my command and that he be brought instantly to me!'

And as Richard still was his king Henry had no choice *but* to obey with a black mark against the score he held for the downfall of Richard…

According to the French chroniclers, more accurate than the Lancastrians who wrote only what their duke told them to write, Henry came accompanied by the Duke of York and his son Rutland, Duke of Albemarle.

At sight of his uncle York and his cousin Rutland, Richard flew into one of his violent tempers. The blood rushed to his forehead as he accosted his uncle: 'Here's a viper I've nursed and trusted as regent! You, York, are as great a villain as your precious son!' Then turning on Rutland: 'As for you, Albemarle, *Duke* Albemarle on whom I bestowed the strawberry leaves — you damned treacherous cur who held back my supplies from England thinking to kill off myself and my army by starvation! I'll see you hanged for that!'

At which Rutland flung down his glove as challenge saying, 'I'll fight you, not hang you for that!'

Richard glowering, kicked aside the challenge shouting, 'I don't cross swords with a traitor!'

York had sheepishly retreated after Richard's outburst. Nor was Henry anxious for a brawl between his two cousins, and one the King, should Richard's supporters take the chance of arresting both York and his son for treason, which would defeat his purpose of immediate seizure of the throne. He therefore ordered Rutland: 'Stand back!', then enacted the part of peacemaker, reassuring Richard of his goodwill and that of their uncle York who only had the King's interest at heart.

'I assure Your Grace,' Henry pacifically purred, looking as it may have struck Richard, like a well-satisfied cat glutted with a saucer of cream. 'I assure you,' he repeated, 'that you need have no fear. You are the King. No harm shall come to you if I can prevent it.'

To which Richard expressed his opinion of Henry's goodwill by telling him, 'You're a damned liar! And as much a traitor as our Uncle York and his accursed son!'

Having spent his wrath on all three of them, who stood as if lost for words with which to reply to these insults, Richard demanded that his young queen be brought to him. Henry, finding it as difficult to control his temper as Richard to govern his, reminded him that the council now in charge of the King during his, er, temporary retirement in the Tower, could not permit...

'Could not permit?' interrupted Richard, again in blazing fury. 'Who dares permit or not permit the King to command that his queen be brought to him?' He raised a threatening fist. 'I'll flay alive any man who dares oppose me!' And he made a dash for Henry, who backed in fear of him who, as he chose to report, 'was in a sudden maniacal fit'. He would always refer to the late Duke of Gloucester's suggestion of mental disorder to account for the King's assertion of his rights when under the stress of imaginary wrongs.

'Try and calm yourself, my poor Richard,' soothingly said Henry. 'We know that in your tempers you are not responsible for what you say or do. Go now to your bedchamber. I will call a physician to see you. He will bleed you of your overheated blood...'

He was paving the way for Gloucester's insinuations to be noised abroad that the King if not entirely demented, would never be sufficiently responsible to conduct his kingdom as sovereign. He played a careful hand with his eyes moving the pieces — his well bribed supporters of knights and bishops — on *his* chequerboard until he could call — 'Checkmate!'

What chance had Richard against this pyramid of lies and invention? Yet if Bolingbroke thought to break his spirit by systematic undermining of Richard's popularity during the last fifteen years since the Londoners had first hailed a young lad as a hero and saviour from the persecutions of their overlords, he must have been sadly shaken by the stormy scene of defiance in the Tower where he held the King his captive.

As Henry, with Richard in tow, rode through the streets of London to the Tower, citizens hailed him, as Jean Cretan reported who had followed the King when captured, that *the joy-bells from all the churches and monasteries rang so loud and joyous a greeting to the Duke of Lancaster that you could not hear God thundering in his Heaven at the degradation of His Anointed.*

But Richard whom Henry intended to bring to his knees as a miserable poltroon pleading for mercy, had shown himself to be a man who would fight, as he said, 'to the last drop of his blood' for his rights and his kingdom. Nor, as Henry had noted, did the King lack supporters. Maudelyn, having arrived at the Tower before Lancaster and his prisoner at once contacted Richard to tell him that Cretan, 'Your Grace's ally and friend of the King of France, has taken the queen this very day across to Paris. Her father, King Charles, will meet the queen and her retinue at Calais.'

Henry's spies having reported Maudelyn's audience with the King which Lancaster could not forbid since Richard was still, in effect, King of England, he realised that he would not find his intention to seize the throne and its hereditary royal occupant so facile an undertaking as he had foreseen.

Although Richard was his prisoner, the Londoners were demanding the King's deposition as the result of Henry's and the late Gloucester's years of poisonous accusations that, like a virulent epidemic, had spread not only through the capital city but the whole countryside. It had now become evident to

Henry that the deposition of an anointed king must be decided by Parliament.

For the whole of September 1399 England had no Parliament and virtually no king, but all proclamations and statutes were still issued in the name of King Richard.

It was in this confusion as to who were the arbitrators to appoint honours or dishonours that the new Parliament assembled. Thus Richard's 'duketies' were to lose their titles and revert to their former earldoms: Albemarle to Rutland, Huntingdon to Exeter, and Richard's nephew Surrey to the earldom of Kent. Executions and banishments were the lot of those who were loyal to the King.

Henry, now more than ever wary, would not endanger his prize by giving any of the King's supporters the chance to frustrate his lifelong dream to find it a nightmare. No!

What of the King of France whose young daughter, the Queen of England, was now safe in his custody? Would he not avenge his son-in-law's wrongs to see him, the King of England, righted, and his daughter beside him on the throne as his consort? Charles would not scruple to attempt an invasion with a strong armed force — and then what?

'They are giving it out that Charles of France is insane,' Richard told Maudelyn, 'because of his wife's numerous adulteries, just as my enemies have named me a lunatic! But Charles is well recovered and Henry can think himself lucky if France does not invade England and restore me with my wife to the throne. You'll see! I can count on Charles.'

A forlorn hope.

Northumberland, whose conscience may have nagged him on account of his solemn oath before the Host that Henry had no treasonable intent against the King had reverted, after confession, to Richard's side and again he swore, before the

Host of his devotion and loyalty to the ruling monarch. All this gave Henry some disquiet. He must insist that Parliament assemble at once!

The official records state that Henry, Duke of Lancaster, with a deputation of the Law and the Church visited King Richard in the Tower accompanied by the Duke of Northumberland who seemed to have changed his loyalties with the variability of a weathercock.

A document of abdication was then produced, to be duly signed and sealed by Richard and witnessed by the authorities of the Law and the Church.

Richard, who had been prepared for this, demanded that he be given time to read and consider the document before he signed away his Crown and his kingdom to any lawful or unlawful successor. After a hushed conference, heads together in a corner of that Tower room, Northumberland as spokesman announced that the request of the, er, he hesitated before he repeated, 'the King', was to be granted a limit of twenty-four hours.

Precisely on the stroke of ten the next morning the restored Archbishop Arundel arrived with the Bishop of York and Henry of Lancaster and presented the King with the document of Abdication for his signature. He, the first King of England who could write his name, made one cool unemotional remark.

'I, Richard Rex in this enforced Abdication sign away my Crown and my Kingdom.'

As usual there were Lancastrian tales of how Richard had spurned the challenge of Rutland, had scorned and abused his uncle York and his two cousins, Lancaster and Rutland, which, as Henry gave out, was uttered in the frenzy of a madman.

The only one of Lancaster's supporters to query the veracity of these rumours was a monk of Westminster, Adam of Usk, who told how he had dined with the King a few days before the Abdication and reported how bitterly Richard spoke but with no sign of mental derangement.

'My God! What a wonderful world this is which exiles, destroys, and ruins a king and the great men of the past, the present, and possibly the future and is ever tainted with strife and envy…' He went on to say, according to Adam of Usk, 'None of my own servants is appointed to attend me, but strangers who spy on me … Who is to be trusted in the fickle fortunes of this world?'

On the last day of September 1399 a vast assemblage gathered in Richard's Great Hall of Westminster. That tumultuous meeting of Parliamentarians and the citizens of London cannot properly be called a Parliament since the throne was empty in the absence of the King. Determined to end any opposition to the seizure of the throne Henry appointed a Speaker of his choice and ignored Richard's insistence, sent in a message from the Tower, for a fair trial before judges.

He was refused trial.

The Abdication, signed and sealed by Richard and read both in Latin and English, contained thirty-three articles and was accepted and agreed by that great assemblage, including the citizens of London, who had come to see their once honoured and esteemed young king pilloried, the victim of false accusations.

For the few who could understand Latin and for the many who could neither read nor write English or Latin, it was said the King had tricked his Parliament into surrendering its powers to the King's despotic control. He had taken —

'Stolen!' came the interruption from the back of the hall, where stood or crouched for lack of space the citizens who had forced entrance, whereby 'taken' was repeated by the Speaker reading from the heavy parchment sheets — 'the money granted by the Exchequer for war and especially for the Irish expedition, all to be squandered by the King. And he made the unauthorised excuse that none but he could make or break the laws of the land.'

Much of it could not be heard in the storm of disgusted howls at these shocking revelations of the sovereign's evil works. 'To think,' shouted a voice later discovered to be that of one of the Drapers' Guild, rival to the King's favourite Victuallers, 'to think how he robbed and would have ruined us.'

'Yes! All of us,' shouted another voice, 'except his own favourites, and they —'

'Silence!' called the Speaker, and from Henry, 'Order! All your grievances will be fairly heard in God's good time.' Loud cheers to raise the ornamental roof greeted his pacific announcement with 'The Duke of Lancaster, God bless him!'

Further articles, taking almost the whole of that fatal day to read, declared that the King had despoiled the sacred altars of the Church, had taken to himself the jewels that were in the keeping of the Treasury for the King and his successors together with the Crown Jewels.

At which another voice yelled: 'Lies! All this is f—ing lies!'

'Arrest that man!' commanded Henry.

There was a scuffle among the crowd of Londoners and yells of 'Hang him!'

'No! Hang *you*, you bloody traitor!'

At long last when all who had given voice for the Abdication, and those against it had been felled to the ground or rendered unconscious with blows and kicks, the cheers of approval drowned the few hisses and groans as Henry stood that all might see him make the sign of the Cross before that great assemblage, whom he addressed: 'In the name of the Father and the Son and the Holy Ghost I, Henry of Lancaster, challenge the realm of England and the Crown that I am descended by the rightful line of Blood Royal from King Henry III, and by the Grace of God, who has sent me to recover the kingdom which has been undone by fault of unworthy governance…'

Many who listened in awed silence to this momentous announcement were ignorant of the fact that he who claimed to be the lawful heir to the kingdom was directly descended from King Henry III. They may have known that the third King Henry of England, second son of King John, had inherited the throne at the age of nine years old even as had Richard; but unlike the second King Richard, the third Henry Plantagenet was a thoroughly bad lot, as inefficient and unscrupulous a monarch as his father, King John, who had first blinded then murdered the rightful heir to the throne, his nephew Prince Arthur.

One or two voices among the rows of Parliamentarians were heard to mutter, 'A direct descendant of Henry III is scarcely a descent of which to boast!'

After the heavy silence that followed Henry's declaration, the Archbishops of Canterbury and York escorted Henry of Lancaster to be enthroned, and placed on his head the Crown of King Richard II.

Loud applause broke out as Henry, raising a hand to silence the resounding cheers, rose to give thanks to 'Almighty God and all in these lands that I have been persuaded to claim the throne *not* by conquest, for never would I deprive any man of his heritage. But I do swear by the Laws of the Realm that I have been proven the rightful successor for the good purpose and profit of the Realm.'

Although Lancastrian chronicles carefully omit the various accusations made against Richard during the reading of the Articles, only one voice, that of Thomas Merke, Bishop of Carlisle, who had always been a staunch supporter of King Richard, was raised in his defence.

Boldly disdaining the tumultuous applause that greeted Henry's announcement of his rightful kingship, the Bishop lifted a peremptory hand as his voice rang out for silence to hear him speak above the din.

'My lords, consider well before you give judgement on what my Lord Duke has set forth, for I maintain there is not one person competent to judge my Lord the King whom we have acknowledged and revered as our sovereign for the last twenty years and more. I advise you to know that there is in this world no false traitor nor wicked murderer who is not brought to justice before his judges and given a fair trial. My lords, you have heard the accusations made against King Richard, and you have condemned His Grace without hearing his defence or without his presence that he may answer to these accusations. I hereby demand that he shall be given a fair trial. My lords, I maintain that the Duke of Lancaster whom you have seen crowned and unlawfully seated on the throne he usurped—'

Ignoring shouts of assent or denial, the bishop resumed, 'I repeat that the Duke of Lancaster who has usurped the throne has more erred and offended against King Richard than has the King against him. We know full well that the Duke was banished for ten years by the Council of the Realm and that he returned to this country without the permission of the King. Moreover, I declare,' he raised his eyes heavenwards as if addressing the God of Justice, 'that the Duke of Lancaster has seated himself on the throne where none should sit save the lawfully crowned King of England. Wherefore I declare that King Richard the Second be brought before a full and just Parliament to hear what he would say, and if he be willing to relinquish his Crown to the Duke or not!'

The bishop faced a storm of abuse and invective for his courageous speech, but he stood by his defence of the King, and paid for it with immediate imprisonment and the loss of his bishopric.

The Coronation of the First King of the House of Lancaster was necessarily hurried and lacked nothing of the pomp and splendour accorded to his Plantagenet predecessors. From the mob that thronged the courtyard of Westminster Palace craning their necks for a glimpse of the new king heading the procession in and out of the Abbey, the shouts of 'Down with the usurper!' went unheard in the rousing cheers of 'God save King Henry!'

One of the many difficulties Henry had to face came in a report to him from the Chief Justice the day after the Abdication. He, Sir William Thringing, informed King Henry that he had told the captive king as directed by agreement of the council that henceforth the late King Richard would be known and called by his rightful name, Sir Richard of Bordeaux, to which Sir Richard had replied, 'All's one to me how I am called since none but God has anointed and crowned me in the name of King Richard the Second of

England with which name, while I live, I remain God's Anointed!'

This verbal report from the Chief Justice to Henry caused him much unease, particularly as Richard had reminded Sir William that only by anointing with the sacred oil could the true king be crowned.

A disquieting poser for Henry was this, since the coronation had been arranged to take place in the following week. But without the sacred oil, first used at the coronation of Edward the Confessor and poured on the heads of all his successors, no king could be anointed.

The fact that none seemed to know where the sacred oil had been kept during these last twenty years or more when the child King Richard had been anointed, put Henry in a rare state.

'Where is it? And who is in charge of it? How is it kept, in a bottle or a flagon, or — what?'

'The sacred oil is kept in what is called the Ampulla, Your Grace,' offered Arundel, the restored Archbishop of Canterbury whose state of agitation almost equalled that of His Grace, for if anyone could know where the sacred oil was kept it should be the Archbishop.

'I don't care where it is kept and if it contains olive oil or castor oil or *any* sort of oil,' rejoined the harassed Henry, 'but my head *must be* anointed!'

If any sort of oil were finally procured in what Arundel claimed to be the Ampulla containing the sacred oil that had anointed King Richard and which, having run dry in the course of twenty years, had now been sacerdotally replenished, as explained by the Archbishop, Henry was duly crowned and anointed King Henry the Fourth of England, the founder of the House of Lancaster.

That there was no consort enthroned beside the King caused no remark, since Henry of Lancaster had been a widower for several years. His wife was heiress to the great fortunes of the Bohuns for which she had been married, and of whom Henry had little use save in his bed, where she had borne him six children still surviving of almost perennial pregnancies. However, if the absence of a queen at the coronation of a widowed king caused no remark, the absence of his eldest son did not pass unnoticed by some who had accompanied King Richard on his Irish expeditions. One elderly knight, having seen the new king's young son knighted for valour by King Richard, and watched the coronation of King Henry in the Abbey, was heard by a few near him to say: 'Pity 'tisn't this one's son to wear the crown. If he isn't here —'

'He's sick in bed!' interposed a loyal Lancastrian.

'So as 'tis given,' pursued the old knight, 'but young Henry is ever for King Richard as King Richard is for him, and if sick in bed I'll wager 'tis a sickness that won't see his father with King Richard's crown on his head. T'would be better for England and for all of us if the young one were on the throne where his father sits, and better still if the rightful king were back where he belongs!'

It seemed there were many who thought the same — too many for Henry's peace of mind; and if 'uneasy lies the head that wears a crown', this king's head that wore the crown was certainly uneasy.

As Christmas approached with Sir Richard of Bordeaux a prisoner in the Tower of London, the capital city was too near the mouth of the Thames for Henry not to wish him either at the bottom of the river or the sea, across which Charles of France and his army might sail any day to invade England, rescue Richard of Bordeaux and give his daughter back to her husband, the King, as his queen.

Jean Cretan who conducted the little Queen Isabelle to Paris and had seen her safely in her father's arms, returned with more disquieting news for Henry. Cretan, the mouthpiece of King Charles, told Henry how the King of France was determined to invade England and restore the rightful king to his throne with his queen beside him.

'We must get Richard to Pontefract,' Henry decided, in conference with his council and Arundel. 'The further away from London and the coast the more difficult it will be for Charles, even if he landed an army, to march it through England, especially in winter with the roads knee deep in snow. I have ordered the whole of the Kentish and south coasts to be guarded. Charles will find he bites off more than he can chew if he tries to get at Richard.'

On the last day of October 1399 Sir Richard of Bordeaux was forcibly dragged from the Tower disguised as a countryman. With his face stained brown from walnut juice and his hair hidden under a forester's hat pulled well down over his eyes, he was bundled into a hay wagon.

Despite the valiant efforts of Maudelyn and his supporters, who made every effort to save the King, he was taken by devious ways along almost impassable roads and either carted or mounted on any raw-boned gelding that could pass as a rustic's horse, eventually to arrive at Henry's castle of Pontefract. There he was flung half dead into a dungeon and left, chained and fettered, to die.

Henry's first Christmas as king spent at Windsor Castle could scarcely have been a happy one. True, he had prepared a feast of great rejoicing, with music, dancing, mummers and a masque in which he appeared in full regalia purporting to represent the great Edward the Confessor, the first king to be crowned and anointed with sacred oil. Had he not been anointed with oil whether sacred or procured from a grocer, an apothecary or somewhere known only to Archbishop Arundel, but anointed he was and proclaimed King Henry IV by almost half his subjects. As for the other half, apart from the loyal Lancastrians of London and his own provinces bestowed on his father by his grandfather Edward III, it was apparent that Henry had not captured the hearts of all his subjects. Threats of revolt to restore the captive king to his throne were heard throughout the kingdom.

On Twelfth Night the rumours that had tormented Henry in the midst of the Christmas festivities became a certainty. A conspiracy, planned by Richard's supporters led by Maudelyn who resembled him in height and features was to impersonate the captive king supposed to have escaped from his dungeon at Pontefract. Richard's half-brother Kent, with the Bishop of Carlisle — he had also escaped imprisonment — plotted to storm Windsor Castle, capture Henry and his sons and destroy for all time the usurper of the House of the Plantagenets.

But again treachery frustrated the conspirators, among whom was Rutland, late Duke of Albemarle, son of the Duke of York. Having learned of the conspiracy, and purporting to be in support of his cousin King Richard, Rutland treacherously betrayed the plot to his father. As uncle of both kings, York chose the safest course.

That he had acknowledged Henry King of England, and, as York believed him to be prime executioner, he preferred to live with his head on his shoulders for he knew Henry would not scruple to cut it off if he offended. So, with his family, Henry fled from Windsor and found shelter within the walls of London. There he had almost the entire city in his support.

Although Richard's rescuers did succeed in capturing Windsor Castle, Henry — secure in the loyalty of his capital city and more than half the kingdom — lost no time in mobilising a formidable force to advance upon Richard's totally inadequate army under the command of his nephew, late Duke of Surrey, son of his deceased half-brother Thomas, Earl of Kent.

To avoid a pitched battle with Henry's stronger forces augmented by his army guarding the coast of Kent, young Surrey directed his followers westward. Henry feared an invasion from France by Charles VI far less than a rebellion of the western counties in favour of the rightful king.

Surrey's army had now reached Cirencester where, with Salisbury who had fought with Richard in his Irish expeditions, he lodged at the chief inn in the town. The remainder of his soldiers were quartered in the surrounding countryside and villages. But Kent, believing the citizens of Cirencester were for King Richard, he reckoned without Henry's supporters.

It was the turning point. An infuriated crowd of citizens besieged the inn yelling, 'Seize the enemies of King Henry, our rightful king! Down with Richard, the traitor!'

Both Surrey and Salisbury with their servants put up a fierce resistance, but were forced to surrender. Some of their soldiers and the chaplain of both earls attempted to fire the town but were too late to save their leaders. Richard's nephew Kent, and Salisbury were brutally murdered; their heads stuck on pikes in the marketplace gave vast entertainment to crowds of jeering townsfolk.

Richard's surviving half-brother John, late Earl of Huntingdon, Duke of Exeter, made valiant attempts to raise a rebellion in London, was captured while trying to escape downriver, and slain by a mob of Henry's Lancastrians. Almost all who sought to save Richard from Henry 'the Usurper', as they named him, were executed or barbarously hanged, including the faithful Maudelyn.

At Oxford where Henry halted when he fled from Windsor, his supporters were now in the majority throughout the kingdom, thanks to his persistent allegations and malicious calumnies against Richard. When at Oxford Henry executed almost thirty knights and squires known to be Richard's loyalists. In London several who had aided the escape of Huntingdon were hanged and disembowelled while still alive.

The Bishop of Carlisle narrowly escaped the same hideous death for his address to the council insisting that the King should be granted a fair trial. However, the Pope intervened and restored to him his lost bishopric.

The wholesale slaughter at Cirencester was tantamount to a death sentence for Richard. Yet Henry, now in supreme command, was obsessed by the fear that while Richard lived, even though strictly guarded in that dungeon at Pontefract, his throne would be forever in jeopardy. He decided to let it be known that Richard had starved himself to death in a deliberate 'hunger strike', and that his body must be shown to the people. Only by satisfying his subjects that the throne he had usurped could be legally his, was he sure there would be no attempt from Richard's supporters to restore the rightful king to his throne.

Having made this decision Henry ordered the corpse of Richard of Bordeaux to be paraded through the streets of London. At every town on the way from Pontefract the body was exposed to convince all who clamoured to know for certain that the King was dead.

The corpse of Richard, brought to St Paul's in London and seen by thousands of citizens, was taken to Hertfordshire and buried in the Dominican Priory at King's Langley. Yet *was* it Richard's body that had been buried, with no state ceremony, and only the good Dominican friars to pray for him?

Few doubted the death of the late king, save Henry and those of his allies, who had learned a dismaying rumour that Richard had escaped from Pontefract. How?

Some said that Cretan, who always had a great affection for Richard, did effect the King's escape. Whether this were wishful thinking on the part of Richard's supporters has never been discovered, yet it was believed by some that the corpse of Maudelyn had been substituted for that of Richard. Maudelyn in height and colouring could easily be mistaken for Richard by many not familiar with the late king. If by placing the body of Maudelyn in a coffin leaving only the face and its head of fair hair visible, and the ravages of decomposition concealed by careful application of paint and powder, it could well pass for the face of Richard.

But *was* it the face of Richard?

Word had been brought to King Charles of France that his son-in-law, King Richard of England, had escaped from Pontefract to Scotland and received a royal welcome from Robert King of Scots.

This was enough for Charles to send Cretan to Scotland to ascertain if Richard, King of England, did indeed escape. If so, could one of the guards at Pontefract have been heavily bribed by Cretan to manoeuvre the King's release? And who but

Henry would have conceived the substitution of Maudelyn's corpse for that of Richard?

The truth has never been discovered, yet we may hazard a last glimpse of Richard at Pontefract on his knees in prayer for his deliverance before a crucifix of his murdered God.

And as Henry had proclaimed King Richard dead why, throughout his reign, was he haunted by the mortal fear that this Second King Richard Plantagenet still lived — and did not die?

AFTERWORD

Did the Second Richard Plantagenet die in that dungeon of Pontefract or did he escape to Scotland?

The question has baffled historians for six centuries. The majority of us only know the drama of Richard II as presented by the world's greatest dramatist; but Shakespeare was not a historian. He wrote his immortal historical plays from contemporary chronicles, as in the case of his *Richard III*, slain on Bosworth Field by Henry Tudor who crowned himself, as legend gives it, with the crown from the dead Richard's head. Nor could Shakespeare have known more of Richard III than the Tudor Chronicles gave him.

The same applies to Shakespeare's drama of Richard II, which gives us nothing of the child king, or of the fourteen-year-old boy who courageously faced thousands in the Peasants' Revolt led by Wat Tyler. We have been given much of Wat Tyler and that great revolt of the fourteenth century by Froissart, but Shakespeare could not have read Froissart since the first translation of his incomparable *Chronicles* would not have been available in English in Shakespeare's time.

We learn from Froissart, who had it from eye-witnesses, that the thousands of insurgents storming the city of London yelled for their boy king to speak for them. The elders of his Court and his uncles held back and allowed this boy to obey the demand of the rebels who mobbed the gates of the Tower from where he addressed them in a voice which at that age rang the changes between a childish treble and a harsh distressing croak, the first herald of puberty.

When John of Gaunt is dying we see Richard, as Shakespeare gives him, cruelly and heartlessly taunting the uncle whom he always loved and regarded as *in loco parentis.*

Since Richard was in Ireland on his second Irish expedition, he could not have been in England at the time of Gaunt's death; but the poignant scene at his uncle's deathbed is the creation of a masterly dramatist. Nor have we any evidence that Richard, according to the Lancastrians, died of starvation, raving mad in the dungeon at Pontefract.

Yet when at the funeral of his adored wife Anne, the King gave way to hysterical and uncontrollable grief it offered Gloucester the chance to spread the report, at which he often hinted, of Richard's mental derangement. We know, from all accounts, even from his most loyal supporters, that Richard had inherited the hot Plantagenet temper which would break out in sudden ungovernable fits of rage and would as swiftly pass. That he suffered from a slight stammer especially when under emotional stress, was another improbable symptom of insanity for Gloucester to seize upon; and when Richard was eventually rid of his most dangerous enemy, Henry replaced him with even more venom.

As to Richard's death, there have been controversial arguments throughout the centuries that he did not die at Pontefract and that he escaped to Scotland.

If, as was said, Charles VI of France sent Jean Cretan to seek Richard in Scotland where he was supposed to have fled, it is not surprising that Cretan failed to find him. Even had Robert III, King of Scots, hidden Richard in a remote castle it is unlikely he would have divulged his whereabouts to Cretan. Robert, as his father before him, was hoping to include Scotland in a permanent peace between England, France and Scotland. Moreover, he may have believed Cretan to be an agent for the Lancastrians, and Robert III of Scotland had no use for any Lancastrians, still less for a Lancastrian king.

From Froissart, who had personal contact with Richard on one of his rare visits to England, we learn that he had great charm, was an excellent conversationalist and spoke perfect French. His effigy in Westminster Abbey by a contemporary sculptor gives him a sensitive, delicately featured face, that of a dreamer and scholar; his taste in art and literature was manifest during his short life; an ardent admirer of Chaucer, he did himself write poems — none, alas, has been preserved. But he did draw and paint, and as a child he was thought by his doting mother to show great talent. The magnificent roof of Westminster Hall was designed by him.

His father, however, never ceased to deplore that his firstborn, the four-year-old Edward, died, and who so soon as he could lisp his words had wished to be a soldier.

Richard always maintained that he hated war and killing men, and during the short time he could have known his father who came back from the wars to die at Berkhamsted, he was constantly reminded of the dead brother whom Richard, when an infant in a cot, could scarcely have known.

That Henry of Lancaster's son, Henry V believed the body of Richard had been buried in the Priory at King's Langley is certain, for when he became king, Henry caused the coffin to be opened and the bones of Richard (or Maudelyn?) to be brought to Westminster Abbey and buried in the tomb Richard designed for his beloved wife Anne, where he lies to this day.

A NOTE TO THE READER

If you have enjoyed this novel enough to leave a review on **Amazon** and **Goodreads**, then we would be truly grateful.

Sapere Books

SAPERE
BOOKS

Printed in Great Britain
by Amazon